Praise for the books of
Agatha Award-winning Author
Edith Maxwell

"The historical setting is redolent and delicious, the townspeople engaging, and the plot a proper puzzle, but it's Rose Carroll—midwife, Quaker, sleuth—who captivates in this irresistible series . . ."
—Catriona McPherson,
Agatha-, Anthony- and Macavity-winning author of the
Dandy Gilver series

"Clever and stimulating novel . . . masterfully weaves a complex mystery."
—*Open Book Society*

"Riveting historical mystery . . . [a] fascinating look at nineteenth-century American faith, culture, and small-town life."
—William Martin, *New York Times* bestselling author of
Cape Cod and *The Lincoln Letter*

"Intelligent, well-researched story with compelling characters and a fast-moving plot. Excellent!"
—*Suspense Magazine*

"A series heroine whose struggles with the tenets of her Quaker faith make her strong and appealing . . . imparts authentic historical detail to depict life in a 19th-century New England factory town."
—*Library Journal*

"Intriguing look at life in 19th-century New England, a heroine whose goodness guides all her decisions, and a mystery that surprises."
—*Kirkus Reviews*

Books by Edith Maxwell

Quaker Midwife Mysteries

Delivering the Truth
Called to Justice
Turning the Tide
Charity's Burden
Judge Thee Not
Taken Too Soon

Lauren Rousseau Mysteries

Speaking of Murder
Murder on the Bluffs

Local Foods Mysteries

A Tine to Live, a Tine to Die
'Til Dirt Do Us Part
Farmed and Dangerous
Murder Most Fowl
Mulch Ado About Murder

More Books by Edith Maxwell

Country Store Mysteries
(written as Maddie Day)

Flipped for Murder
Grilled for Murder
When the Grits Hit the Fan
Biscuits and Slashed Browns
Death Over Easy
Strangled Eggs and Ham
Nacho Average Murder
Candy Slain Murder

Cozy Capers Book Group Mysteries
(written as Maddie Day)

Murder on Cape Cod
Murder at the Taffy Shop

Murder on the Bluffs

A Lauren Rousseau Mystery

Edith Maxwell

BEYOND THE PAGE
PUBLISHING

Murder on the Bluffs
Edith Maxwell
Beyond the Page Books
are published by
Beyond the Page Publishing
www.beyondthepagepub.com

This book was originally published as *Bluffing Is Murder* under the name Tace Baker, copyright © 2014 by Tace Baker. This edition copyright © 2020 by Edith Maxwell.
Cover design by Dar Albert, Wicked Smart Designs

ISBN: 978-1-950461-69-1

For the members and attenders of Amesbury Friends Meeting,
who have held me in the Light for thirty-one years

Acknowledgments

My fellow writers in the Monday Night Salem Writers Group critiqued most of the scenes in this book and improved it vastly. Thank you to Margaret Press, Rae Francouer, Elaine Ricci, Sam Sherman, and the late Doug Hall. Sherry Harris read and edited the entire manuscript. She once again pointed out numerous plot holes and offered valuable suggestions for improvement. Any flaws in the book are due entirely to my ignoring the comments of these colleagues.

I wouldn't be published at all if it weren't for what I learned through Sisters in Crime, the Guppies, and the New England chapter of SINC, and I wouldn't have had so much fun along the way, either. Thanks so much to Bill Harris of Beyond the Page Publishing for picking up this book as well as *Speaking of Murder* and reissuing them as Edith Maxwell books after they went out of print under my first pen name of Tace Baker.

Readers familiar with the North Shore of Massachusetts will recognize landmarks from the town of Ipswich and similarities to certain news stories from past decades. This story is entirely fictional, however.

Once again I am indebted to my second family, the regulars at Amesbury Friends Meeting, who cheer me on and hold me up. I am grateful to all the mystery readers out there who like to read about Quaker protagonists in these books and in my historical Quaker Midwife Mysteries. I hope you also love my contemporary cozy mysteries published under the name Maddie Day.

As always, thanks and fierce love to my sons, Allan and John Hutchison-Maxwell, and to my main man, Hugh Lockhart.

Chapter One

I turned away from the teller when a man in work clothes pushed open a frosted-glass office door in the Ashford Credit Union and stalked back into the main lobby of the bank. His ruddy face spoke of sun, hard work, and frustration. A beer gut pushed out his shirt.

He pivoted to look at the man standing in the doorway. "Look, Walter. I need that loan for my boat. It's bad enough I can't even afford to live in town anymore. Now you fat cats are cutting off my livelihood, too."

The banker followed him out, dressed in impeccable threads: nicely cut dark suit, pale yellow shirt, perfectly tied gold necktie, shiny black shoes. His thinning blond hair was arrayed neatly on his scalp, every strand gelled into position.

"Bobby, I told you I was sorry." Walter Colby's tone was low, but everyone else in the high-ceilinged room had fallen silent as they watched. "We've known each other forever, but I can't justify this loan."

"It's just to tide me ovah," Bobby Spirokis said in an exasperated tone. He shook his head and rubbed his forehead with a weathered hand.

Walter shook his head. "I can't do it. I have to account to the directors, and they won't approve it. If Charles Heard won't insure your lobster boat, we can't loan you money for it."

"How am I supposed to fix it so's I can insure it if you won't give me the money?"

Walter spread his hands. "That's how the world runs, Bobby."

Bobby stormed toward the door. "Your time's gonna come, Walter Colby. You'll see how it feels," he spat. He paused at the door. "You watch yourself. You and your buddy Heard."

The bells on the heavy door jingled behind him. The teller rustled paper as if to show that she was, in fact, doing her job instead of eavesdropping on the branch president and a client. I stood rooted in place grasping the cashier's check I'd just bought.

Walter smoothed down his tie and his graying hair and then

1

caught sight of me. He walked toward me, hand outstretched. He had a bit of a gut, too, but I'd bet it came from Scotch and lobster and not Bud Lite.

"Good morning, ma'am." He beamed the smile of a salesman.

I shook his hand and wondered when I had gone from a miss to a ma'am.

"Is Tracy helping you with what you need today?"

I nodded.

The smile left his face as he turned back toward his office.

So much for actually getting to know one of your clients. I left the building and crossed Market Street. The late-May air was mild on my skin. It smelled of lilacs and impending summer.

I pulled a letter out of my bag and read it one more time. "If we do not receive full payment within five business days, a fine in the amount of five hundred dollars will be added to your premium, payable immediately." It had only arrived at my condo the day before. My mortgage was also at risk if my insurance lapsed. I shook my head.

One of the many good things about small-town Ashford was being able to walk downtown and pay bills in person. Except that I had been so busy at the end of the Agawam College semester that I'd forgotten to pay my homeowner's insurance. I'm a newly tenured professor there and can easily afford my condo expenses. When I remember to remit them.

I entered the Heard Insurance Agency and greeted the young man at the desk. He wore a long-sleeved shirt and tie and looked like he'd recently graduated from high school. The door to Charles Heard's private office at the other side of the room was closed. Good. I didn't really want to try to be civil to the man who'd signed the letter.

I stood in a small space that featured what looked like original watercolors of the salt marshes and the Ashford River. A bonsai spruce in a shallow rectangular pot sat on a table under the window. I raised my eyebrows. That was a new addition to the office. I cultivated a bonsai elm in my own office at the college.

"Nice tree. Who takes care of it?" All thoughts of my late

insurance bill flew out the window as I stroked a miniature gnarled branch. The tree's form was classic, like it should have clung to a coastal cliff.

"That's Ms. Heard's hobby, ma'am," the young guy said. "She thought the light would be good for it here."

There was that *ma'am* again. I must be showing my age. Since when was thirty-five old?

"It's lovely. I didn't know anybody else in town cultivated them."

He smiled at me with the patient look of the young, waiting for an elder to quit boring him. "Can I help you with something?"

"I simply want to pay my bill." A small nameplate on his desk read *Mark Pulcifer*. "Are you related to Phillip and Samuel?"

He looked up. "They're my great-uncles. How do you—"

The door to the back office opened. Charles Heard appeared with a paper in his hand. He shook his head with impatience and pursed his lips in exasperation. "Mark, did that fax come in from the lawyer for—" He stopped when he saw me.

"Morning," he said. He pasted a smile over whatever he had been upset about.

I returned the greeting and extended my hand. "I don't think we've met before, Mr. Heard. I've had my insurance with you for several years. Lauren Rousseau. I live up on Upper Summer Street."

He shook my hand. "Always happy when people want to keep their business in town. We appreciate it, ma'am." A tune from *Carmen* rang out from the back office. "Excuse me for just a moment." He set the paper on a bookshelf, turned back to his office, and picked up a cell phone from his desk.

I glanced at the paper. Curious. It looked like it was written in Arabic. I took a closer look and spotted two of the characters that were added to the script for writing in Farsi. Maybe Charles Heard had business in Iran, or maybe he had lived there at some point.

I returned to the bonsai. As I stroked its leaves, I heard Charles's side of the conversation. It sounded like a discussion of the current controversy in town, the conflict between the Trustees of the Bluffs and the town. Residents who lived on the Bluffs land trust owned their homes but rented the land under them. The Trustees' three-hundred-year-old mandate required them to turn over the rents to the town for the education of the children. Except the secretive cabal hadn't given the schools money for years. It was all anyone in town talked about lately.

"Listen. The children are fine. They've still got their precious sports." His tone was bitter. "We're managing the property as best we can to simply stay afloat."

In the silence that followed, I studied the bonsai.

"We're going to win, you know. Don't try to stand in our way. Somebody could get hurt."

I glanced at the young man at the desk to see if he had heard the threat. Head down, he appeared to be focused on the paperwork on the desk in front of him.

Charles reemerged from his office with flushed face. He looked startled to find me still there. "Thank you for coming by. If there's ever anything I can do for you, just call, all right?" He straightened the knot on the bright blue tie he wore over a white dress shirt that still bore fresh creases from the laundry.

"Well, actually, don't you think it's pretty harsh to threaten me with a fine? My insurance payment is only a few days overdue." I waved the letter as my voice rose.

The smile slid off his face. He took the letter and perused it. He looked at me. "Our recommendation is for you to fold the home-owner's policy into your mortgage. For customers who choose to pay it themselves, we need to be sure coverage is kept current. It was clearly stated on the application packet you must have filled out."

"I have been current! This is the first time I've ever been late with the check. You don't give more than five days' leeway for local residents?"

"Ma'am—what was your name again?"

"Lauren Rousseau."

"Mrs. Rousseau—"

"It's Dr. Rousseau."

He rolled his eyes. "*Doc*tor Rousseau." The stress on the first syllable of my title sounded exasperated. "Look, we're trying to protect our clients. It's to your detriment if you are an uninsured homeowner. We've found that knowing about a financial penalty encourages people to pay on time. How long have you lived in town, anyway?"

"What does that matter?"

He consulted the letter, peering at a code in the top margin that I had never been able to decipher. "Around here, Doctor, buying a condominium and living in it for a few years hardly qualifies you as being from here." His tight smile was topped by cold eyes. The bell on the door jingled.

"Look, I can take my business elsewhere if you can't be decent enough to allow a grace period." Appalled to hear my voice shaking, I turned toward the door. "I've never heard of such a fine."

Charles's eyes darted away from mine, and he tapped the letter on his left thigh.

"What's this about decency?" A sturdy man with a shiny pate strode in. He wore a dark gray shirt with a navy tie, and over it a maroon sweater vest with a moth hole near the shoulder. A round pin proclaiming Rotary membership was fixed to one side of the shirt collar. "You giving people trouble again, Charles?" He looked back and forth between Charles Heard and me.

Charles cleared his throat. "Only some business with a customer, Chief Flaherty. Dr. Rousseau here seems to want special treatment."

"Just some business? I think threatening to fine me an exorbitant amount if I don't pay in five days is heartless," I steamed. "There are plenty of other insurance agencies that are more understanding."

"Not in this town, there aren't," Charles snapped back. He folded his arms and stood with his feet apart like Mr. Clean. Except he wasn't tall and bald and didn't sport an earring. And he didn't smile.

"Now, now," the police chief said. He looked at me. "Ah, yes. Dr. Rousseau. We've met before." He extended his hand.

I shook his hand, glad for the diversion. Glad for a chance to catch my breath and cool down, despite the reminder of the circumstances under which I had met the chief of police a couple of months earlier. What had come over me, to yell at someone in public? I realized my other hand still gripped the envelope with the cashier's check in it. I might as well pay up. I proffered it to Charles.

"You'll take my money, I assume? And not cancel my policy?"

He nodded, then extended his chin toward the young man at the desk, keeping his arms folded as if as a shield in front of him.

Young Mark, meanwhile, kept his eyes firmly on the papers on the desk as if two adults hadn't just embarrassed themselves in front of him.

"Here, Mark." I handed the envelope to him.

He looked up and smiled with what looked like relief on his smooth, pale skin. "Thank you, ma'am."

"Can I have a receipt, please?"

Mark nodded and wrote one out.

I thanked him. I told the chief it was nice to have seen him again and walked out. Charles Heard said nothing and neither did I. I felt his eyes burn holes into my back. I did not turn around.

• • •

I stretched and checked the clock the next afternoon after working on my paper for the East Asian Linguistics Conference. Five o'clock at the end of May still left enough time for a run on Holt Beach before it closed at sunset. I changed into stretch shorts and a T-shirt, grabbed the keys to my truck and a water bottle, and headed out. Another blessing of the town was a gorgeous wild beach on the Atlantic a fifteen-minute drive away and an annual town resident's parking sticker for only twenty dollars.

At the end of the raised boardwalk over the dunes, I headed left, inhaling salt air. The tide was out, and I ran along the water's edge where the sand was the most firm. A breeze picked up, blowing straight into my face as I headed west. A dark cloud temporarily blocked the sun. It looked like today might prove the old adage about New England weather: if you don't like it, wait an hour and it'll change. A family started to pack up plastic toys and beach towels, and two women walking toward me picked up their pace.

I ran past a plaid cloth with its corners anchored in the sand. A classic woven picnic basket sat open. The top of an open wine bottle poked out. A seagull pecked at the remnants of a plate of several cheeses, with wrappers that looked like the ones from the best deli in town, the Coastal Greengrocer. A box of expensive crackers skidded away on the wind. The picnickers must have been out strolling the beach.

I wished I'd worn a light jacket. And then wondered how many additional calories I was burning running into the wind. I pushed on, thoughts as insistent as the whitecaps on the dark sea. When I immersed myself in a research paper, the topic tended to occupy my thoughts day and night. I couldn't find my stride, slowed down, caught my breath, watched the boats across the channel at the Bluffs Yacht Club, where the Ashford River met the ocean. A small boat—it was always the small ones—was about to come unmoored by the turbulent water.

I turned around. The wind now pushed me along but also chilled the sweat on my back. More dark clouds blew in. On a whim, I decided to head up the path that stretched into the woods so I could do some hill work. I was curious about exactly where it ended, whether it would afford a better view of the Holt mansion on the hilltop. Plus, I'd be out of the wind for a few minutes. I left the sand. After several yards of crushed seashells mixed with sand the footing turned to packed gravel.

As I pistoned uphill, the trees closed in until the canopy joined overhead. A branch cracked to my right. I had to hop over a sapling blocking the way. The path was like running in a tunnel, with the overgrowth and the lack of light. The gravel turned to weeds that reached mid-calf because of the recent rains. A root caught my toe and I stumbled but managed to stay on my feet. Ahead it looked a little lighter. The path took a bend as it leveled out and then opened up all of a sudden.

I stopped in surprise. A wide swath of mown grass stretched up a hill in front of me. Conical evergreens lined the edges of the woods on either side of the grass. At the top in the distance I spied low hedges and a stone fountain. And beyond that, probably a quarter mile distant, a mansion held court over the hill. I stood on the Grand Allée.

I'd seen pictures but had never managed to squeeze in a visit to any of the summer concerts that were held on the lawn of the Holt Estate, at the other end of the same lawn I stood on. From the beach I could tell the Holt mansion was a large building, but this view highlighted its massive, ornate construction. I'd read that Holt, a plumbing magnate in the early 1900s, had built the mansion as a summer cottage for his family. Some cottage.

In the distance a man in work clothes walked away from me between the fountain and the house. They must have employed quite a few gardeners to keep these grounds up. Otherwise no one was in sight. The Allée looked like it needed Victorian women with parasols strolling in white dresses on the arms of men wearing white linen and bowler hats. I stretched a little and then turned back toward my path. A crow, cawing its lungs out, flapped by and preceded me into the woods.

I ran through the trees thinking about the estate, wondering how many rooms it held. I wondered how much its current owners, the state park system named the Department of Conservation and Recreation, must have to pay to keep it minimally warm in the frigid Massachusetts winters.

Something sharp hit my face.

I cried out. I brought my hand to cover my right eye. It stung. What in the world was that? I took my hand away, and through blurry vision saw blood on it. I cursed as I closed that eye.

I heard a branch snap. My skin went cold, and my heart beat fast and hard. It wasn't from running. Someone was watching me. I was sure of it.

With my hand over my eye, I turned my head with a quick movement. I didn't see anyone out of my left eye. I turned all the way around. No one. I realized I was taking fast, shallow breaths and made myself slow and deepen them. Then I saw who was watching me. Perched on a branch was my corvid friend. The crow cocked his head but kept those dark eyes trained on me.

I laughed weakly. Then what had hit me? I looked around again, feeling my heart return to normal, although my legs felt wobbly. I saw a thorny branch at about eye level. I must have been so distracted I ran right into it. Once a klutz, always a klutz.

With caution I opened my eye again. I blinked several times. It still hurt and was a little blurry, but I could see. I was grateful nothing serious had happened to my eye, or at least I hoped so.

I didn't feel up to running anymore but set off at a fast walk back down the hill, glad when it opened up to the beach again. I crunched down the shells and made my way through the rocks toward the main part of the beach. The wind had not abated. I was glad it was now at my back. I hugged my arms in close.

The growth clinging to the hillside on my right was rough and scraggly. For brush and trees to survive the salt wind and poor soil, they had to be tough. I spied a mass of something white on a shrub half hidden behind a cypress tree most of the way up the bank. I was curious about what could be flowering. Maybe I could bring a sample leaf back to my sister and ask her what it was. Jackie knew everything about plants. It seemed early in the season, though, for anything wild to be in bloom.

My eye felt a little better. I decided to see if I could reach the plant. I scrabbled up the hillside. I grabbed on to roots and branches where I found them. I focused on my immediate path.

Looking up, my eyes widened. Even with a scratched cornea, I could see that that was no flower.

It was a shirt. A white shirt. And it was on Charles Heard.

I froze. My hands gripped the root that kept me from sliding down. He sprawled faceup at an odd angle in a small clearing. His head pointed downhill, his eyes open in a look of terror. He didn't move. I couldn't see him breathing. I opened my mouth to call his name when I saw a thin red line on his neck.

Chapter Two

His collar looked soaked with blood. The dried leaves near his head appeared darker than those a few feet away.

My stomach roiled. Charles Heard was dead. Someone had killed him. I climbed up a few more feet until I stood beside his body. I reached out and touched his cheek with a tentative finger. I drew it back in a hurry. Skin wasn't supposed to feel cold.

I shivered. He'd been a nasty man, but nobody deserved to die like this. I reached for my cell phone and then cursed. I wore stretch shorts. No pockets, so my phone was elsewhere. I tried to think if I'd left it in the truck. How was I going to find help?

I looked down the hill. Should I slide down and run to the lifeguard station? I shook my head. It was too early in the season for lifeguards. I looked back at the body. How had he come to be here? I glanced around. A narrow path led into the woods. Branches were broken at its edges. I wondered if Charles had been killed elsewhere and brought here, or if someone had followed him to this clearing and cut his throat. I shook my head to clear it. That wasn't my business. But finding a phone was.

Leaves rustled and I froze again. Goose bumps jumped up on my arms. Was the killer still here? Watching me? I wished I'd never come up this hill.

"Hello?" I called out. My voice barely croaked out the words. I swallowed, took a deep breath, and called again in a stronger voice. No one answered. More branches cracked. I started. And then breathed again when I saw a deer move away from me.

I squinted at the narrow path. It was probably quicker to try to follow that back to the estate than to go along the beach. That person I'd seen could call the police. I looked back at Charles's body. I wanted to split myself in three: one part to watch over the body, one part to get help, and one part to go into hiding and never encounter a dead body again. I sighed and took my one self up the path.

I kept a hand up so a branch wouldn't scratch my eye again and hurried along. It wasn't much of a path and was too overgrown to really run on. It looked like it was only an animal travel-way and not a human trail.

I sniffed. Great. The air smelled like rain. It had been a dry spring and the ground needed water. But I didn't need it on my head.

I walked for a few minutes until I came out onto the wider path I'd been on earlier, the one that led to the Grand Allée. I turned and looked back. I never would have known there was an opening to that path. I jogged uphill toward the estate. Fat drops splashed on my head, penetrating even the canopy overhead.

When I was free of the trees, I ran up the long wide hill of grass toward the mansion. No one was about. When I neared the fountain, I stopped and waved my arms in case someone was watching from the mansion. No one appeared. At the edge was an outbuilding. Maybe that was the maintenance shed. Maybe I could find that worker I'd seen earlier. I ran to the door and pounded on it. The rain had soaked my shirt, and I was chilled. A grimy window up high looked like a light was on behind it.

No one opened the door.

I didn't know where to turn next. I stared at the door, as if wishing it would produce someone. When I heard a faint noise from within, I pressed my ear against the thick door. My hopes soared. But I heard nothing.

I felt desperate for help, any kind of help. I looked farther up the hill at the mansion and cursed. I had to do it. I started to run. At least it might warm me. The rain lightened and stopped. My heart pounded as I reached the tall glass doors. Their ornate ironwork might have protected them from breaking, but it looked like the entrance to a fortress to me. It was dark inside. I banged my fist but barely made a sound.

I trudged back down the wide curving steps. I was wet and miserable. How far was I going to have to walk to locate help? I rued my decision to take this route instead of the beach. I made my way around to the front and started down the drive. At least if I could reach the road, a car might pass by. And if not, I could head back to the gatehouse at the entrance to the beach parking lot. Poor Charles Heard was going to have to wait.

Dusk was already falling. It seemed darker than the time indicated because of the cloud cover. I didn't dare run on the gravel for fear that I'd trip. Once I cleared the road, then I could sprint. And since the beach closed at sundown, I'd have to hurry.

"Hey, lady," a voice called out from behind me.

I stopped so fast I skidded as I whirled. I could barely make out a man who stood at the top of the drive. I waved my arm as I headed back up. "Hello! I need help," I shouted. "Do you have a phone?"

The man did not answer. He looked like a monolith uphill from me.

I hailed him again. He remained silent as I approached in the gloom. I stopped some yards away. What was going on? Why didn't he speak?

"Sir?" I said one more time. Maybe I should start running back to the road in a hurry.

"What kind of help you need?" The hair on his square head was matted down by the rain. His shape was solid, like a boxer or a weight lifter.

Finally. "I need a phone. I need to call the police." I walked toward him.

"Why's that?"

I stopped again. I wasn't sure I should tell this stranger about the body in the woods. "I need to report something, um, that I found," I stammered.

He leaned his shoulder against the tree trunk he was next to. Keys jangled. "What's that you found?"

I still could barely see him, so I continued in his direction. "Do you have a cell phone I can use?"

"No, ma'am. I don't."

Oh, no. This was bad. I was glad I hadn't told him about Charles, though. I turned to go. "I have to find a phone," I said over my shoulder. "Thanks, anyway."

"You can use the phone in the office."

I turned again, starting to feel like I was on a carousel. "You have a working telephone here?"

He nodded and beckoned me to follow him. Now that I was close,

I saw he wore a dark blue cotton work shirt tucked into matching pants. A weathered brown belt held a jumble of keys. The pant cuffs were frayed and one back pocket hung down at its corner.

We walked around the other side of the mansion. He stepped past a small unlocked door in a low addition that looked like an afterthought to the massive building it was attached to. I hesitated to follow him into the small room. Then a light illuminated the inside, like a beacon to safety, and I walked in.

A black rotary phone, the kind made out of real metal, sat on a wide wooden desk. The man gestured toward it as he leaned on the doorjamb. I looked at him closely for the first time. I was surprised to see it was the guy who had begged for the loan in the bank yesterday morning. What had his name been? Bobby somebody?

"Thank you so much, Mr. . . . ?" I raised my eyebrows along with my intonation.

"You can call me Bobby. Everybody in these parts does."

I thanked him again. "But would you mind if I have a little privacy for the call? It's sort of confidential."

He gave me a look like I was a crazy woman, then shrugged and stepped outdoors. He pulled the door most of the way closed after him. I couldn't do anything about him listening through the crack, but I'd have to take that risk.

I dialed 911 and reported what I'd found to the dispatcher who answered. I told him that, no, I wasn't with the body, and no, I couldn't return there to guard it any faster than they could. I said, when asked, that I thought it was Charles Heard, and explained where I was now. When he asked if I was alone, I said that someone named Bobby was there and had let me use the mansion's office telephone.

"Bobby Spirokis?" the voice asked.

I said I didn't know. The dispatcher asked to speak to him, so I called Bobby in and handed him the receiver.

I looked around for something to keep warm with. I was freezing and knew if I checked my toes, they would be an unhealthy shade of yellow. I didn't have good circulation in my extremities, despite my habit of running. A wooden coatrack of an era to match the telephone stood in the corner, and among the garments on it hung a thick beige cardigan.

After Bobby hung up, I asked if I could wear the sweater.

He shrugged again. "Belongs to Miz Lopes. The secretary. Ugly as sin. You can wear it."

I didn't know if he was referring to the secretary or the sweater, which was, in fact, a really unattractive shade of coffee cream with a hint of mustard. I was so cold I'd have worn a moth-eaten coat from the Salvation Army if I'd had one. The sweater was thickly knit and long enough to reach the tops of my thighs. It felt like heaven.

"P'lice are coming." He cocked his head. "We best wait outside. Time to close up here, anyway."

At my look of angst, which I accompanied by grasping the plackets of the sweater and wrapping it more tightly around myself, Bobby snorted.

"You can keep the rag on. Bring it back tomorrow. She's away. She won't care."

Those were the most words I'd heard him string together since yesterday. I didn't care if he was naturally taciturn or as eloquent as an orator, I simply felt grateful to warm up at last, and hoped he was right about the sweater's owner not caring. We left the sanctuary of the office and walked out into the twilight. I heard sirens in the distance as he locked the door. I realized I hadn't introduced myself.

"I'm Lauren Rousseau, by the way." I extended my hand and then brought it back when he kept his in his pockets.

He nodded without looking at me. He stood with feet apart and gazed down the drive, much as he had when he had first called to me.

I stood in silence next to him. As a member of the Society of Friends, I was comfortable with silence.

The sound of sirens drew near, and the drive filled with blue flashing lights, the rumble of a fire truck, and the white shape of an ambulance. I shielded my eyes with my arm.

"Dr. Rousseau?"

I brought down my arm. Chief Flaherty stood in front of me. "Yes."

"You the one called in a dead body? And you think it's Charles Heard?"

"Yes, and it is."

He raised his eyebrows. "Bobby says you didn't want him to hear you calling. Why was that?"

"I don't know. I thought, well, I don't know." How could I explain that something about Bobby made me feel uneasy? I looked around for Bobby. He seemed to have slipped away. His disappearance didn't appear to bother the police, though.

The chief regarded me. "Looks like you've been in a fistfight this afternoon."

I bristled. "No, of course I haven't."

He pointed to my face. "Your eye is puffy and you have blood on your face."

"Oh, that. A branch scratched my eye. That's all."

"Right. Quite sure you didn't continue your disagreement with Charles Heard up here?"

"Yes, I'm sure."

"Why don't you show us where this body is." He crossed his arms.

"Sure. Do you have a flashlight?"

His tolerant smile and slow nod made me feel a little foolish. Of course the police would have all kinds of equipment.

I led a parade of the chief, three officers, and two EMTs with a stretcher back down the Allée and through the path in the trees. The long dusk of spring cast a blanket of shadow that made everything look different from before. I hoped I could find the way through the brush. As we walked without speaking, I had a strange thought that maybe the body wouldn't be there. The darkness made me wonder if I had imagined the whole thing. I glanced at Chief Flaherty and decided to keep these thoughts to myself. He probably thought I was a bit crazy as it was. Or maybe he was thinking the same thing: did this lady really find Charles Heard dead?

But apparently I was not nuts. I found the opening. I led them through the brush and pointed. Same Charles Heard, same white shirt, same absence of life. I stood back with my arms wrapped around myself as they did their work. One officer, a young guy I had met earlier in the spring, set up a portable floodlight, while another took pictures from all angles. The EMTs pretty much didn't have a job. There was no one to whom they could administer emergency medical treatment. Except me.

"Let me clean up that cut for you, ma'am." A helpful-looking young man offered his services.

I agreed and winced as he swabbed it clean and applied a bandage.

A green-khaki-clad state park worker strode in and conferred in low tones with the chief. He must have come from the beach in one of the ATVs they drove up and down patrolling for beer parties or lost souls. The worker looked at me from under his DCR hat and continued to talk. I hoped I'd be able to extract my truck from the parking lot. It was past sunset.

My stomach growled and goose bumps ran up and down my arms. I was sorry Mr. Heard was dead but figured my civic duty had been done. I wanted to go home. I walked toward them, but the chief held up a hand to forestall me. Great.

A woman pushed her way through the bushes followed by a slim female police officer. For a minute I thought it was Natalia Flores, an officer I knew and my sister's current amour. A friendly face would have been a welcome sight about now, but when the officer turned toward me, it was someone I had never seen before.

The other woman carried a black bag. I had read about medical examiners in mystery books and this woman looked exactly the type. An all-business attitude, trim gray hair, sensible black slacks. The only thing that didn't fit the image were her hot pink blazer and a set of oversized dangling silver earrings with turquoise beads at the ends. The woman shook hands with the chief and knelt by the body.

The chief moved to my side. "I'd like to hear your story now, Dr. Rousseau." His tone was alarmingly polite.

I repeated the sequence of events. How I had been running. Clambering up the bank to see what was blooming. Finding the body. Trying to find help.

"I thought I heard someone in the shed, but no one answered my knocks, and no one seemed to be around the mansion. I was heading down to the road. And then this Bobby guy appeared out of nowhere.

He let me call."

"You and Charles Heard argued yesterday." His eyes bored into mine.

"It was only about my insurance payment. No problem, really." I waved my hand in dismissal. "So can I go home now? I'm freezing and—"

"It sounded serious. You both seemed pretty upset."

I stared at him. "What? You think I killed Charles Heard? Over my insurance? Then why would I have called you about the body?"

The woman in the blazer joined the group. "I'm all set, Dick. I'm heading back to my dinner, if that's all right with you." She looked me up and down. "You found the deceased?" Her tone was brisk to the point of a winter wind. "I hope you didn't touch anything."

I felt distinctly underappreciated. Here I'd gone out of my way to be a good citizen, and instead they were accusing me of, what? Having a reason to murder someone? Tampering with a crime scene? Really? And while I was still shaky from having found a local citizen dead.

"Yes, I found him. And I went some distance to report it as soon as I could."

"And why didn't you go back along the beach?" The chief looked at me with a polite little smile.

"I thought since I was already up on the hill, it'd be faster to go up to the estate. Thought someone would be around."

His face didn't register much belief, but he let the explanation pass.

The ME wasn't going to let her question go unanswered, though. "Did you or did you not touch anything, move anything?"

"No." I faced her. "I didn't. The only thing I touched was the ground with my feet." I remembered I had touched poor Charles's cheek. Did I need to say that? I decided not to.

"So can I go?" I asked the chief.

"I'll need to speak with you later about your altercation with Charles. I was there, you remember. It was more than nothing. You'll be at home?"

He wasn't going to let me off about that stupid disagreement. I wasn't famous for my tact, and blowing up at an officer wouldn't help anything. I nodded. "I will be at home. Or nearby, anyway."

"Good." He turned to the ME. "Thanks, Lydia. We'll be in touch.

Hey, Frank, take Dr. Rousseau back to the parking lot, will you?" he said to the man in the DCR uniform. To me he added, "Frank Jenkins'll run you back to your vehicle."

I'd never been so glad to leave somewhere.

Chapter Three

I poured a glass of Scotch and sank onto my couch. Wulu, my black cockapoo, jumped up next to me. I stroked his curly fur while I sipped. I'd gone for a nice beach run and found a dead body. I tried to report it and was basically accused of murdering Charles Heard. What a fine start to a summer.

"What do you think, Wulu?" I asked.

He looked up and barked like I hadn't fed him in a week. He hopped down and ran to his dish.

Oh, yeah, dinnertime. I filled Wulu's dish and gave him fresh water. I wandered the confines of my condo, glass in hand. I ended up in my guest room that doubled as an office. I could fire up the computer and see what else I could find out about Charles Heard. But since it was my dinnertime, too, and since I didn't cook much, maybe heading down to the Dodd Bridge Pub was a better bet. Not only did they offer excellent fried food and local ales, I was also pretty much guaranteed to ingest some good gossip.

I took off the Ms. Lopes sweater and changed into jeans and my own sweater, this one black and slightly more stylish. I stuffed some money, my cell phone, and my license into a pocket, and headed down the steep hill that was my street. The rain clouds had moved out to sea and left a windy, cool night. Stars polka-dotted the darkness. It took barely ten minutes to walk through the historic part of town. I passed houses built mostly in the 1600s and 1700s, with the occasional early-1900s cottage tucked in between. Some were in better repair than others, but most sported an Ashford Historical Commission plaque proudly announcing their birthdays.

When I passed the stone building that was the library, I paused. The lights within looked comforting and safe in the dark air, as if each lit window was a mini-lighthouse offering shelter from a storm. The tempest that now pummeled me was not going to be pushed away by a few compact fluorescent lights, though. How the chief could think that I had anything to do with Charles Heard's murder was completely beyond me. Chief Flaherty had been in the office. It wasn't like I'd threatened Charles Heard or anything.

I shook my head and made my way down Town Hill. From the outside, the pub smelled of sizzling meat and fried clams. My stomach grumbled in response. I pulled open the door to the bar area and looked around. Added to the aroma was now hops and ketchup. My favorite waitress, Katie, waved from the back. I decided to sit at the bar. I'd be more likely to pick up news there than in a booth by myself. The huge American eagle that hung overhead scowled at me in two dimensions, but I ignored it and perused the menu. I didn't need anybody else frowning at me today.

The bartender was a tall man I hadn't seen before, a youngish guy with curly black hair and a Vandyke beard, also dark. The gold stud in one earlobe gave him the air of a pirate; the long white apron he wore around his waist, not so much.

I ordered the fish and chips and an Ipswich IPA. I asked the bartender if he was new to the pub.

"Pretty new. Not to bartending, though. Been doin' that for some time." He smiled as he slanted a pint glass under the tap and drew the ale with care. "Katie over there's my sister. Got me the gig."

"Oh, I didn't know she had a brother. Are there more of you around?"

He nodded. He placed a cocktail napkin in front of me and set the beer on it. It was full to the brim. An entire pint for once. "We're a regular gang. Six in all."

I wasn't really surprised that I didn't know this since I hadn't grown up in Ashford. I watched him under my eyebrows as I sipped the brew, trying to figure out how old he was. I knew Katie was in her early twenties, and thought he was a bit older than that. But not as old as me, I was pretty sure.

"My name's Lauren, by the way. Lauren Rousseau."

"Nathan Eames. Spelled with two *E*'s."

I raised my eyebrows.

He sighed and spelled, "E-a-m-e-s. Most people hear it, think it's A-m-e-s. Not that you probably even care. So d'ja hear the big news?"

"I'm not sure. What news was that?"

He leaned in. "Body found out at Holt. Near Steep Hill Beach."

Deciding to play it innocent as long as I could, I said, "When?" I hoped the look on my face conveyed surprise and not shock that even the newly hired local bartender already knew.

"This evening. Katie heard it from her friend Ashley, who works with Chief Flaherty's daughter, Colleen, at Salon 36."

My head spun with the connections. From the times I'd sat and had my hair carefully cut by Ashley at Salon 36, I knew local news always filled the room.

"That's terrible. Do you know who it was?"

"They're saying one of the Trustees." He rubbed the countertop with a cloth.

I shook my head, hoping to convey sorrowful commiseration with the victim and not let on that I had discovered the body. That news would be out soon enough.

Nathan nodded and turned to three men who had recently taken stools across the horseshoe-shaped bar from where I sat. I took a long drink from my glass. The first swallow was always the best taste of the bitter hops. I rubbed my tongue against the roof of my mouth, savoring the flavor. And then yawned. It had been a long day. I needed dinner and bed.

My pocket vibrated. I pulled out my phone and checked the number. My boyfriend, Zac.

"Hey, Zac. How's it going?"

"Marie-Fleur wants to talk to you." Marie-Fleur, his preteen Haitian niece, was living with him for a few months.

"What's up?"

"She heard about something bad happening. I guess some guy was killed. She's upset about it."

I shook my head. I stared at the phone. How in the world did news travel so fast that an eleven-year-old already knew it? "Put her on, then. Although I don't know what I can do."

"You're a woman. She misses her mom. I feel kind of helpless, *bebé*."

I rolled my eyes and waited for him to put the girl on the line.

21

• • •

I arrived home the next morning from my run along the river. The air had chilled my hands and face. My gait had been off. Remembering the sight of Charles Heard's lifeless face had shadowed every step.

I was just out of the shower when the phone rang. Chief Flaherty asked me to come by the station as soon as possible. I knew I had nothing to hide but felt nervous about the interview nevertheless. I dressed in black pants and a sweater, which had to look more respectable than the running clothes and borrowed sweater the chief had seen me in the day before. Which reminded me that I needed to return the sweater to the mansion.

A short time later I stood gazing at the Ashford Police building. I walked up the stairs and extended a hand to the heavy door. It opened fast toward me, whacking my hand in the process.

Bobby Spirokis stormed through the opening. He muttered as he clomped down the stairs. "Damn police. Damn town. They know where they can stick their damn Trustees."

I rubbed my stinging hand and watched him go. I didn't think he'd even seen me. I approached the door with more caution this time in case someone else burst out of it. I rapped on the thick glass window that separated the lobby of the Police Department from the inner office and gave a little wave to the officer who stood within.

"Can I help you?" His voice sounded disembodied coming from a speaker above my head.

"Chief Flaherty wants to see me. About the, uh, body out at the Holt Estate." I was alarmed to hear my voice creep upward. I cleared my throat and tried to calm my nerves.

"Your name, please?"

"Lauren Rousseau."

The man picked up a phone, spoke for a minute, and then motioned me to a side door.

I waited until the gray door swung open.

The officer asked me to come with him. I followed him down a dingy gray hall. He didn't speak, so I didn't either. Voices from around a corner drew near, then Walter Colby strode toward us. He seemed to fill the hallway and didn't appear to be looking where he was going. He also didn't appear as genial as he had in the bank two days ago. I wondered what he was doing there. Had he been questioned about the murder, too?

The officer in front of me stopped. Colby pushed past him without acknowledging his presence or mine. After the door to the lobby slammed shut, the officer turned to me.

"Real polite, that one." He raised his eyebrows.

I nodded and smiled. His friendliness settled my nerves. I waited while he knocked on a door farther down the hall. He pushed it open and held it for me.

Chief Flaherty sat behind a wide desk. He stood, dismissing the officer with a waving salute and a nod. "Good morning. Please sit down, Dr. Rousseau." He gestured to a chair in front of the desk.

I returned his greeting and sat. I held one hand firmly with the other in my lap, silently instructing them not to fidget.

"So, don't you think it's unusual, finding two bodies in as many months?" His voice was quietly insistent.

I tried to keep my tone casual. "Sure, it's unusual. It was complete chance that I discovered them both. Most people don't even find one body in a lifetime."

He kept his eyes on me as if he could somehow induce worry. Concern upset my stomach like a couple of sparring crustaceans, but I wasn't going to tell him that.

"Do I have your permission to record this interview?" Flaherty pointed his head at a small black device on his desk. A cable connected it to a desktop computer on the floor.

"Yes." I wanted to keep my answers as simple as possible. "That's a digital device?"

"It is. Lots easier to use than having all those cassette tapes to keep track of. It even works with speech-recognition software. I can dictate a report and print it out instantly." He beamed at the little machine as if he were its proud father. He looked up at me and cleared his throat. He clicked the device on with a mouse. He said his name, the date, and that he had my permission to record the conversation.

"This is an informational interview with Lauren Rousseau. Please state your address, date of birth, and occupation."

"Eight Upper Summer Street here in Ashford. November 14, 1985. I am an associate professor of linguistics at Agawam College in Millsbury."

"So that's why you go by Dr. Rousseau."

I shrugged. "It's only a title."

"But you're not a real doctor." He raised his eyebrows.

I returned his gaze in silence. I'd had this discussion before and didn't need to defend my doctor of philosophy degree.

"Please relay the events of May twenty-fourth."

I wondered why a lesser officer wasn't the one to babysit me and the voice recorder. Surely the chief of police had better things to do. I started talking. I went through the whole afternoon again. The beach. The thing I thought was a flower. Finding Charles Heard.

Flaherty held up a hand. "Describe in detail how he looked. What you touched."

"He was lying downhill. I mean, his head was lower than his feet. Pretty much on his back. Well, you saw him." I released my hands and extended both with palms up above the desk. Did he really need me to repeat all this?

"Please, this is for the record."

I sighed. "His left arm was up kind of over his face. His shirt—it was white, that was why I saw it—had blood on the collar. His neck looked like it was cut. I only touched his cheek. It, he didn't feel alive."

"Did you move the body? Search it?"

"No."

"You didn't see any weapon around? A knife? A razor?"

"No, nothing. I didn't look around. I had to find somebody to help."

"Why didn't you run back to the beach?"

"I thought somebody would be at the estate." The agitation I had felt the day before thrummed through me again. My voice shook. "I wasn't sure I'd find anyone on the beach at that hour. I just thought . . ."

"Continue, please." Flaherty folded his hands on his desk. He drilled his eyes into mine.

I tried to calm myself. "I ran up the Allée. I thought someone was in a shed, I heard a noise there, but nobody answered. I made it to the mansion but it was locked." I kept my voice flat and even. "I was heading down the main drive when that Bobby guy appeared."

"Appeared?" The chief's eyebrows went up along with his intonation.

"Yeah. He wasn't there and then he was. I have no idea where he'd been. He told me, eventually, that I could use a phone in the office. So I did."

Flaherty continued to gaze at me.

I'd read enough crime stories to know this was a tactic. Stay silent long enough to make the other person nervous and they'll make a mistake. I have no mistake to make, I thought, and nothing more to say. Two could play at this. Particularly when one was a Quaker.

Flaherty cleared his throat. "Do you have anything else to tell me? For example, about your fight with Mr. Heard two days ago?"

I met his eyes. "As I mentioned last night, sir, it was not a fight. I disagreed with the Heard Insurance policy of giving very little grace time for paying homeowner's insurance. That's all."

"How long had you known Charles Heard?"

"I didn't know him!" Oops. Now my voice was rising. Down, girl. "I had my insurance policy with his company. That's it."

"Was anyone in your family acquainted with him?"

I stared. What did he mean by that? "I very much doubt that. I suppose it's possible, but I never heard anyone mention his name. My sister Jackie also lives in town. You can ask her, I guess. But it's pretty unlikely. She works a lot."

"Her last name is Rousseau, as well?"

I nodded.

"Thank you for your time." He switched off the device. "If you think of something else you'd like to tell me, please call anytime." The chief's voice took on a warm, friendly tone. "People can remember details days later that they hadn't realized they'd seen at a crime scene."

Edith Maxwell

I stood and said I would call if I thought of something. "Do you have any suspects? It's creepy to think a murderer is walking around out there."

"Thanks again for coming in."

Ah. Stonewalled. "When's the last time you had a murder in Ashford?"

"Why do you want to know?"

"I'm curious. I'm a voting resident. Don't I have a right to ask my friendly local police chief a question?"

It was his turn to sigh. Turning to the door, he said, "1986." He ushered me down the hall. At the exit, he said, "Please don't discuss the details of the crime scene around town."

In the street outside the building, I wondered how a small-town department that hadn't experienced violent death in so long was going to be able to track down a killer at large. The chief must have been a fresh recruit the year of the previous murder. The year after I was born.

26

Chapter Four

"Kaliméra" I called out as I entered Iris's Bakery a few minutes later. I sat at a little table by the front window.

Iris returned the greeting in Greek and said, "What, you on vacation now?" She smoothed her bottle-blond hair and tugged a pink apron down over hefty black-clad hips.

"Semester's over. And not a minute too soon. I'd much rather be here than in my office at the college preparing a linguistics lecture. You know, I love my job and the students. It's just nice to have a break."

"Good. Coffee?"

I ordered my usual: double espresso with steamed milk and a scone. "How's business?" I asked. Which was a dumb question, since the small shop was full and several take-out customers waited in front of a glass display case full of delectable pastries, breads, and Greek pies.

"It's good." Iris delivered a blueberry scone glistening with a sugary egg wash.

I opened the latest *New Yorker*. I had work to do this summer, but it could wait a few days. I made my way through several paragraphs, then closed the magazine when Iris brought my coffee. "Join me for a minute?"

Iris looked around. "Sure. Joey can handle the counter." She took the chair across from me, smiling as she watched her teenage son in action.

"Shouldn't he be in school?"

Iris shook her head. "It's some teacher in-service day."

"He's really growing up. He's going to be a senior in the fall, right?"

Iris nodded and then frowned. "I hope he makes it."

I raised my eyebrows.

"He likes cooking a lot more than studying. And those friends of his, they just want him to go drinking all the time. I tell him he has to finish high school." She sighed and then brightened. "Some news, yeah? A murder in Ashford."

I nodded. Should I tell Iris I had found the body? If I did, it'd be all over town in an hour. If I didn't, my friend's feelings would be hurt when she found out.

"I hear you the one found his body." Iris's eyes widened.

So much for that decision. "The police chief asked me not to talk about the details. So don't ask."

Iris nodded sagely, then cocked her head. "Who do you think did it? You know . . ." She made the universal slashing gesture across her throat and uttered a high-pitched *keek*.

I shuddered. Did Iris know how Charles Heard had been killed? Had even that detail traveled the gossip lines? Or was she only making the iconic gesture and sound effect for murder?

Iris leaned in. "You know, him and Walter Colby got some history don't have nothing to do with the Trustees." She looked around the room and lowered her voice to a level I could barely hear. "You shoulda seen Charlie in here yesterday morning, too. Him and Mr. Wojinski—you know, he's on the school board—really got into it. And Charlie's sister . . ."

"Ma!" Joey yelled from behind the cash register. He gestured with a rolling motion at the line of customers. "Oh, hi, Dr. Roo." He waved at me.

I'd known Joey since he was seven, when he'd shortened Rousseau to a simple Roo.

Iris stood. Adjusting her apron again, she returned to work. "Tomorrow we go walking on the beach, yeah?" she said over her shoulder.

"You bet." In the summer, I visited Holt Beach almost daily. Late May wasn't quite summer, but it had been balmy recently. I thought I'd stay out of the trees and in the open for the foreseeable future, though.

I resumed reading. The coffee shop bustled around me. The stream of customers ebbed and flowed, the murmur of conversation punctuated by a laugh here, a whisper there. A number of the faces were familiar, since I came here often, but I was still a relative newcomer to town, having lived in Ashford for less than a decade. In this corner of New England, if your grandmother wasn't born in town, you were still from "away." Even my children, should I ever be ready to have any, would have a distance to go on that yardstick.

When the crush lightened, Iris ambled back over and perched next to me. Leaning in, she said, "Mr. Wojinski was steaming yesterday. He told Charlie off, all right, said them Trustees were making the children of his former students suffer. He talked to Charlie like he was still a kid." She checked around the room and went on, "Then Charlie, he says, 'Mr. Wojinski, you can keep your nose out of school business and out of my business. You're not my teacher now.'"

I shrugged. "Local politics. Sort of bad timing for this Mr. Wojinski, though, right? I mean with Charles turning up dead a few hours later?"

Iris nodded. "You bet." Joey gestured from the counter. "Oops," Iris said, and returned to work.

A fit man with neatly trimmed white hair held the door for a woman with her brows drawn together. She was thin, with a short cap of salt-and-pepper hair.

"Why are we here, James?"

"Fiona, this is Iris's Bakery. You remember Iris." He led her to a table. "Now sit down while I buy our breakfast."

The woman sat and began to tap two fingers on the table. "I know where I am, James." She didn't look at him.

I watched her. The woman's hands were weathered, and her thick fingers looked like she did physical work with them. Perhaps she was a weaver or a farmer.

James greeted Iris, and I glanced up when I heard Iris address him as Mr. Wojinski. He looked pretty mild-mannered to be accosting one of the fabled Trustees. He wore a short-sleeved plaid shirt tucked into belted jeans. His tan and his trim physique brought to mind a lifelong tennis player or maybe a runner. I turned my head back to my magazine.

"What can I get you today, Ms. Heard?"

I raised my head again.

A slim woman in linen slacks and a silk blouse stood at the counter. She appeared to be around fifty, but she'd clearly taken the advice not only of her beautician but also of her dermatologist. Her few wrinkles were fine and her skin pale and without age spots.

"Only coffee today, Iris. Black." Her large green eyes pulled down at the edges.

She must be Charles's wife. Widow. Why was she already out fetching her own coffee?

"I'm so sorry for your loss, dear." Iris leaned across the counter and patted the woman's hand.

Mr. Wojinski, still at the counter, murmured the same.

"Thank you, both." The woman lifted her chin as she picked up her cup. She handed money to Iris and left. She eased the door shut behind her.

From my vantage point by the window, I saw the woman carry the coffee across to the parking lot that bordered the former mill buildings. She walked with straight back and measured stride, like a queen. She climbed into a silver Jaguar.

I returned my eyes to my article. Enough with the small-town intrigues, including a murder that was none of my business. I had a vacation to enjoy.

• • •

I spent the afternoon puttering in my condo. I walked Wulu, read, and tried to do anything but think about dead bodies. On my way to Zac's for dinner, I remembered to drop the sweater at the mansion. Wednesday was our usual dinner night. I used to look forward to it, but now with Marie-Fleur there, it felt a bit awkward. And I certainly couldn't spend the night.

As I drove up the hill to the mansion, a group of people crossed the road. It looked like a tour of some kind, with an outdoorsy kind of man leading the way and gesturing. I parked and found my way to the office where I'd used the phone the day before.

Bobby Spirokis opened the door at my knock.

"I'm Lauren, from yesterday. You let me use the phone."

"Okay." He stood blocking the doorway with arms folded.

"I'm returning the sweater."

He didn't reach for it.

I finally extended the sweater and he accepted it, but he didn't look as if he wanted to.

"Thank her for me, please," I said. He was an odd bird, I thought, as I climbed back into my truck.

When Zac met me at the door of his apartment, he pointed his eyes into the room behind him. Marie-Fleur sulked on the couch, twisting her Justin Bieber bracelet, her hot pink high-tops firmly planted on the coffee table.

I greeted the girl. "What's going on, Marie-Fleur?"

She ignored me. She stared out the window as only a tween could.

Zac came up behind me. Putting his arm around my waist, he said, "The school canceled her class field trip. To the Museum of Natural History in Cambridge."

"Oh, no. Why?"

Marie-Fleur finally met my eyes. "They lied to us. They broke their promise."

I knew how much the girl loved all things animal and how much she'd been looking forward to this trip. I also knew how much the eleven-year-old missed her mother and, while living with her favorite uncle for a few months was fun, it wasn't the same as being at home.

"That's terrible, honey." I resolved to take her out for some girl time before Zac accompanied her back to Haiti after school was out for the summer.

"Marie-Fleur, they didn't lie," Zac said. "It was because of the Mother's Day flood—they had to spend money to clean up, and that was the money that was supposed to fund the field trip."

Marie-Fleur tucked her feet up on the couch and looked away.

"It's pretty bad at school, though." Zac shook his head. "They're out of paper, out of supplies of all kinds. They're even canceling foreign languages for next year."

"They are? That's terrible."

"I know. Don't you read the *Chronicle*? They have an article about this stuff every week. You know, about the Trustees not paying up what they're legally obliged to."

"I've been too busy to read the paper. And all that business this spring, with Jamal killed and me trying to put a muderer behind bars. I was a little preoccupied. I guess I'm catching up on local news all at once."

"Well, it's nuts. As are the major players, except for that, what's his name? Wojeski or something?"

"Mr. Wojinski. He seems like a good guy. Taught at the high school for years, Iris told me. Recently retired." I turned to the girl. "So, Marie, when is school out?"

"My name's Marie-Fleur." She sighed and picked up a purple cell phone. When it was clear that she was determined to text her friend rather than talk, I turned to Zac. He steered me into the kitchen, where smells of pasta and tomatoes greeted us.

Zac stirred a pot on the stove. "She's really disappointed about that trip. You know, it seems criminal that the schools are taking this hit when they don't have to."

I agreed as I perched on a stool. I inhaled. "Smells good. What're we having?"

"Your basic spaghetti and meatballs. Haitian-style, of course."

I wondered what Haitian-style meatballs were, but since I'd yet to be disappointed by Zac's cooking, I decided to wait and see. It was very convenient to have a sometime boyfriend who could cook, especially since I couldn't. Or didn't usually, anyway.

"How's work been?" I addressed his back.

"Had an interesting case where I had to demultiplex about twelve cameras. And then on camera ten I spied the guy just strolling down one of the halls. I used the height standard to figure out his size, too."

Video forensics jargon was only partially intelligible to me, but I knew he liked his job as a civilian with the police department, and he'd helped to find my student's murderer only a month ago. He was entitled to use as much esoteric language as he wanted, in my opinion.

"So I bought our tickets to Port-au-Prince." Zac waved his spoon and bits of tomato sauce flecked the cupboard door. "Oops."

"When are you guys taking off?" I knew he had planned to escort Marie-Fleur home.

"Soon as school's out, which is supposed to be June fifteenth. We fly the seventeenth." He looked at me. "Sure you don't want to go? You could meet Gran."

I smiled and shook my head. I wasn't sure I was ready to meet the grandmother who had partly raised him. Yet. "I won that grant to develop a new course this summer. My travel's going to be from my condo to the beach and back. Next time."

I helped him set the table, and the three of us sat to eat. When I stretched my hands out to each of them for a moment of silence, Marie-Fleur surprised me by putting her small cool hand in mine and accepting the hand Zac had offered her, too. She usually rolled her eyes and said something about dumb Quakers. I closed my eyes and counted my considerable blessings, then squeezed each of their hands before letting go.

Marie-Fleur crossed herself before she picked up her fork. She tasted a bite and her eyes widened. "Tonton, this is just like Mama's!" She chewed with a smile on her face.

"Of course! She's my twin. We both learned to cook from Gran."

I savored the spicy sauce. "Why does it taste so, I don't know, Caribbean?" I asked Zac.

He winked at Marie-Fleur. "Secret. We can't tell regular Americans, can we?"

Marie-Fleur nodded with a conspiratorial air.

I bet the girl would have an apron on next time I came for dinner and would have cooked half the meal. Zac adored his twin sister's only daughter. I knew he didn't approve that Pia had felt the need to send the girl away for a few months, because she'd recently remarried and wanted time alone. But he was glad for the time with his niece and wanted to make her happy. Zac wanted to make everybody happy, including me. Who wasn't quite ready for that.

• • •

Iris and I met in the resident-only parking area at Holt Beach the next morning. This early in the season, it didn't matter that a special parking lot was reserved for Ashford residents, but later in the summer, it was a real perk to be able to bypass the hundreds of cars waiting to park on a sweltering Saturday.

We set out on the boardwalk that led over the dunes. I paused at the top and took in the warm breezy air as I surveyed one of my favorite vistas. The beach stretched out to the right for several miles, with the edge of Rockport across the water in the distance. To the left the beach curved around across the sound from Sandy Point on Plum Island. The strip of sand on this side narrowed where the woods came down to almost meet a cluster of smooth rocks. The woods where Charles Heard might have taken his last breath.

A tern dive-bombed the gentle swells and came up with a fish in its mouth. I looked at Iris. "Did you see that?"

Iris nodded and inhaled deeply. "This place always makes me feel better, you know?"

I agreed as we continued. "You sure you can take the time away from the bakery?"

"No problem. Morning rush is already over and my helper can handle it for an hour."

We left our sandals at the bottom of the stairs.

"Left or right?" I asked.

Iris pointed left. I frowned. Did I really want to walk past the murder scene? I'd have to someday, might as well make it today.

We set out across the sand, catching up on each other's news. I never minded running or walking the beach alone, but it was always more fun with Iris. The warmth of the midmorning sunshine was a balm. A sea breeze riffed our hair. A group of teenagers played Frisbee. Couples sat reading, children dug in the sand by the water, and two young women enjoyed a snooze on a blanket as they tanned, but the beach was largely quiet this early in the season.

The tide was in, so the water almost covered the rocky area. We managed to weave our way around the bend to the last stretch of sand before the Ashford River joined the sea. I shuddered as I glanced up the hill to my left at the thick woods that separated the beach from the grand Holt Estate above it. The lowest trees barely hung on to their perch on the sandy cliff. The dark underbrush presented an ominous contrast to the light on the ocean and the carefree feeling of walking on vacation. Especially with the image of Charles Heard's dead body superimposed on the arboreal forms.

"See why they call it Steep Hill Beach?" Iris asked as I examined the hill.

"It's definitely a steep hill."

"That's where you found Charlie Heard, right?"

I nodded.

"What'd he look like?"

"Chief Flaherty asked me not to talk about it, Iris. It was pretty awful. I don't really want to even think about it, to tell the truth."

We picked our way through the rocks and came out to another stretch of sand. The cottages on the Bluffs, the source of all good and bad that stemmed from the Trustees' oversight, marched up the hill across the channel. A water tower kept watch from atop the hill and was probably a lifesaver to the residents of that tiny peninsula.

"What's that?" I pointed to shrubby undergrowth on the dune behind us. "I've seen them forever, but I don't know what they're called."

"Beach plums. Those plants'll take over if you let 'em. Them and the Rosa rugosa."

"Don't you make jam or something out of them?" I remembered a little jar of a sweet, clear, tangy spread Iris had given me at Christmas one year.

"Both the rose hips and the beach plums make great jelly. Because they're so tart."

We continued our walk all the way to where the smaller beach ended and the river merged with the ocean. Marshy green flats lined the waterway as it stretched inland. An intrepid local in a wet suit paddled his way past in a long red kayak, raising one end of the double-edged paddle in greeting. I heard an engine and saw a fishing boat approach the small wharf on the Bluffs side.

"So what is the deal with the Trustees and the town?" I asked Iris. "Everybody is so upset about it. On both sides."

"I'm surprised you don't know more about it."

"You know, I've been so busy getting tenure I haven't paid much attention to the town I actually live in. That's going to change from here on out."

Iris shook her head. "I been hearing about this business since I was a little kid. Some guy, Payne I think was his name, gave the Bluffs in trust to educate the children of the town in the 1600s. It was only boys back then, but it used to be simple. The Trustees are supposed to give any rents from the land to the town schools."

"The schools seem to be struggling these days."

"Well, the trust worked for about three hundred forty years of the three hundred fifty Then the Trustees just stopped giving money. And now since the economy's gotten worse, you know, the state isn't sending us much and everything costs more. My Joey's good at languages, but they cut his German teacher. Cut French and Latin, too. Now all's they got is Spanish."

I looked over at some of the houses across the water. "They call those cottages, but some are pretty fancy. The Trustees are collecting nice rents off those, right?"

Iris shrugged and leaned down to pick up a horseshoe crab shell. "Weird thing is, the tenants own the houses. They only pay rent on the land. And there was some big water project a few years back. But anyway, those Trustees still oughta pay money to the schools. And they aren't."

"Nothing? That's outrageous."

"Not a cent the last few years, and only peanuts for ten years before that." Iris threw the shell into the water with a strong arm and looked satisfied when it landed with a splash some yards out. She checked her watch. "Oops, it's ten thirty. I gotta be back for lunch prep."

We turned and retraced our steps. As we passed the woods, an osprey flew overhead with a desperately struggling fish in its enormous talons. The powerful bird of prey landed on a dead tree that reached stark branches above the tree line. I felt its keen eye watching me.

• • •

At home an hour later, I pressed the End button on my cell phone. Wow. I gazed out the window. Zac was leaving that afternoon with Marie-Fleur for Haiti. Something to do with his sister's health. I hoped she'd be all right. I'd agreed to run over for a quick farewell lunch with them. Then the summer could stretch out as a blank slate. That was a nice prospect. And a month or two without Zac. That might be a good thing, too. It was going to happen anyway, but now he was leaving sooner. The intensity of his feelings had been increasing. So had my discomfort with being the focus of his emotions.

I hoped missing the end of the school year wouldn't harm Marie-Fleur academically. Or socially, for that matter. Then I thought about what the last few weeks of any given school year had been like for myself and laughed. My mother had been a middle-school teacher before she retrained as a technical writer. She used to complain that the stretch between Memorial Day and the start of summer vacation was a complete waste of time.

I surveyed the mess that represented my home office. During the semester I never had the chance or the energy to file papers and clear up clutter. As soon as I got home from lunch, I'd get on it.

• • •

At four o'clock that afternoon, I was hard at work in a karate dojo downtown. After a set of basic karate punches, I wiped the sweat from my forehead with a quick swipe. I settled deeper into the horse stance—legs wide, knees above feet, pelvis tilted under—and resumed punching as the martial arts class counted in unison.

"*Ichi! Ni! San! Shi! Go!*"

Sensei Dan Talbot strolled behind the rows that started with little six-year-old Josh in the front and ended with me, the newcomer, in the back. I felt my left elbow strike the teacher's wide palm as I jabbed it back, at the same time twisting and punching forward with my right fist.

"Tuck that arm right in at your side when you strike backward. More power that way."

I nodded. I knew that but was a few years out of practice. I switched sides. This time my elbow knocked into his hand with more force.

37

"Good."

"*Roku! Shichi! Hachi! Kyuuu . . .*" The class extended the vowel of "nine" in unison. "*Juu!*"

"And sit," the teacher said.

We all dropped to sitting on our knees on the mats, backs erect. I was impressed by the students' discipline.

"Now for kicks." Sensei strolled to the front. "Rousseau," he barked. He beckoned me forward. "You remember your round-house?"

I nodded. I ran to the front. I faced the teacher and bounced in a less wide stance than before for a few beats, fists up in defensive position. I lifted and turned my right knee, twisted my lower leg up, and as if sweeping the top of a table while I leaned to the left, connected the top of my bare foot on Sensei's defensive arm.

My lower back twinged as I returned to standing. Running used an entirely different set of muscles.

"That's pretty much the idea." Sensei bowed to me.

I bowed in return, elbows out, one fist in the palm of my other hand. I headed back to my place. But I barely saw the other white-suited participants. Instead my body remembered the last roundhouse kick before this one. I'd sent my attacker tumbling down a flight of steps only weeks earlier. I shook off the memory as I knelt in the present.

Sensei turned to the children in the class. "Maddie, want to give it a try?"

A little green-belted redhead trotted to the front.

"Let's see a left front kick followed by a roundhouse with your right. Make sure you keep your guard up."

Her gap-toothed smile flashed at the teacher, then she bowed, instantly serious, keeping her eyes on the teacher's. She bobbed on her feet for three beats as I had, then spun into motion. Her lightning-fast kicks were perfect, as was her upward-swept arm that blocked Sensei's punch.

They bowed to each other. Maddie dropped back into her place, smiling again. If I ever have a child, I thought, I'd want one like that. Strong, sweet, fearless. And way cute.

Sensei ordered us to pair up and practice kicking and blocking. "We're not sparring yet. I want you to go for precision and strength. Kickers, aim well and follow through. Blockers, turn your opponent's energy away from you. Use their strength against them. *Hajimemashoo.* Begin."

Ten minutes before the end of the session, after a final demonstration featured Sensei sparring with an aspiring brown belt, the teacher called us all to sit. He took his place facing the class. He placed his hands on his knees and murmured words in Japanese that I didn't catch. The room fell silent. Oh. Meditation. That I could do. The energy of thirty students winding down from an hour and a half of learning to fight was very different from Sunday mornings sitting in silent worship with Friends. My previous sensei had been all business, all about fighting. I'd had trouble integrating that with my Quaker belief in nonviolence. I loved the discipline, the exercise, the self-defense readiness that karate gave me. It spoke to me. But this sensei's more spiritual approach to the martial arts was welcome.

After class, Sensei approached me as I shrugged into my jacket.

"And?" He smiled, gesturing with arms open.

I looked into hazel eyes. He had been a treat to watch. Long fluid legs in loose white pants. Strong forearms sliding out from the sleeves. A black belt cinched around a slim waist. His neck and chest now glistened with exertion, or what I could see of his chest under the V of the quilted *gi* top. When sensations fluttered inside, I admonished them with a deep breath.

"Great. It felt great. You know, it's been a long time . . ."

"Did you say ten years?" His thick dark eyebrows rose. "You haven't practiced karate in that long?"

"Not since I lived in Japan." I stretched my arms and winced. "I'm a runner, I think I told you, but these muscles? It's like they remember how to kick and how to punch, but they aren't in shape to actually do it."

"Show up at every class and you'll be caught up in no time. And we'll get you caught up on your belts, too. See you Monday?"

I agreed as I fingered the white belt wrapped twice around my own waist, a color befitting a student showing up at a new dojo. I'd been a brown belt in Japan, nearly ready to test for black, when I'd received the acceptance letter from Indiana University and had headed off to graduate school. Achieving first a PhD and then tenure back home at Agawam College left me little time for any exercise except solitary runs I could fit in at any time of the day or night.

Now tenured Associate Professor Rousseau had the summer off. I'd nearly been taken hostage in the spring. My memory of how to execute a roundhouse kick had been the only thing that saved me and put my attacker behind bars. And after finding Charles Heard's body, I'd decided it was finally time to regain my identity as a *karateka*, a student who practiced the ancient art of "empty hand."

Plus, a teacher as good to look at as this one was extra motivation. Ouch. I frowned as I left the dojo. The twinge this time wasn't from my back but from my conscience. Wasn't I committed to Zac? Was I?

Chapter Five

I heard my house phone ringing and raced to unlock the door of my condo. I fumbled with the keys and dropped them. I cursed and started over. The phone went silent right before I reached it inside.

Sighing, I filled a glass of water at the tap and drank it down. I sank into the chair next to the phone, my body alive and relaxed in the way that only an exhausting, sweaty ninety-minute workout can produce. The sore muscles and stiff joints would come tomorrow or, more likely, right in time for Monday's class.

I pressed the phone message number. It was Zac, from the airport, wanting to tell me goodbye one more time before he boarded. I considered calling him right back. No, we'd had our goodbyes earlier. Better to let him go.

Wulu, after circling my chair several times, looked up and gave a pert bark.

Oh, yeah. Dinnertime for doggies. Maybe a quick walk first, although I'd much rather just sit. Sip a glass of wine, savor a plate of pasta, and read a good mystery. Instead, I checked my reflection in the hall mirror, resecured my auburn hair in a ponytail, and grabbed Wulu's leash.

"Come on, buddy," I said. The sun, a month before the summer solstice, still hovered well above the horizon. I didn't need any more exercise today. I let Wulu poke around the edge of the woods across the road. I marveled at my dog's ability to explore a world of smell inaccessible to the person at the other end of the purple leash.

I looked down the road at my condo, one of four in an antique house. It sat about halfway up a steep hill that peaked in an under-maintained park. The trees and underbrush across the road from me grew densely, a tangle of sumac, northern spicebush, and mountain laurel amid the tall maples, plus the occasional donation of a crumpled coffee cup or somebody's fast-food lunch bag. Sometimes I scooped up bits of trash in the same plastic bag I used to pick up Wulu's leavings.

As the dog made up his mind where to do his business, I tilted my head back. I searched the treetops for the Baltimore oriole I heard pealing its full, clear call. I held up one hand to shield my eyes from the sun. Surprised by the roar of an engine, I nearly fell over.

A pickup truck raced down the hill. It knocked and clattered over the uneven pavement. It headed straight for me.

"Hey!" I leapt sideways into the brush at the same time I yanked Wulu in close. Branches raked at me. Wulu yelped.

The truck, a dirty red, flew by me with inches to spare. After it passed, I twisted to look. It careered around the corner at the bottom onto High Street. I heard brakes squeal and a horn blare. I winced. I expected a sickening slam of metal on metal, but it didn't come.

Wulu scrambled onto the road. He pulled up to his full height of twelve inches and barked down the hill where the truck had been.

I swore as I extricated myself from the berm. My knee ached. Scratches reddened my hands. A spot on my cheek stung on the same side as the eye I'd hurt in the Holt woods.

"What was that, Wu?" I inhaled deeply and tried to calm my angry, upset center. I strolled with Wulu up and down in front of my house. When he stopped, I stopped. I closed my eyes in a moment of prayer, struggling to hold myself and Wulu in the Light. I ought to hold the driver, too, but I wasn't a saint, and extending forgiveness to some stranger with whom I was still furious was too much for now. Maybe later.

When Wulu tugged on his leash, I cleaned up after him, dropped the plastic bag in the trash barrel, and let us back into the condo. Time for that glass of wine. Better yet, a glass of Scotch.

I stood at my front window and looked up the road. Who would want to run me down? I'd tried to see the license plate number, but the plate had been covered with what looked like dried mud. I shook my head and sipped the whiskey. The smooth liquid warmed my throat and my core.

I set down the glass and picked up the phone. I pressed the numbers for the nonemergency police number and several minutes later was still talking.

"Listen, this person was some kind of maniac. Somebody else could get killed. Why can't you put an officer on it?" I'd been trying the whole time to convince the police dispatcher that the crazed driver posed a danger to the town.

"Ma'am, like I said, I'll file a report. And I'll get the word out to a cruiser, but they're currently occupied on other calls."

Maybe Natalia Flores could help track down the red truck. The local officer had helped me after Jamal was killed. I pressed the speed dial for Jackie on her cell phone. Natalia and Jackie were usually together when they weren't working.

"Natalia happen to be around?" I asked. "I almost got run down by some maniac on my street. I called the station, but it seems like only the dispatcher is there now. She said she'd let the cruisers know, but—"

"Are you all right?"

"I am. So's Wulu. We had to leap into the woods to avoid being run over. I'm still shaking."

"Good. But Nat's not here. She's off to the big city for TDY. Temporary officer training or something. For a couple of months."

"She is? Which big city?"

Jackie laughed. "Boston. I guess it's like being an exchange student. Except one of theirs doesn't come up here. She's even staying down there, because of the weird shifts they pull."

"So she won't be back until the end of summer?"

"Nope."

"Darn. It was like the truck was aiming straight for me. Me and Wulu."

"Why would someone try to run you down? Maybe the sun glared in the driver's eyes and they couldn't see you. Or whoever was driving was late for work or had an emergency or something?"

I held the phone at arm's length and stared at it, then brought it back to my cheek. "You don't believe me! Crap, Jackie. I was almost run over."

"Calm down, Lauren. I'm sure the police will look into it and they can figure out what to do. Right?"

"I guess. It's been a tough week. Did you hear I found Charles Heard's body?"

"Yeah. How are you doing with that, *Schwesterchen?*"

I smiled at the nickname Jackie had used for me since high school German class, then grew serious. "It's pretty creepy. I even had to go into the station to file a report after I'd already told them what happened."

"Standard operating procedure, I'm sure."

I heard the click of a lighter. "Are you getting high?" My own voice was high, too. Here I was upset, and my sister not only didn't believe me about the crazed driver but was blowing me off by smoking some pot.

"Yes, Lauren." Jackie spoke slowly as if to a child. "I am getting high. You know I can't when Natalia is around. Very sorry if this inconveniences you."

"I'll talk to you later." I disconnected. My relationship with my big sister somehow never went smoothly, despite how close we were. Maybe we were too close.

• • •

I sat up in bed Saturday morning and yawned. Sunlight buffed the wide pine boards in my bedroom with a golden glow. An early golden glow. The curtainless windows made sleeping in at this time of year difficult. But I preferred seeing what Mama Nature was doing out there every morning to hiding behind dust-gathering draperies. My second-floor windows faced a majestic old horse chestnut tree instead of the windows of nosy neighbors, so undressing at night wasn't a problem, either.

I whistled as I puttered in my kitchen. A good night's sleep had diminished my anger from the night before. Jackie could be right— the maniac might have been late for work. Desperate to get to a wife in labor. Blinded by the sun in the west.

I ground Peruvian dark roasted beans from Zumi's and brewed a pot of coffee. Zac always insisted a French press made better coffee. I like my java hot, though, and the French press let it cool off too much. I stuck with my little four-cup drip machine.

A familiar slow warble sounded through the open window. I leaned into the screen and smiled. There was that oriole I'd been looking for, right at the outer edge of the chestnut. He flashed his brilliant orange breast and flew off to court his baby mama for the season.

Still whistling, I cleaned Wulu's bowls. When I filled them with water and kibble, the curly figure raced up in a blur of black and started to munch. I wiped down the counter, poured a mug of coffee, added a dash of milk, and sat at the round table I had refinished the summer before. It, too, gleamed in the morning sun.

"Wu, why do I feel so happy?" I asked, chin on hand.

Wulu, busy with breakfast, did not respond.

I decided I might as well admit to myself that I felt at peace because I felt free. Zac was going to be in Haiti until August. For the moment, or for a couple of months, commitment and accountability were at bay. I realized I was whistling the classic "Summertime, and the livin' is easy . . ."

Oh. That had been Daddy's song. My summery mood dissipated like a cold river current colliding with a warm stream. No one had ever explained my father's disappearance and subsequent death to my satisfaction. I was only nineteen when it happened. My mother, despite her incessant good cheer and ubiquitous intelligence, seemed to wear blinders when it came to her late husband. My sisters weren't much help, either. One was estranged from the family and another was residing in a state prison for a few years. And Jackie, a successful computer scientist whose only vices appeared to be marijuana and a penchant for competent women? Jackie refused to talk about Daddy.

• • •

I loped down the last hill of Toil-in-Vain Road. My running route was a hilly three miles and was virtually traffic-free. The woods opened up to the tidal creek that shared the road's name and the salt marshes that kept most of the town's borders with the sea from being beachfront property. It was going to be another sunny spring day. Light glistened on the creek water as it rushed under the bridge.

I sprinted over the bridge, heading for the extension. The narrow roadway bisecting the marsh often flooded at extreme high tides. It dead-ended in the Holt sisters' white gate, the gate across a road most maps and GPS systems showed as going through to Argilla Road and then the beach. I slowed at the small blue colonial tucked in a grove of tall pines at the corner. I'd found my friend Elise nearly dead of a heroin overdose in this house in March. It still gave me the creeps. It was almost always empty. The owners seemed to occupy it only for a couple of weeks in August.

A green panel van sat in the drive. Halting my run, I walked cautiously toward the home weathered from age and salt air. The driver's door of the van stood open. Strains of Bruce Springsteen blared out into air usually accompanied only by the whoosh of wind through treetops, the cries of gulls and hawks, the barking of a dog from the neighbor farther down the road. An electric saw keened, then stopped.

I peered around the corner of the house. A tall dark-haired man wearing jeans, a T-shirt, and a carpenter's leather tool belt hammered nails into a clapboard. Humming to the music, he turned with a graceful move, and then started as he caught sight of me.

"Hey!" Recognition crept over his face and he smiled. "Lauren-san. You startled me there for a minute."

It was Sensei. Dan Talbot. Carpenter Dan, by the looks of it. "Hey, yourself." I returned the smile. I grabbed the corner of my T-shirt sleeve and wiped my forehead. "I guess teaching karate isn't your only job."

"That's right. This is what I really do." He gestured toward the table saw set up on the scraggly grass and the pile of clapboard.

"The place needs some improvement." I shook my head at the peeling paint. Rotted wood at the bottom edges of the screen door competed with cracked glass and chipped glazing calling out to be repaired.

"Yeah. The owner recently passed. His daughter asked me to whip the house into shape for sale." He stuck a pencil behind his ear. As he raised his arms, folding his hands atop his head, a band of taut skin flaunted itself between his shirt and the top of his jeans.

I looked, and then looked away. "That's sad." I bounced on my heels so my muscles wouldn't tighten up.

"So what are you doing sneaking up on me out here?" Sensei's yellowy green shirt matched his eyes. He ran those eyes along my bare legs and up to my face.

A face that concealed nothing. My half-Irish skin blushed hard and easily. I cleared my throat. "I was, um, this is . . . I run. My route." I shook my head again, this time at my own peeling façade, at being tongue-tied like a teenager in front of this man.

He picked up another board and turned to his saw, laughing. He glanced up. "Well, better get back to it." He winked. "The run."

Dismissed. Fine. The snick and thwap of his tape measure on the board resonated in my ears. I turned and ran on toward the white gate. I kicked at a pebble. It went flying into the newly sprouting points of salt marsh grass that poked up from marshy water. When the tide was high like this, the creek flooded the marshes. I stopped and stretched at the gate, then headed back.

"All he was doing was checking out my legs," I muttered as I ran. "I'm the one who put on running shorts. It's not like he asked me out on a date or something."

As I approached the blue house again, I whipped my head to the left. I caught a smooth streak of movement in the sky. I smiled. "Sensei! Come look. Quick."

Dan dashed out onto the road. His eyebrows were drawn together, his eyes alarmed. He was about to speak when I grabbed his arm and pointed with my other hand.

"Great blue heron," I whispered. The huge bird flapped its slow graceful wings across the marsh, then extended long legs and landed on a high spot. "It's the first one I've seen this spring. A special omen." I turned and looked up at Sensei.

He was gazing at me, not at where the heron had lit. It felt like those hazel eyes swallowed me up and took me dancing in a pavilion on a steamy evening.

"Speaking of special," he said. "You know, you should call me Dan. I do have a name, after all."

"Oh-kay, then." I detached my hand from his arm. I looked back at the heron but it had flown on. I looked back at him. His eyes now crinkled with a private joke.

"As you said, I'd better get back to my run. Dan." I turned and took a step.

"Oh, Lauren." Dan held his hand up to stop me. "After class I remembered Monday is Memorial Day. I'll still hold class, but don't worry if you can't make it."

"Got it. Thanks for letting me know."

"Have a good weekend, then." He stood with his hands in the tool belt pockets.

I waved. I ran back over the bridge and up the first hill. I flashed on an image of Dan Talbot wearing nothing but the tool belt. I groaned and made myself pick up the pace to a point where all I could think about was my breathing and the state of the pavement in front of me.

• • •

I showered, doing my best not to think about Dan Talbot. I threw together one of my few special dishes to take to Jackie's holiday weekend cookout. I drained crab meat from a can, then layered it with cream cheese, salsa, and sharp cheddar in a flat ceramic dish. I'd run it under the broiler at Jackie's and serve the dip with scooper tortilla chips as well as carrot and celery sticks. People always raved about it.

The windows darkened. I hoped my sister's party wouldn't be rained out. When I stepped out onto my tiny back deck, though, the bright sun was back. An antique lilac bloomed dark purple and smelled like a letter from my childhood, like my grandmother Rousseau. I pictured playing under the lilacs at Grandmere Helen's house, my laughing father holding the hose in a spray of water, Jackie and me holding hands and shrieking as we ran through. Where had that sunny man disappeared to?

He had vanished and then turned up dead. No one ever figured out the reason for either his disappearance or his death. After sixteen years, my heart didn't ache quite as much. And I wasn't quite sure why these questions were rising up now. Maybe because I'd helped solve more than one crime in the spring and had discovered the satisfaction of bringing about justice. Now, because of my stubborn curiosity, I was even more determined to delve into what happened until Way opened to the answers I needed.

I laughed, remembering once when I had uttered the old Quaker phrase in one of my classes. "You should work ahead on your term papers throughout the semester as Way opens." My students had never looked so confused. And I resolved to keep Quaker ways of speaking to myself.

I checked the clock. If I hurried, I could arrive at Jackie's early. Jackie hated to talk about Daddy's death. She was the oldest sister, though. She might have seen something or could remember a detail about the events that nobody else had.

I slipped foil over the dip and put the six-pack of Ipswich IPA and the chips into a bag. I hurried to change into a pink T-shirt, my white Capri pants, and leather sandals. A pair of dangly silver earrings and a silver bracelet were enough decoration for a cookout. Grabbing a jacket and the bag, I ran down the stairs to my truck.

"Oops." Wulu. I deposited the bag and ran back up. I opened the door and called, "Wu, we're going to Jackie's."

Wulu barked, looking at his leash. Jackie had a fenced yard and loved Wulu's company.

When we arrived, Jackie's rotund cat, Athena, was not so pleased. After hissing at Wulu a few times, she retreated to a spot under Jackie's Prius in the driveway.

"Hey, Jack, we're here," I called. I let myself and Wulu in the garden gate.

Late bulbs bloomed around the edges of the green lawn. Several groupings of garden chairs looked ready to host conversation, and a gas grill stood open and scrubbed. A long table sported a red bandana-print tablecloth and shaded a chest cooler under one end.

"Yo, I'm in here." Jackie's voice sailed out of an open kitchen window.

I set my bag on the table. I transferred the beers to the cooler, keeping one aside, and carried it and the dip in through French doors on the deck. I embraced Jackie with one arm.

"Brought my world-famous dip." I extended the dish to my sister.

"Good," Jackie said. She nodded and shoved a hand through already messy short dark curls. "I'm still finishing up some stuff in here." Stuff apparently being a platter of ribs, a wide bowl full of tricolored potato salad, a watermelon shell filled with balls of red melon and blueberries, and a tray of brownies.

"You expecting the whole town or something?"

"Only the usual suspects. A few friends, some colleagues, couple of neighbors. I asked Mom and Luke but they were busy."

"Can I help?" I figured I was safe, since Jackie never wanted help in the kitchen.

"Nah. Just pour yourself that beer and watch me do my magic."

I poured the ale into a glass and settled on a kitchen stool. I traced the condensation on the glass as Jackie puttered with ingredients in a bowl that looked destined to be sauce for the ribs.

"So, you know tomorrow is Daddy's birthday."

Jackie, her back to me, grew still.

"Finding that body out at Holt on Tuesday made me think about Daddy's death all over again."

Jackie pivoted in slow motion. She faced me and gripped the counter behind her with white knuckles. Her eyes burned.

"I am not going there," Jackie bit off, word by word. "You are not ruining my party. We are not discussing this. Not now, not ever again."

"Jack, listen," I implored. I set down my drink and stretched both arms toward my sister. "You might have seen something you don't remember. Can't we please discuss it? I know he didn't die of an accident. I just know it!"

Hands on hips, Jackie glared. "What gives you that idea? You're smarter than the police now?"

"They never told us why he vanished like he did. He wouldn't have done that, Jackie. You know that."

"I have no idea. Neither of us really knew what went on in his work life, who his banker buddies were, did we? Anyway, it's been sixteen years, Laur. Let it go. Let him go."

A knock sounded at the glass door. "Hallo? Jackie?"

Jackie shook her head fiercely and hissed, "No more. You hear me?"

I took a deep breath and let it out, nodding. I put on my party face, telling the new arrivals I was happy to meet them, too. I went through the motions of heating up my dip. Helping Jackie carry food outside. Inviting Jackie's friends to help themselves to beer, a glass of wine, or a cup of lemonade. Knocking a striped wooden ball through croquet hoops.

I took a break from socializing a couple of hours later. The afternoon had heated up, and I retrieved my Boston Red Sox hat from the truck before returning to the backyard. Wulu rested in the shade of the sugar maple in the corner of the yard. I sank down with my brew to sit next to him. Oh, no. An out-of-shape guy with pasty skin wearing a polo shirt in a size too small squatted next to us. Judging by the logo embroidered on the shirt, he apparently worked with Jackie. All the shirt lacked was a pocket protector. He'd been eyeing me all afternoon.

"Hi, I'm Brian," he said, extending a hand.

I shook it and introduced myself as Jackie's sister.

"So, do you have a boyfriend?" Mr. Subtle's eyes were bright under brown hair cut short and parted on the side. I bet he'd worn the same style since first grade.

Truth or dare? I decided to fudge it. "Yep. He's on the West Coast right now talking to some venture capitalists."

"Do you have any sisters?" He leaned forward and raised his thick eyebrows like he was channeling Groucho Marx.

"Three. You work with the lesbian."

The man's eyes opened wide.

"Come on, like you didn't know that about Jackie?" I knew Jackie didn't hide her sexual orientation. "Other than her, you want to meet the manic-depressive or the one in prison?"

The man's eyes widened until they looked like they might explode. He stumbled to his feet and mumbled, "Sorry, sorry," as he turned toward the rest of the group.

Darn. That wasn't a very kind thing for me to say. Too late now. The rest of Jackie's friends seemed nice enough. But my heart wasn't festive. Every time conversation lulled during the afternoon, my thoughts wandered to the day my father never came home.

The killing at Holt, and my questioning by the police, had triggered all the old questions about my father's death. I had to find a way to discover the truth.

Chapter Six

Despite the sun, the wind coming down from Plum Island Sound two hours later blew cool over Holt Beach. Wulu loved it. I shed my sandals as soon as we stepped off the long boardwalk over the dunes. It was the last weekend dogs were allowed on the beach until after Labor Day. That, and a nice day on a holiday weekend, made the beach appear to harbor more dogs than humans.

I looked left, then right. Which way to walk? Right, toward Gloucester and Rockport, the sand and dunes stretched out for a couple of miles. Left, I'd be right back at the Holt Estate with the view of the Bluffs. Drawn to the long expanse to the right, I sighed and headed left, the leash-free area. At least for a couple more days. I unclipped Wulu's leash and stashed it in my pocket.

Wulu ran off. He danced with the edge of the water. He picked up a small piece of driftwood and trotted toward me, carrying it in his teeth.

I laughed. I wrestled it out of his mouth and threw it. This was more like it. The party full of folks I mostly didn't know had exhausted me. I'd managed to extricate myself after thanking Jackie for the excellent lunch. I was surprised to receive a firm hug in return followed by a beery kiss.

"Don't worry about the past, little sister. It's all good," Jackie whispered in my ear.

I hugged back. I very much doubted that. But this wasn't the time to keep picking at Jackie. I had grabbed my empty dip dish and called Wulu.

Now the sheer joy of being by the ocean lifted my spirits. Playing with my dog amid other dog lovers was fun. Feeling the still-icy Atlantic on my toes perked me up. I broke into a jog.

Hearing a familiar yip, I turned and jogged back the way I'd come.

Wulu was engaged in a mock attack with a large golden retriever. The two dogs ran at each other and barked. The retriever backed off, then ran circles around Wulu. They ended up sniffing each other and racing off in separate directions.

"Wulu! Come on, buddy," I called as I jogged in place then turned, keeping my eyes on him. "Oof!" followed. I had collided with someone. Staggering, I turned.

"Hey, watch where you're going!" a red-faced man yelled at me.

"Sorry. I wasn't looking." He hadn't been, either, apparently. I decided not to point that out.

"Damn right, you weren't. You dog people are all alike." Thin blond hair blew straight up from his head.

Wulu ran up to my side and barked at the man.

The man walked off, shaking his head. He muttered something I didn't catch. I tilted my head as I watched him go. "Hey, Wu," I said, squatting down and petting him. "If he doesn't like dogs so much, what's he doing on this part of the beach? They ought to call it Dog Weekend instead of Memorial Day weekend."

Wulu yipped his approval.

We made our way down the beach. I threw the now slimy stick. Wulu raced and bit it. I tugged it out of his mouth and threw it again. At water's edge he was distracted by another dog. A wave carried the stick off, and his look of puzzlement made me laugh out loud. The tide was low, so it was easy to pick our way through the rocky area even though we walked into the sun now approaching the horizon. I purposefully did not look up the hill into the woods.

At Steep Hill Beach, I stretched my arms up high. I clasped my hands atop my head as I gazed across the water at the Bluffs. With the low tide, the distance was short between the mud flats on this side and the rocky harbor on the other. A simple spit of land that had provided happy vacation memories for so many families was now the source of apparent hatred and division.

An open boat motored down from Great Neck and around the bend of the Bluffs toward me. The sound of the engine slowed. A tall woman in a black baseball hat and a matching jacket stood at the helm. She steered with one hand and peered into the water ahead of her. She was alone in the boat.

Something about the woman looked familiar to me. I resumed my walk, slowly now, keeping an eye on the boat. Its motor slowed further. The woman pulled it up right near the shoreline and cut the engine. She threw what looked like a small plow head on the end of a thick rope into the water. The woman shrugged on a knapsack and climbed off the front of the boat. She hopped into the shallow water wearing tall black rubber boots. Right in front of me.

"Hello there," the woman greeted me.

I returned the salutation. The woman didn't seem surprised to see me. Looking around, I saw how many other people strolled the beach. Why should she be surprised?

But I was the surprised one. This was Mary Heard. From Iris's bakery the morning that seemed like a month ago now but was only a few days prior.

"Mrs. Heard, right? I saw you . . ."

Mary held up her hand. "That's Ms. Heard. I am not married at present."

"Oh, I'm sorry." I must have looked confused, because Mary went on.

"Charles is my brother." Her face, which a moment before had been politely animated, now darkened. "Or was, I suppose I now must say."

Her brother. And why not? "I'm very sorry for your loss," I murmured, but I felt foolish uttering the trite phrase.

Wulu ran up and emitted a happy bark at Mary. Her face lightened again.

"Who's this sweet pea?" She bent to scratch him behind the ears.

Wulu wriggled in happy acceptance. He could tell a dog person a mile off. And Mary had gone up a notch in my esteem, as well.

"His name is Wulu. It means 'dog' in Bambara."

Mary uttered doggie endearments for another moment before straightening. "Where do they speak Bambara?"

"In Mali. It's in West Africa."

Mary nodded as if that was public knowledge. In my experience, it wasn't. Lots of Americans knew next to nothing about Africa.

"And Wulu's person is?" Mary asked.

"Oh, sorry. I'm Lauren Rousseau."

Mary's face sobered again. She fixed my eyes with her own. "You found Charles."

"Yes, I did. I . . ." I stopped. Deep breath. "Yes. Is there anything I can share with you about that? I mean, I don't want to add hurt. But, well, I know sometimes people want to know the details." I was thinking not of Charles Heard, though, but of hearing the news about my father's death. Wanting always to know more.

Mary shut her eyes. Her lips pressed tight as if to prevent them from trembling in front of a stranger. She seemed to master her emotions and opened her eyes. "I came across the channel because I want to go up there. To see where he was found. I brought my camera. I need to see it." Her perfectly arched eyebrows drew down at the outer edges.

"I'll take you. We can go up together." I worried for an instant about entering those woods with a person I knew nothing about. Mary seemed like a bereaved sister. She was well groomed, sounded educated. So bad people were never educated or well groomed? I shook off my doubts. I laid my hand on Mary's arm for a moment. When she flinched, I quickly withdrew my hand.

She cleared her throat, then nodded at me. "Let's go."

We walked up the beach to the beginning of the wide path. I pointed down toward the rocky area. "I went up from there when I found him. But we should go by the path."

She stopped. "Why did you go up that way? How did you even see him?"

These were the kinds of details Mary needed. The kinds I had never learned about Daddy's death. I drew a deep breath.

"I saw a splash of white. I thought it was an early flower. I wanted to identify it. Actually, I wanted to be able to describe it so my sister could identify it."

"I see."

"So I climbed up the bank through the brush. When I moved closer, it wasn't a flower. It was his shirt. His white shirt." I felt that chill again of realizing I'd seen a person, not a native plant. And not a live person.

"Thank you." Mary didn't meet my eyes. "Let's keep going." She followed me on the path as it narrowed.

I searched the left side until I spied the smaller pathway through the trees. "This way," I motioned, holding a branch for my taller companion. Wulu followed along. We walked in silence for several minutes.

"I saw a nice bonsai spruce in the insurance office last week." Maybe chatting about a neutral topic would put Mary at ease. "Young Mark said it was yours."

Mary nodded. "It is."

"I take care of one, too. Mine's an elm."

Mary raised her eyebrows.

At her nonresponse, I let the topic go, thinking I likely wouldn't want to make small talk, either, if my brother had recently been murdered. If I had a brother.

Soon we arrived at the trampled path barred by a wide yellow police tape strung between two trees. I pointed. "It's right through there."

"They can't still be searching here," Mary said. "Let's go around the tree."

In a minute we stood side by side at the edge of the clearing. The sounds of the ocean lapping, dogs barking, and people chatting as they strolled the beach below seemed only feet away.

"I found him there, Mary." I pointed again, then realized Mary was no longer next to me. The silence of a sudden pause in the noises below roared in my ears. I couldn't see or hear Wulu, either. Spooked, I turned slowly.

Mary stood back by the yellow tape. Her right hand was in her pack. A weird expression coated her face like a mask. My heart thumped. It beat faster. What was Mary doing? Where was Wulu?

Mary pulled a professional-looking camera out of her bag, and her face returned to its usual genteel look. Wulu ran up with wet leaves stuck to his head. The ambient sounds resumed. I took a deep breath and told myself to get a grip.

"I want to record this. For myself," Mary said. She removed a lens cap and began to take pictures. "By the way, you didn't kill Charles, did you?" Her eyes remained on the viewfinder. The camera clicked repeatedly.

I stared at her.

Mary stopped shooting and looked over the camera. "Well, the chief seems to think you might have. And he doesn't have diddly-squat for other ideas."

"No, I did not kill your brother. I barely knew him. I bought my insurance from him. Why would I kill him?"

"I didn't think you did." Mary resumed her photography. "It'd be pretty stupid of me to come into the woods with a killer, don't you think?"

I agreed as I backed out of the scene, amused and a little disturbed that each of them had had the same thought. "Who do you think would have wanted him dead, though? Did he have enemies? People who disliked him that much?"

Mary lowered the camera again. "You're not from here, are you? Charles had trouble getting along with almost everybody. Got in fights in high school. Couldn't stay married. Sure, he was a successful businessman, and a Trustee. But my little brother was not well liked. He and I had our own share of disagreements."

"For someone to go so far as to murder him—that's way beyond not getting along." I leaned against a tree and folded my arms.

Mary shrugged and started snapping pictures again. "I'm leaving that to the experts."

Wulu bumped my leg. I reached down and ruffled his head. "Where did you go, little guy?"

Wulu yipped and ran back into the woods, then back to me. He looked up at me.

"What? Do you have something for me?" I followed him a little ways into the underbrush, where he stood expectantly over a mound of leaves and sticks. Light from a gap in the tree canopy shone on small green shoots of something popping up nearby. And on something shiny that gleamed in Wulu's pile of leaves.

I knelt. I picked up a stick and poked around the shiny thing, uncovering it. It looked like a cigarette lighter. An old-fashioned one, not the throwaway colored plastic ones I saw on sale at the convenience store. I extracted a tissue from my pocket and fished down to pick up the object. I knew enough from cop shows not to touch it with my fingers. This could be a clue to Charles's killer. I slipped it in my pocket. I'd call the chief as soon as I arrived home. Wulu gave me his What-a-Good-Dog-I-Am look. I patted him and whispered my thanks.

I straightened and looked back to the clearing, deciding I wouldn't tell Mary about the find. Not now, anyway.

"I'm almost done here," Mary said. She'd crossed over and stood a down the slope I had originally climbed up to find the body. "What'd the dog find?"

"Dead baby squirrel," I lied. "Nice, what dogs get into."

• • •

I typed "The Bluffs Ashford" into Facebook's search bar an hour later. I took a bite of the peanut-butter-and-lettuce sandwich that was my dinner tonight, chasing it down with a sip of seltzer. I gazed at the results. So the Bluffs had its own community page. I clicked the link.

It looked like an announcement board for social events. Tide Pool Camp sign-ups were due by June 1. The Spring Cleanup at Half Moon Beach was successful, and all volunteers were gratefully thanked. And so on. I clicked the info tab and scrolled down.

A section on the Trustees. Just what I sought. I knew Charles Heard had been a Trustee, but I didn't know who the other lifetime members were. It looked like quite the cozy club, if you thought middle-aged white men were cozy. A picture featured four males standing on a dock. To a one they adhered to a uniform of pastel-colored polo shirt, khaki Bermuda shorts, and dock shoes without socks. One was taller and younger than the rest. Besides Charles, there was Walter Colby, the slick banker I had met earlier in the week, another older man I'd never seen before, and . . . I peered at the picture. Dan Talbot. The sexy carpenter-sensei. A Trustee? Really? How did he earn that position? I'd heard it was virtually a dynasty, that the Trustee positions were handed down from father to son. His father must have been a Trustee, then.

I clicked the link on his name. His personal page opened. I clicked the photos area, curious if he had a wife or girlfriend in his life. I gazed at a beaming sensei standing behind a little *gi*-clad boy who grasped a trophy. Dan hammering at the growing skeleton of a house behind a Habitat for Humanity sign. Dan and a tall older man sailing a small boat in front of what looked like Holt Beach.

I closed my eyes and tried to picture Dan's left hand. Ring? No ring? I didn't remember seeing one, but I also knew men who worked with their hands who said it was dangerous to wear any jewelry. They said that a protrusion or a tool could hook on to a ring and cause serious hand damage.

I clicked back to his home page and didn't have to think long before clicking Add as Friend.

As I stood up to refill my glass, I felt a shape in my pocket. Oh. The cigarette lighter from the woods at Holt. I hadn't called the police. By the time Wulu and I had returned home, the sun had set and I'd forgotten all about it. I checked the time in the corner of the computer. Wow, time flew when you wandered through the Internet. It was already nine o'clock. No way Chief Flaherty would be on duty on a Saturday night. Someone would be at the station, though.

But would they know what to do with the lighter? How could I explain traipsing around behind crime-scene tape with Mary Heard?

I thought the wiser choice would be to wait until I could talk face-to-face with the chief and hand the lighter over to him directly. Less room for error that way. I extracted a fresh ziplock bag from the kitchen and carefully slipped the lighter from the tissue into the bag. I switched on a lamp and held the bag in the pool of light. It appeared to be an antique silver lighter, like the one my grandmother always clicked to light her cigarettes in a matching silver cigarette holder. I looked closely. One side held engraved initials in a curly script, but I couldn't make them out.

I switched from seltzer to red wine and returned to my office. In a spare spot on the bookshelf, a relaxed Zac beamed out from a wavy glass frame. He squatted with his hand on Wulu. The Toil-in-Vain Creek sparkled behind them. I'd snapped that picture soon after Zac and I had met the fall before. That had been a sunnier time for us.

I thought if I visited a shrink, he would probably tell me I had abandonment issues. My father had disappeared when I was nineteen. When I was just starting to learn what loving a man meant. Since then, whenever a relationship grew too close, I grew itchy and claustrophobic. Which didn't bode well if I ever reached the point where what I wanted was a life of intimacy and family.

I sighed. Letting a sip of the dark liquid comfort me, I sat back down. I could think about Zac later. On the monitor was a message box. Dan Talbot had approved my Friend request. Was he sitting at home alone, too?

• • •

Wulu pulled me toward the condo after our walk in the park at the top of the hill the next morning. It was going to be a busy day, so we'd gotten our walk in early. I'd be off to Friends Meeting soon, then lunch with my mother. And Charles Heard's funeral was this afternoon. I thought it would be respectful to show up, even though I'd barely known the man. Finding his body had forged a macabre link between us.

The ancient stucco mansion on the left was the first house on the narrow road after the park. I had often wondered what the story was behind the large house, which faced away from the road with a view over the marshes beyond. It had to have been a splendid summer estate a century earlier. Now it was in need of repair. Water stains marred the walls, and paint peeled off the woodwork. A nearly equally ancient Mercedes was parked in the circular drive. A beat-up red truck sat behind it. Was it the truck that had almost run me down, which had come from this direction? I thought the house was occupied, because of the cars and lights I sometimes saw through the windows, but I had never met the inhabitants or even seen them outside.

As we passed the house, a man emerged from the back and slammed the screen door behind him. He glanced at us but didn't seem to recognize me.

I raised my hand in greeting. The man was Bobby Spirokis. So that was who lived there. He stumped over to the red truck, climbed in, and spun gravel as he drove away. I lowered my hand. Maybe he hadn't seen me. That truck was definitely the one that had driven straight at me a couple of days earlier. Surely it hadn't been on purpose, but Bobby needed to work on his driving safety.

• • •

I locked my bicycle outside the Millsbury Friends Meetinghouse an hour later. When I'd left my condo to ride to Friends Meeting two towns away, the sky was clear over Ashford. The morning sun seemed to shine into all the dark corners and sweep them out. Half an hour later, clouds had blown in and the temperature dropped, making me wish I'd worn a heavier jacket for the ride home.

I exchanged greetings at the door with Dorothy, an angular elder who, despite her tendency to be something of a grouch, was one of the most politically active people I knew, always writing letters to the editor and standing weekly in silent peace vigils. I took a seat on one of the plain wooden pews arranged in a rectangle. I faced the simple white walls free of any adornment and the nine-foot-high windows that had let light into this room for nearly two hundred years. I closed my eyes.

Images of my father washed over me. This was his birthday. He had been the Quaker in the family and had brought me here with him for many years. My other sisters hadn't been drawn to it like I had, so it had been a special thing to do together, only Daddy and me, on Sunday mornings. I had taken a break from weekly worship for a few years in high school, when I preferred the company of my peers to any kind of time spent with either of my parents. I had begun to attend again, sitting in the silence next to my father on weekend visits home from college, until he vanished.

After the room filled and quieted, the silence deepened. I struggled to quiet my own thoughts and join the communal prayer. I pictured a circle of light around the benches, around the community gathered there with me. But my mind would not hold still. It raced from image to image: That strange moment when Mary stood with her hand in her knapsack. Discovering that Dan Talbot was a Trustee. Jackie's angry refusal to discuss our father's death. My encounter with Dan at the house on Toil-in-Vain Road.

I finally gave up and simply watched the branches outside the windows as they danced in the wind. The new bright green leaves contrasted with the ever-darkening sky. Rain was coming.

During fellowship after Meeting for Worship had ended, Dorothy pulled me aside.

"Today was your father's birthday, you know." She looked somber. "I have been holding Harold's memory in the Light this morning."

"You knew this was his birthday?"

Dorothy nodded. "We were old friends. I knew him before your mother did."

"Where did you meet?"

"Right here in Millsbury Meeting. We were children in First Day School together. I was a bit older, of course. I was an only child, so I decided Harold was my little brother. I even asked my mother if I could take him home with us."

"I didn't know you'd been friends."

"Well, we really grew up together. He went off, you know, to college and so on. We were all surprised when he brought Miriam to worship with us the first time. And pleased," she acknowledged with a frown, as if being pleased went against the grain.

"I thought my mother never came to Meeting."

"She did at first. I believe her Buddhist studies might have swayed her more in that direction after a time. And then when your sisters weren't interested, you know, she stayed home with them."

"I remember that. It's funny you mention Daddy's birthday. I have been thinking about him so much recently. I feel like no one will tell me the truth about his disappearance and his death."

Dorothy gazed at me. She nodded again. "That was a very difficult time for all." She swayed and reached out to me for support. "I'm sorry, I must sit. I haven't been feeling as strong as usual lately. Low iron, I daresay."

I helped the older woman to a chair, then sat across from her. I'd never thought of Dorothy as frail, but the pale arm I'd just held was thin and her skin looked like parchment.

"Can you tell me anything about when Daddy went missing? I don't know if you remember, but I was in my first year at Wellesley and I was pretty absorbed in that."

Dorothy shook her head. She folded her hands in her lap. "I don't really know any details, Lauren. But why do you feel you must bring it all out into the light now? After all this time?"

"I'm curious, Dorothy. Something seems hidden. There's a darkness about his death that makes me uncomfortable, and I want to open it, know it, bring it into this world."

Dorothy continued to hold my green eyes with her own pale blue ones. "You're still hurt because he left you." Dorothy reached for my cheek and laid her hand against it for a moment.

At the uncharacteristic gesture as much as from hearing the truth, my eyes filled. My throat thickened. I nodded instead of speaking.

"Let's hold that in the Light together." Dorothy took both of my hands in her own and closed her eyes.

I closed mine, as well. The social chat swirled around us. Small feet ran by, and a child giggled from across the room. Coffee cups clinked. A chair scraped on the floor. Dorothy wasn't going to tell me anything, that was clear. For the moment, it didn't matter.

• • •

I tried to dodge the rain as I dashed from my truck into my mother's cottage on Plum Island. I'd been drenched enough for a month on my wet and windy bicycle ride home from Millsbury. Everything I'd worn was soaked by the time I arrived at my condo. Once a day was plenty.

"Hey, Mom," I called. I shook out my hair and hung my raincoat on a hook.

Miriam Rousseau emerged from the back and gave me a hug.

"Lunch is all ready, sweetheart. Hungry?"

I nodded. I followed my mother through a hallway crowded with bookshelves and souvenirs from her travels.

The kitchen faced the back of the property, which nestled on a sandy hill behind the beach. A wall of glass doors showed the rain falling on a disheveled garden of beach plants, potted herbs, and bird feeders. A statue of a peaceful Buddha gazed across the yard to a wickedly grinning gargoyle. A small St. Francis of Assisi with a bird perched on his shoulder stood in the bowl of a birdbath.

Mom set bowls of chunky lentil soup on colorful Indian place mats. "Sit down, honey." She brought a board with a loaf of fresh bread to the table with a bread knife. "Here, slice that while I pour the wine."

"Thanks. This is really nice." I sank into my chair, suddenly ravenous.

"We don't spend much time together lately, just the two of us. Luke's off on one of his junkets, so I thought we should seize the moment." She set a juice glass of red wine next to each place and sat.

I didn't mind that my mother's boyfriend was away. I reached my hand out to my mom's. I closed my eyes and savored the moment of blessing. The jewel of quiet extended until my stomach rumbled. I squeezed her hand and laughed as I opened my eyes.

We chatted as we ate. Buttering my second piece of bread, I said, "Mommy? Can I ask you something?"

My mother put her spoon down. "You haven't called me 'Mommy' since you were twelve. Unless you want something." She raised dark eyebrows.

"It's Daddy's birthday. Will you tell me one more time about when he disappeared?" My voice shook. Was this cruel? Would my mother be willing to dive back into a painful past? "Please?"

She sank her face into her hands, elbows on the table. When she looked up, her brown eyes sagged. "Why?"

"Because it doesn't feel clear to me. Because I was away at school. Because when I heard about it, all those emotions of grief and confusion scrambled up my memories. Because nobody will talk about it! Not you, not Jackie, not even Dorothy at Meeting." I sipped my wine, then continued. "And mostly because something feels cloudy about those events, like I'm looking through frosted glass when I think about it. You know? You can see someone moving, you make out colors, but details are obscured. Like in a dream."

Mom took a deep breath. She stood and looked out at the garden, arms crossed. When she turned, her eyes blazed. "Don't you think maybe there's a reason you don't know? You put me in an impossible position, Lauren. You were close to your father. You went to Meeting together. He took you sailing. Jackie always got seasick, so she hated it. Alma and Gwen were too little. You had a special bond with Harold."

She took a small framed picture from a shelf over the door and handed it to me. "Look at this."

I held it in both hands. I remembered that sunny day. I was about fifteen in the photo. My father and I had returned from an afternoon of sailing. We smiled for the camera, ruddy, windblown, the same auburn hair, the same green eyes. My throat tightened.

"Do you think I wanted to destroy that?" Her voice shook. Her face flushed. She paced the small room like an animal seeking escape. "Are you sure you want to know what happened?"

I looked up. She was scaring me now. But I had to know. I nodded.

"Lauren, your father left me. He didn't vanish. He didn't disappear. He told me he was leaving. That he had to. And it wasn't for some bimbo, or for his rediscovered first love. He left me for a man." Mom sank into her chair. Her eyes welled with tears. "Satisfied?"

If I'd been knocked into a wall, I couldn't have felt more stunned. Everything I'd ever known now stood on its head. People—my mother, news reports, Friends—had always said my father's disappearance was a mystery. His subsequent death, an accident. My head felt light, unsubstantial. I stared at my mother. What if the accident wasn't true, either?

"How did Daddy die?" I separated each word as if each were a story unto itself.

She stared at the table and shook her head. "That part? As far as we know, he died in an accident. He was found floating with his safety line attached to the boat. It looked like he'd had a heart attack. Truth? I hadn't seen him in a week. I don't know who his lover was. I don't know if he went out on the water alone." A tear edged down her cheek.

I reached over and wiped it. Her skin burned under my cool fingers. Then an even worse thought beset me. A possibility I never would have conceived of before now. "He didn't kill himself, did he?"

"Oh, honey. I surely don't think so. That man had a George Fox spirit. 'Then you will come to walk cheerfully over the world, answering that of God in every one.' Your father walked cheerfully if anyone ever has. Except when he told me. And even then he was answering a call to be true to himself."

"Aw, Mom." I reached my arms around my mother and held tight. "I wish you had told me at the time. You're right, it would have made me see him as a real person and not my perfect father. But I was nineteen. I could have handled it. And I could have helped you maybe."

"I would have been grateful for that." She nodded. "Jackie was furious with him."

"Jackie knew? You told Jackie but not me!" I felt like I'd been whacked again.

"I thought she'd understand." Mom implored me with sad eyes. "You know. Even then I could see she preferred girlfriends to boyfriends. But she was a daughter first. She said she could have killed him for leaving us. And because of her fury she couldn't see how sad I was to lose Dad. I mean, even before the accident. I knew how much I would miss him."

I sat in silence. I watched a goldfinch in bright summer plumage nibble on black thistle seed in the narrow feeder on the other side of the glass. The bright little body did nothing to lighten my heavy heart.

"I'm sorry. I haven't even been thinking about you. You thought you were going to grow old with your soul mate, I bet. Play with your grandkids together."

She examined her hands as if they were strangers. "We had grown apart a little in those last couple of years. But I didn't know I'd never see him again," she whispered.

Chapter Seven

I checked my watch as I parked several blocks from the All Angels Episcopal Church. I'd stayed at my mother's too long, and now I was almost late for the funeral. Judging by the number of cars, it looked like it was going to be full, too. At least the downpour had ended. I hurried to the stone church and ran up the stairs. A man in a dark suit entered the open red pointed-arch doors ahead of me. I slowed as the somber strains of organ music invited me in.

A black-coated usher extended his arm toward the pews on the left. I slid into the end of one in the back. The church was indeed full. On a sunny day the tall windows featuring saints in colored glass would no doubt beam inspiration to the worshippers. Today the overcast sky outside made the ornate windows almost threatening and cast a sobering atmosphere for the mourners. The rest of the church was equally ornate. Gilded carvings and deep red velvet drapes hung behind the altar. The contrast with the simple Millsbury Friends Meetinghouse was sharp.

I closed my eyes. Despite the music and now the voice of a priest in the front of the sanctuary, I took a moment to be silent. I held Charles in the Light, along with his sister Mary. I held my mother and the memory of my father in prayer, too. Sitting in worship calmed me, even when disturbing events swirled around me like angry wasps.

As the priest intoned a prayer, I felt someone staring at me. I glanced across the aisle. Walter Colby, in the dark suit that had preceded me into the church, twisted sideways in his seat. His eyes burned into mine. I whipped my head back to the front. Why was he looking at me like that? What had I done to garner such attention? It occurred to me that it was also curious that he sat in the back. He'd been a Trustee with Charles. I would have thought Walter would have taken a seat in the front with special friends and family. Maybe it was because he'd arrived as late as I had. Maybe the Trustees weren't necessarily friends with each other. Or maybe he'd been the one who had ended Charles's life.

The service was a busy one. Silence did not seem to be a part of the Episcopalian ritual. The congregation participated in a communal call-and-response. Everyone present seemed to know when to speak and what to say, when to stand, when to kneel, the words to the hymns. When the priest spoke, finally, about Charles, it was in generalities, as if he hadn't actually known the deceased personally, although he gestured repeatedly toward the coffin draped in white at the head of the center aisle.

I had attended several Quaker memorial services, including the Memorial Meeting held for my father. Friends gathered in silence, as usual, and then in turn rose and shared memories of the person whose life they celebrated. No one spoke who hadn't known the person. I far preferred that kind of funeral.

At last the service ended. The coffin was wheeled by a somber Mary and several men in black down the aisle. The priest swung a metal sphere on a cord, the ball emitting puffs of incense, as he followed the coffin. Several acolytes trailed behind him. I tried to avoid looking directly at Walter Colby, but I noticed that he joined the procession right at the beginning. I waited until the end of the line of mourners was in sight before I rose and joined them. I didn't need an encounter with someone who felt the need to glare at a funeral.

At the door, Mary and the priest stood together in greeting. Mary's eyebrows went up as she spied me, and then she smiled. It was a small sad smile, but a smile nonetheless.

"Thank you for coming, Lauren." Mary took both of my hands. "Won't you join us in the hall for something to eat and drink?" She gestured to a building to the side of the church. The sun had emerged and was casting long shadows behind them.

"Oh, I couldn't. You'll want to spend time with your friends, and—"

"Please, Lauren. As a favor to me?"

I wondered what kind of favor I would be doing Mary. The only reason to stay was to see who else showed up, and maybe to overhear a bit of information that might give me a clue about who killed Charles. I guessed that was a good enough reason.

"Yes, I will. Thank you. I'll see you over there."

Mary nodded as she turned her attention to the next person in line.

I spent several minutes strolling the grounds of the churchyard. A black iron fence enclosed a small cemetery. Rays of late-day sunshine sparkled through the remaining raindrops on shrubs and trees. A bed of bleeding heart bloomed next to several clumps of a silvery foliage. Grassy areas were neatly edged, and the flowering plants were trim. Someone had devoted serious attention to the grounds.

As I examined an ancient gravestone, I heard voices behind a hedge. I listened more closely. They were speaking in the Quebec dialect of French.

"I told you not to go blabbing about the plan. Can't you keep quiet?" A male voice spit out the words in a pitch so deep I thought I could almost hear the individual beats of his laryngeal folds.

A female answered him in a husky voice that sounded smoke-damaged. "Listen, *chéri*. I'm talking to whoever I want to talk to. Got it? Where's it written you can tell me what to do?"

The male voice lowered to a fierce whisper so I couldn't make out the words, then the female barked out a laugh.

I decided it was time to head into the reception. As much as I wanted to see who was speaking—and about what plan—I thought it more prudent to clear out of there. The two must have thought they were using their secret code language. Too bad French was one of my languages, too. I turned and nearly bumped into Bobby Spirokis.

"Oh! Excuse me." I wondered if he'd been trying to catch the hidden conversation, too. Or was he spying on me? And if so, why?

The look of alarm on Bobby's face became a blank visage as he backed off a few paces. "Pardon. You looking for the reception? It's over in the hall." He pointed to a stone path. The full key ring that hung from his belt jingled as he moved his arm back to rest on the handle of a rake.

A rake. "Is this your artistry? The grounds are lovely."

A beam spread over Bobby's face. "That it is. The plants sorta speak to me. I'm glad you appreciate it, ma'am."

"It creates a peaceful atmosphere. Thank you." I waved as I headed down the path. Curious. He must supplement his lobstering income with maintaining the church gardens and the Holt mansion.

I pushed open the heavy door of the hall at the end of the path. Warm air and fragrant smells mixed with the buzz of low conversation. Several townspeople held coffee cups and saucers, but most seemed to be hitting the wine instead, balancing plastic glasses with their small plates of hot appetizers and tiny sandwiches.

I found the drinks table and selected a glass of Chardonnay. A young woman in a white shirt offered a platter of small meatballs in sauce. I toothpicked several and laid them on a proffered plate. I surveyed the crowd, not seeing anyone I knew well enough to chat with.

"Hey, Dr. Roo!" Joey materialized at my side sporting a wide smile. He wore the white shirt of the serving crew and carried a mostly empty platter of tiny quiches. "How about some pie?"

"Hi, Joey. You work for a caterer now?" I was fond of the lanky young man.

"Yeah. I'm saving up for a car. And Mom says it keeps me out of trouble."

I took two of the quiches and thanked him. I watched as he skillfully slipped among the crowd, holding the tray level, smiling again, and offering as he went. He was the only young person I was close to. It had been a real delight watching him grow up into this cheerful, motivated teenager.

As I popped a quiche in my mouth, I looked for Mary and finally spied her in a group near the sliding doors at the back. Dan Talbot's head stuck up from the assortment of mourners around her. Well, he was a Trustee, and so had been Charles. Walter Colby walked by me but either didn't notice me or chose to ignore me. Chief Flaherty stood talking with someone, looking ill at ease in his dark suit and tie. His eyes roamed constantly over the crowd. He was probably working, watching for suspicious behavior.

By the time I emptied my plate as well as my wineglass, people were drifting toward the door. I didn't know if I should try to maneuver closer to Mary, if only to say goodbye, or if I should leave. I certainly hadn't overheard any juicy conversations beyond the unknown speakers behind the hedge or picked up any new pieces of information, other than that Bobby was the church gardener.

I felt a tug on my elbow. A thin woman stood there looking angst-ridden.

"We have to go now." The woman's voice made it sound urgent.

"Hello, Mrs. Wojinski. Where's your husband?" I smiled at her and looked around the room. I waved at Mr. Wojinski as he made his way toward us. I looked at his wife, whose hands shook and whose brows were knit over eyes wide at some unseen danger.

"It's not safe here." Mrs. Wojinski darted her eyes around the room.

"Your husband is coming, Mrs. Wojinski. He'll be right here."

James Wojinski looked to have been waylaid by a man in a well-cut gray suit. I couldn't hear what they were saying, but from the shaking fist of one and the red face of the other, it didn't look like a friendly conversation.

Mr. Wojinski finally broke away and strode over to where his wife and I were standing. "Vincent Waters threatened me! He's the one at fault, him, his precious Bluffs, and their rotten Trustees."

"We should call the authorities, James." His wife glared in the direction of Waters.

Mr. Wojinski seemed to finally realize who he was talking to. His voiced calmed as he said, "Don't worry, Fiona. Everything is fine."

Fiona shook her head. "We need to go home. Right now. It's not safe here."

Mr. Wojinski took her elbow. He turned toward me. "I'd watch out for that slime lawyer Waters, if I were you. He's evil and he's dangerous." His eyes beamed into mine. "We all need to be vigilant against people like that."

I watched them walk toward the door. I gazed back at the group around Mary, which the man in the suit had now joined. I decided to take Mr. Wojinski's advice and leave well enough alone. I could catch up with Mary later. This day had been long enough.

• • •

Glancing down at the last remaining noodle on my plate a couple of hours later, I shook my head. I'd been so absorbed in my book I hadn't even realized I'd finished the entire plateful of take-out pad thai. And the Bangkok Palace container on the counter was still half full.

Wulu butted my leg with his head. "Good idea, my friend," I said. I rose and clipped his leash to his collar. I laced up my sneakers, donned a sweater, and headed out in the direction of the cemetery.

It was only a few blocks to the graveyard that had been the original town burial site. Wulu and I wandered through gravestones carved beginning in the mid-1600s. I bent down to examine a thin, dark gray stone with the skull head of an angel of death watching over the remains. The letters in the slate were barely legible in the dusk, but I thought I made out the inscription:

Here Lyes Buried the Body of Mr. Jebediah Winslow
Aged 51 years
Departed This Life 23, May 1796

The stone next to Jebediah's bore a slightly fresher carving about Mrs. Patience Winslow, wife of Jebediah, who had not departed until 1832.

I pulled Wulu close. I perched on a stone bench across from Jebediah's grave. What a period to have lived through. Born in 1745, Jebediah saw the creation of a new country. Maybe he'd enlisted in the Ashford Minutemen who had marched to join the Battle of Lexington and Concord. Perhaps he had ultimately died as a result of some injury suffered in the Siege of Boston or at the Battle of White Plains. What about Patience? Had she stoked the fire in the wide colonial fireplace while he was gone? She'd surely have tended a vegetable garden or taken in mending to feed their children.

Fifty-one. That had to be about Charles Heard's age. It had been five days since his murder. A killer likely still roamed the town. How long would it take before the police made an arrest? It seemed to me that finding the motive for the killing must be key. The only murder I'd been involved with had had money and drugs at its root. I didn't know of any drug connection with Charles Heard, but money? Highly possible.

He was a Trustee and a businessman. He'd had conflicts over the disposition of the Bluffs rental income. He hadn't been a very pleasant insurance agent, at least in my experience. Who else might he have crossed? Mary didn't seem overly upset about his death. She'd said she'd had disagreements with him, arguments perhaps about money or property. But kill her own brother? Yikes.

Maybe Iris knew something about his personal finances or even his personal life. Nobody had mentioned a grieving widow or children. Mary had said he hadn't stayed married long so an ex-wife was somewhere. A weeping bereft girlfriend could be somewhere in town.

I heard the crack of a branch to my left and whipped my head in that direction. Dark had approached while I'd imagined Jebediah's life. Who was out there? I stood, feeling in my pocket for my phone. I swore. It was at home. Exactly the thing I'd promised myself never to do again, go out without a phone.

Shapes moved in the gloaming at the other end of the graveyard. Wulu yipped.

"Shh, Wulu," I whispered, my heart thudding. I made my way as fast as I could toward the path that led back to High Street and the safety of its streetlight, pulling Wulu on his leash. He strained in the direction of the shapes. "Come on," I urged, still whispering.

A hoarse laugh came from one of the shapes, and then a high giggle. I glanced over. Two red spots pierced the dark. I blew a breath out. It was only teenagers having a smoke.

Despite danger being transformed into innocence, relief washed over me when I trod on the sidewalk again. "Time to be at home behind a locked door, Wu," I said as we picked our way over pavement buckled from the roots of decades-old trees.

Wulu barked his agreement.

• • •

As I ran along the salt marshes the next morning, I still felt scrambled by what my mother had told me, like a giant hand had shaken the little snow globe that was my life and rearranged everything. Daddy hadn't disappeared. He was gay. The only constant was the accident. But even that seemed murkier than it had. And then the voices in the churchyard, followed by the altercation between James Wojinski and Vincent Waters after Charles Heard's service. What had happened to my peaceful summer vacation?

I finished my morning run by stretching my calves at the steps to my condo. Yesterday's rain had blown out to sea. The town's Memorial Day parade and town picnic would have clear skies and probably a heavy dose of sunburned faces by day's end. But all I could think about was the past.

I shook my head. I had to move on with my day. I'd lost enough sleep over an event almost two decades ago that I couldn't change. I'd asked for the truth and received it. I resolved to start coffee, shower, and work on the paper I needed to write.

Several hours later, through the open window I heard the thumps of drums and the high strains of flutes. The parade. I'd become so involved in Japanese phonology that I'd forgotten about one of the highlights of living in a small New England town.

I grabbed my Red Sox hat, stuffed money and ID in my pocket, clipped Wulu's leash on, and ran with him down the hill to High Street. We joined a crowd of residents who watched from the narrow sidewalk. An elderly woman sat in a lawn chair gripping the handle of a tiny American flag. A boy with tousled blond hair looked on from his father's shoulders.

I made it in time to catch the start. The veterans' honor guard led the way, a uniformed man holding on with both hands to the staff of a large flag holstered at his waist, accompanied by a group of male veterans of all ages. One tapped a cane as he held another man's elbow. The five selectmen marched next, two of whom were women looking sharp in white slacks and navy blazers. Walter Colby was part of the group. I had forgotten he was a selectman as well as a Trustee.

The next group was female veterans. I shook my head. Still second-class citizens in this day and age? I knew the young women currently serving in the armed forces underwent as much danger and trauma as the men. A group of Ashford police officers marched by. Even Chief Flaherty wore a uniform. Right as he passed me, his eyes veered onto mine. Was that a scowl? I gave him a little wave and smiled.

Which reminded me that I still hadn't given him the lighter. I promised myself to do it the next day. I checked on Wulu, who sat alert and panting, excited by the music and the crowd.

When I looked up again, I stared. This had to be the oddest section of the parade. About a dozen middle-aged men walked along, waving and smiling. Wearing aprons. Stiff-looking half aprons. The men's cooking club? It had to be something else. But what? The banner in the front of the group had already passed by. I'd have to ask Iris.

I tapped my foot as the slightly ragtag high school band marched by in white shirts—some tucked in, some not—and black pants. The young musicians were mostly in tune on the Marine anthem and marched somewhat in unison. I had played the clarinet in my high school marching band, which won awards for its music and its precision. Awards this ensemble was unlikely to qualify for. Still, military music always plucked a fond, if ironic, chord in my pacifist heart.

The procession lasted another ten minutes. There were vintage convertibles with flags and a motley troop of boys in khaki Scout shirts followed by smaller Scouts in blue. After them, taking as example the placement of the veterans, no doubt, walked the Brownies and the Girl Scouts.

Finally, fire engines brought up the rear, sirens a roar. I pushed an index finger into my right ear to protect my hearing and drew Wulu in closer with the other hand. What looked like every resident who had been watching farther up the road now took up the rear as if following the Pied Firefighter. Strollers, bicycles, kids on skateboards. Everybody headed to the field in front of Town Hall for the ceremony and the picnic.

I looked more closely at the skateboarders. "Hey, Joey!"

He hitched up his pants with one hand and waved the other without losing his balance. "Hi, Dr. Roo," he called.

"See you down there," I replied. Iris had said she'd save me a spot on their picnic cloth. Wulu and I joined the crowd strolling down

High Street. It had been the original road of the town back in its inception. Many of the homes now proudly displayed plaques declaring the name of the first owner and date of construction. The Josiah Lord House, 1658. The Old Manse, 1727. The Whitehorse Inn, circa 1658. A wide restored building at the corner of North Main was the Day-Dodge House, 1737.

I liked to picture residents of that era walking down the road or riding on a horse or in a wagon. The route would have been narrower, without pavement, without power wires, without even glass in the windows at that time. Woodsmoke would have wafted from every chimney. Every yard would have had its kitchen garden and a shed for the owner's cow and horse.

The modern-day walkers turned onto County Road. Two blocks down at the corner where it intersected Green Street, I spied a tall man on the sidewalk. He seemed to be arguing with someone. I pulled Wulu to that side of the road. The man's short dark hair looked like Dan Talbot's. As I grew closer, I saw that it was Dan. He looked down at Bobby Spirokis and shook his head. The fire engines still blared right ahead. I couldn't make out what the two were saying. I started to wonder how they knew each other, then gave up, a small town being synonymous with familiarity.

As I watched, Bobby pushed Dan. Bad move. In an instant Dan had Bobby neatly on the ground with his arm twisted at an unnatural angle.

Bobby's face was red and it looked like he swore in Dan's face. Dan leaned in close to him and said something.

The parade followers nearest to that side of the road stopped. I tried to move closer but couldn't weave through the thick crowd. I stood on my tiptoes. What was Dan doing to Bobby? Two men from the street approached the two on the corner. As fast as Dan had wrestled Bobby to the ground, he now had him up and standing. He kept hold of Bobby's arm. At the same moment, the sirens fell quiet.

"It's simply a disagreement, gentlemen. Not to worry. Right, Bobby?" Dan's face was somber, but his voice was calm. He seemed to tug a bit on Bobby's arm.

"Right. Yeah. No problem." Bobby waved the men away. He

glared as he wrenched his arm out of Dan's grasp. I guessed that happened only because Dan let it.

By the time the crowd swept me along with it to the corner, Dan and Bobby had disappeared. What kind of bad blood did those two have? Bobby didn't seem to get along with many people. That evening at the Holt Estate, he had acted strangely. It seemed like yesterday and a lifetime ago. It had been six days.

Still, the sun shone. I surveyed the people around me. Children waved small flags and ate candy. Residents of the Green Street nursing home sat in chairs and wheelchairs along the side of the road. Some wore red-white-and-blue sun hats and watched the procession, others slumped in oblivion. None of these people were concerned about a body discovered above the beach.

It was only another block to the field in front of Town Hall, a broad three-story brick building next to the Ashford River. As I approached, I heard a band of a different kind amplified through loudspeakers. This was no martial marching music, but rather an Eagles tune my parents used to dance to. Oldies rock for all generations.

The town picnic was under way. An irresistible aroma of grilled hot dogs and burgers wafted by. The band music mixed with children's gleeful screams and the mumble of hundreds of people chatting, arranging blankets, throwing footballs, and probably discussing town politics.

I caught sight of the Tapmobile, an antique red truck fitted out with taps from the Ashford Brewery. A line of adults waited to buy tickets for tall plastic cups of draft ale.

I scanned the crowd for Iris. Coming up empty, I joined the beer line. Wulu barked as a deep voice spoke close to my ear.

"Don't forget we have class in a few hours, Dr. Rousseau."

I whirled as Dan Talbot straightened, hands in pockets, a crooked smile on his face. "Sensei! You startled me."

"A good *karateka* isn't startled. Always stay aware of your surroundings."

"That's good advice, actually." I shifted my gaze to the red truck ahead. "Anyway, one beer will be out of my system before class." I knew my thirst wasn't simply physical. When I looked deep inside, I realized I probably drank too much. I should probably figure out why my thirst was great. I knew Quakers traditionally frowned on the consumption of alcohol because it muddled the clearness of life they strove for. I tried not to look deep inside too often.

"Hey, I'm in line, too." His tone was light. "Beautiful day for a picnic, isn't it?" Dan swept his arm out, as if gesturing to the world. His face was a mask of contentment, but his alert eyes moved over the crowd like a proctor's.

I looked up at Dan. "I saw you wrestle Bobby Spirokis to the ground. What was that about?"

Dan didn't meet my eyes. "Only a disagreement. He's not happy about the clam flats at the Bluffs. And doesn't really know how to play nice." He stood with arms folded. He no longer smiled. "Don't worry about it."

I didn't feel worried. Curious, definitely. I didn't think I'd accomplish anything trying to find out the real story, though.

The line inched forward. I realized it had been a mistake to bring Wulu. The field was filled with way too much activity for a small dog on a leash. Wulu strained this way and that, his eyes on a Frisbee sailing overhead, then on a sweaty Cub Scout who tore across their line in pursuit of another boy.

"I have to take this guy home," I said to Dan, pointing at Wulu. "I don't live far, and I run." I dug a five-dollar bill out of my pocket and proffered it. "Get me an IPA? I'll be back in five minutes."

Dan nodded, accepting the money. "Meet you over at the edge by the Riverwalk." He pointed across the field to where the grass met a row of trees.

"Thanks. I'm supposed to eat with a friend. We can find her together. Come on, Wulu." I eased out of the line and through the crowd until we reached the street. I ran with Wulu the few blocks to my condo, made sure he had food and water, then locked the door and ran back in the heat. That beer was going to hit the spot.

Dan was exactly where he'd promised, two tall plastic glasses full of ale in his hands. As we headed in search of Iris, he halted. Walter Colby strode toward us.

"Dan, I need to talk to you." The banker's voice was low and urgent. Dan shook his head. "No, you don't."

I looked from one to the other. Dan's eyes were icy. Walter's pleaded.

"After our last meeting—" Walter began.

"We don't need to talk. Come on, Lauren." Dan gestured to me and turned his back on Walter. He strode in the opposite direction without waiting for me.

"Is this a Trustees issue?" I looked at Walter Colby.

Walter stared at Dan's back, then turned and left as if I hadn't spoken.

Did the Trustees not agree with anyone, including each other? I wandered through the crowd until I spied Iris, who waved and patted the empty space on the Indian bedspread she'd spread on the grass. The middle of the cloth held a half dozen containers of food as well as several plates of items from the grill.

Dan appeared a moment later. "I try to avoid people with negative energy," he murmured in my ear.

I started to introduce him to Iris and Joey.

Iris put up her hand. "I know Dan Talbot. How are ya, Danny?"

Dan appeared to wince at the nickname but said, "Good. You, Iris?"

We chatted in between bites of grilled sausage and Iris's special potato salad. Joey seemed impressed with Dan's karate credentials before he sauntered away to hang with his friends.

Iris mentioned a couple of mutual friends and inquired about the karate studio. Then she said, "And aren't you a Trustee, Dan?"

"Yes, I am."

Had Iris read my mind? I had been dying to ask Dan about the Bluffs. But surely Iris had already known that Dan was a Trustee?

"Do you mind telling me how you get to be part of that group?" Iris's alert eyes did nothing to disguise her curiosity.

Dan shrugged. "I'm not really supposed to talk about it."

"I saw your picture on the Web with the rest of them," I chimed in. "Aren't you a little, you know, young for that?"

"I guess." Dan surveyed the assembled residents. Some lingered over lunch, others danced in front of the band. Children ran everywhere, and two teens tried skateboard maneuvers on the concrete steps to Town Hall before a police officer waved them away. Dan looked back at Iris and me with a somber face. His dark eyebrows nearly met in the middle.

"You must not have heard. My father moved to San Francisco some years ago." He frowned, as if concentrating on the memory. One hand picked at a spot on the back of the other. "The rest of the Trustees asked me to carry on." He spread his hands. "I was pretty young, but they wanted the continuity, I guess."

"Why did he move?" Iris asked with innocent perkiness.

I stared at my friend. What did she know that she wanted confirmed?

"Tired of the winters, I suppose. I haven't really seen him since then."

"And now you have to pick a new Trustee. 'Cause Charlie's dead. Hey, maybe you saw the killer," Iris said. "My girlfriend said she saw you heading onto Holt Beach the afternoon of the murder."

"Your friend needs to get her eyes checked. I wasn't anywhere near there that day." An incoming Frisbee headed for Dan's head. Staying seated, he scooped it out of the air and airmailed it back to its teen sender in one fluid motion.

Iris shrugged. "Yeah, she must have been mistaken."

"So, how's the bakery business?" Dan asked. "I hear your new cinnamon rolls are to die for."

Chapter Eight

I pulled my karate *gi* off a stack of clean laundry. I'd grabbed a twenty-minute catnap after I walked home from the picnic.

I glanced at the clock on the wall. Speaking of karate, I was almost late. I donned a turquoise tank top and tied the loose pants snugly around my waist. I folded the *gi* top and my belt into a bag.

I walked with brisk steps to the dojo downtown, a storefront next to the bank whose clock read 4:05. Inside, the studio was empty. Then I heard Dan's voice. He must be in the alcove where he kept his desk. I narrowed my eyes as I listened. It sounded a lot like Farsi, which I'd studied for a year as an undergrad. The language of the note in Charles Heard's office. I listened but couldn't make out what he was talking about.

When Dan emerged, a smile spread over his face. He kept his eyes on me as he walked forward like he was checking out my very snug sleeveless shirt and what was under it.

Great. I turned my back toward him. I scrabbled in my bag for my *gi* top. I slipped on the rest of the *gi* and white-belted myself in with a firm knot before I faced the center of the room. Dan had his back to me now and was launching kicks at a long heavy bag hanging from the ceiling.

"Shoma chetur hastin?"

He spun, eyes narrow. "Why did you say that? And how do you know—"

"Weren't you just talking on the phone in Farsi? I studied it as an undergrad."

He nodded, frowning, and turned back to the bag. "Did you understand what I was saying?"

"Not really."

"Good." He delivered a strong forward kick and followed through with three quick punches.

"Nobody else here yet?" I sat on the mats and started to stretch.

"Well, it's Memorial Day. I probably should have canceled class." He grunted as he connected a roundhouse kick that sent a long punching bag swinging into the air.

"I'm here." I glanced in the wall of mirrors opposite me. Dan smiled to himself and nodded, as if he'd planned this solo class. What was up with that? "And I need the workout after that lunch."

"Let's do it, then." Dan walked next to me as I stood. "A class of one. You'll have my undivided attention."

Not sure if that was a good thing or not, I swung my arms and torso back and forth. I decided to play it as straight as I could. "I'm ready when you are."

We spent the next hour practicing punches, kicks, and combinations. I spent some time with the bag myself. Dan held it steady as I pushed through with punches and put all my weight into forward kicks.

He called for a water break. "Is it coming back to you?"

"It is. It's like riding a bike, except that you need a lot less flexibility and fewer muscles to remember how to pedal down the street."

"How about some kata?" Sensei wiped his brow. "Do you remember any?"

I nodded. I remembered the names of a few of the stylized fight patterns and thought I could probably walk through the basic movements of the first one, *Heian Shodan.*

"Show me." He gestured to the middle of the room. He stood with fists on his hips.

I took a deep breath. I bowed, announced the name of the kata, and began the series of slow, fluid moves that mimicked actual fighting. A downward block. A forward punch. Whirl one hundred eighty degrees. Downward block. Upward outer block. Face forward. Three alternating overhead blocks moving forward, punctuating the third block with a cry from the *ki*, a sound I pushed out from my core.

Dan stopped me. "I'll do the opposite set."

I raised my eyebrows. "I've never done that. We didn't —"

Dan held up his hand. "It's something I developed to teach students what they are really doing. And why it matters. I'll perform the corresponding attacks and defensive moves to yours. Also in the kata style, though. Slow. Deliberate. With strength and grace." He shrugged, as if explaining too much would detract from doing the routine correctly. "Simply execute *Heian Shodan* again. You'll get the hang of it."

I bowed while Dan did the same. I lifted my fist and forearm in the first block. This time I deflected a ritual punch from his strong arm. As we continued, I had to fight arousal. He was right next to me. He moved with my moves. Our sweat mingled. His *gi* top pulled open almost to his belt, and he didn't wear a tank top under it. His smooth skin emanated a warm scent that made me want to bury myself in his arms and not come up for breath for a long time.

Time slowed. We fought in tandem, as smooth as a waltz and as stimulating as a tango. I swept his punching arm up and to the side with a striking hand in the last move. The end of the kata came too soon. We stood face-to-face, inches between us. My hand remained in contact with his arm. I was stunned, my breath shallow and fast.

Dan cleared his throat and stepped back. He brought his fists to his sides. He began to bow, then stopped. "Lauren?"

"Right." The bow was de rigueur. My legs shook. My *gi*, damp, clung to my skin. My body was damp elsewhere, too. I bowed, meeting his eyes.

He threw his head back and laughed.

That broke the spell. Of course. He did this with all his students. He'd said so. He was used to it. I turned, chagrined. I definitely was not used to this. I doubted I should be. Zac would be back at the end of the summer. And I didn't know anything about Dan Talbot, really.

• • •

I switched on the desk lamp in my office a couple of hours later. Dusk melted into dark while I sat at my computer in a solitary pool of light, Wulu asleep at my feet. I took a sip of Chardonnay. The cool wine soothed and buffered my nerves. I meandered through my Facebook friends. I caught up with Aiseta in Mali and my former karate buddy, Rumiko, in Japan. I wrote an email message to Zac and had clicked Send when my eyes fell on the silver lighter.

I clicked back to the Facebook tab and navigated to the Bluffs community page I'd visited before. This time I noticed a message board link and clicked that. It looked like a super-localized For Sale and Wanted page for the Bluffs only. Clammer4Ever asked if anyone had found a red oar, extra long, with the initials DT carved in it. Another post offered tickets to the first Holt Estate concert of the summer at half price. The next entry wanted a Bluffs resident to partner in buying a recreational boat. From the description, it sounded to me like one of the party boats I'd seen on Plum Island Sound, usually inhabited by adults who'd had too much sun and too much alcohol.

I was about to shut down the computer when I glanced at the next post. Also signed by Clammer4Ever, it was a personal ad. "Tall athletic 40 year old SWM interested in walks on the beach, quite dinners, and nights on the town seeks attractive lady 25–35 looking for same."

I would have thought the Bluffs was a small enough community that this single white forty-year-old with imperfect spelling might have already met all the attractive women, but apparently not.

I heard a voice. It seemed to come from my back pocket. I pulled my phone out and glanced at the display. "Hi, Iris. What's up?"

"What do you mean, what's up? You called me." Iris sounded sleepy.

"No, I didn't."

"Yes, you did!"

"Well, I just heard your voice from my pocket and—oh, wait. Crap."

"What?"

"Well, after all the stuff that happened this spring, I downloaded an app that keeps an emergency call button in the center of my phone's screen. But to keep it available I had to turn off the screen locking."

"Which means you butt-dialed me."

"That's about it. I try to remember not to put the darn thing in my pocket, but—"

"You forgot."

"I forgot. Sorry. Go back to sleep! See you in the morning." I disconnected and sighed. I placed the phone very carefully on my desk.

• • •

"No, stick it in deeper." Iris motioned with her clamming fork. She dug in the damp mud with one smooth motion. "Like this."

I leaned on the long handle of my borrowed tool. My back already hurt, my hands cramped with the chill, and we'd only been out on the flats for an hour. The sun just now crept high enough in the sky to provide a little warmth.

"How often do you come out here at dawn?" I asked.

Iris pried the fork up, extracted five clams from the muck on it, and straightened. She tossed them into her bucket. "Whenever the tide is low at dawn, I'm here before the sun comes up. Got to head to the shop pretty soon, though. So get a move on." She raised her eyebrows, but softened the order with a smile.

I peered into my own bucket. A measly dozen clams were my haul for an hour's work. Great. "Next time I ask if I can come along, simply say no, okay?"

"No way. You're not really from Ashford if you don't go digging once in a while. You'll see." Iris plunged her fork into the muck again. "You'll apply for your own license pretty soon. Bet ya lunch at Ithaki."

I groaned. Our standard bet. Well, it was a Zagat-rated restaurant, and the food was always outstanding. Not to mention the exquisite fresh floral arrangements. I couldn't lose, really. Even if I went down in defeat on the bet, I'd still eat a superb lunch out with my friend.

"You're on. Why should I go through all this work for a dozen clams?"

Iris looked out at the water. It danced ever closer with the rising tide. "Wait'll you cook them up. You'll be begging Town Hall for a license to dig."

I also checked the approaching water, then noticed two men who worked down the beach a ways. The stocky one looked a lot like Bobby Spirokis. The other was taller and thinner. Something about his movements made me think he was young.

I shook my head. It didn't matter. Anybody with a recreational license could dig on any of the town clam flats. I shoved the tines of my fork into the mud. I tried to mimic Iris's experienced motion. This time I brought up five. I smiled as I bent to extract the clams.

"Ouch!" I drew my hand back from the fork. "Those tips are sharp."

Iris rolled her eyes and kept working. The fork's shape, with the tines at a right angle to the handle, wouldn't have done much good on a giant's dinner plate, but it was perfect for prying under the top layer of the wet muck where the clams had buried themselves.

I pried away until I heard a vehicle crunch the gravel at the side of the road where Iris had also parked, maybe fifty yards away. I paused and looked up. It was a cream-colored sedan that had a look of luxury about it. A Lexus, maybe? I didn't track car brands too closely.

My eyes widened. Walter Colby strode toward us, bucket and fork in hand. Somehow he didn't seem like the clamming type. He wasn't quite dressed for it, either. He wore new jeans with a crease pressed into them and a yellow polo shirt. The only nod to the excursion was a pair of green rubber boots without a scratch or a trace of dirt on their shiny sides.

"Good morning, ladies." His voice boomed toward us. "My alarm didn't go off. Hope the tide isn't too far in yet."

I looked at Iris, expecting a roll of the eyes. What was a banker doing on the mud flats, after all? Instead, Iris sported a satisfied little smile and cheeks much rosier than they'd been a few minutes earlier.

"Glad you could make it, Walter."

Walter? I thought I was on a confide-all-in-your-girlfriend basis with Iris, but I'd never heard my friend talk about Walter before. "Glad you could make it" made it sound like she'd invited Colby to join us. Well, Iris was divorced, so why not invite a reasonably attractive and likely wealthy man on a dawn excursion. Because he was married, maybe? I did a quick check of Colby's left hand. No ring.

"You know my friend Lauren Rousseau?" Iris smiled at me, then shifted her eyes back up to Colby's face.

"We bumped into each other in the bank last week." I wiped my muddy hand on my pants and extended it.

"Ah, yes. How are you, Lauren?" Walter extended his hand, but he didn't look happy about it.

I shook hands. Colby's was warm and smooth. He must not dig for clams very often. As to how I was? Tired of people who smiled without involving their eyes, that's how I was. I didn't have room in my life for insincerity.

Iris's happy face was sincere, though. I decided this was a good time to take my clams home and leave the two alone to dig in happy coupledom.

• • •

After a hot shower, I scrubbed and steamed the clams. As I scrubbed, I thought about my father. How close we had been. All the time we spent together on the water. I sautéed the clams in butter, per Iris's instructions. Savored on toast with a hot mug of French roast coffee, they made a delicious breakfast.

I carried my coffee into my office, determined to put all thoughts of murder out of my mind. That was the job of the police. As for me, the conference fast approached at the end of June, and my paper still wasn't finished. Just because I'd secured tenure this year didn't mean I could stop publishing.

• • •

I shifted in my seat at Town Meeting that evening. I had already sat for more than two hours, after sitting in my office all day, in an uncomfortable auditorium seat with Jackie and much of the Ashford voting population. Most waited for Article 22 on the warrant: a vote to restructure the Trustees of the Bluffs and bring their hidden dealings under public scrutiny. Town Meeting hadn't completed the warrant the week before, although an earlier article regarding the school budget had also raised tempers for and against the Trustees of the Bluffs. The meeting had been carried over to tonight. The Article 22 discussion was finally under way. With some vitriol. James Wojinski stood at the microphone in the aisle with Vincent Waters next to him.

"Gentlemen!" The moderator put up her hand in a forestalling motion. "Mr. Wojinski has the floor."

Waters straightened his silk tie and blinked behind designer eyeglasses. At least he stopped interrupting Mr. Wojinski.

The former schoolteacher pushed up his glasses and straightened his spine to his full height. "Madam Moderator, I simply want to make sure the record shows that the School Committee has received no funds from the Trustees in years. Our children are suffering. This group acts like a medieval cabal. Secret meetings. No public accounting. No responsibility to its own charter of educating the children of Ashford. This has to change. And soon."

The high school auditorium erupted into applause as he returned to his seat. I looked around. Not everyone clapped. Most in a group in front of me sat with quiet hands in their laps or arms folded in rigid anger. Several shook their heads in disgust, and two leaned their heads in for a whispered discussion.

Vincent Waters took his turn at the microphone, wearing a tailored and expensive-looking light gray suit.

"Madam Moderator?" His voice was a deep bass.

My eyes widened. His had been the voice behind the hedge. The one with the "plan."

The florid woman behind the lectern on stage recognized him and instructed him to stick to his three minutes. And to civility.

"Madam Moderator, Vincent Waters, Twelve Neck Road. I am a simple citizen. While I happen to be a lawyer, I speak as a resident of the Bluffs and for my neighbors. We're tired of having our rents raised every time the town needs more revenue for the high school band. We simply want to own the property our homes occupy." He went on to describe a litany of complaints with the town, with persecution by what he described as "off-Bluff" town residents, and with what he described as the biased coverage of the *Ashford Chronicle*. "We've had it! Let the Trustees sell the Bluffs to us."

Another wave of applause resounded, but one rather smaller than that which approved Mr. Wojinski's comments. This time the clapping was mixed with an undercurrent of muttered remarks from throughout the seats.

The moderator gaveled the podium. "May I remind you, Mr. Waters, that sale of the Bluffs is not part of this article? Now, does anyone have anything *new* to contribute to the discussion?"

I turned to Jackie in the next seat. "Geez. Is Town Meeting always this turbulent?"

Jackie smiled, keeping her eyes on the stage. "It can be pretty wild. Democracy in action isn't necessarily a pretty sight." She turned to me. "Why didn't you ever come before this spring?"

I shrugged and said I didn't know. "I guess I didn't feel like they needed me here. Now I do. This Trustees business is too bizarre. And when the schools decide to cut foreign languages because they don't have the money that some cabal is supposed to be paying them, well, that's the last straw."

The woman sitting next to me looked up from the sweater she was knitting and nodded. "That's right. It's a darn shame. A crime, more so," she said in a low voice as she leaned in.

I checked the stage. One of the selectmen, a white-haired woman in a blue pantsuit, was droning on about something.

I looked back at my neighbor. "What I don't understand is how the Trustees can get away with this."

"No one quite understands." She stopped when a man in front of us swiveled to glare.

We listened in silence to the continued discussion.

"Call the question!" a voice shouted from the back.

"Second!" Several others chimed in from around the hall.

Ayes and nays to the resolution resounded in almost equal volume, so counters were appointed. "All those in favor of Article twenty-two, raise your hand high and keep it up until the counter has passed your row," the moderator instructed. Two men and two women walked slowly down their appointed sections, making eye contact and pointing at each raised hand. The procedure was repeated for the nays, then the counters reported their numbers to the stage.

It looked to me like it had passed.

"The ayes have it. The resolution to instruct the selectman to bring the Trustees into accountability by restructuring the board has passed, two seventy-two to two thirty-four. We move on to Article twenty-three. Shall the town approve and appoint the sum of five thousand dollars to replace the sidewalk snowplow?"

Several people from the nay-voting group rose and made their way out of the auditorium. Their personal interests appeared to be the only reason they had attended. I looked at my watch and groaned at the hour. It was past eleven. I was relieved when the question passed with no discussion and the meeting was adjourned.

I rose. I extended my hand to the woman next to me and introduced myself.

The woman said her name was Sheila Beaton and that she lived out on Pineswamp Road. "I taught high school English for many years. My granddaughter goes to the Winthrop School now, and I'm damned if I'll let those Trustees ruin a public school education for her."

"We're lucky the meeting wasn't continued to yet another night," Jackie said to me as we moved up the aisle. "Glad you came?"

"I wouldn't have missed a night at the theater for anything. Really, it's almost more entertainment than it is government."

We moved through the lobby. Small clumps of people looked like they were still conducting the business of the town. I heard shouts through the open doors from the steps outside the building.

"We have a right to our homes. My family's been there for three generations."

It sounded like Vincent Waters's voice. He didn't sound happy.

"Our children have a right to a decent education, Vince."

I slid through a gap in the crowd. I pulled up the hood on my jacket as rain began to fall. Vincent and Mr. Wojinski stood face-to-face on the sidewalk. Vincent towered over the older man. Vincent pointed a finger at Mr. Wojinski.

"Listen. The children are fine. All their little field trips and enrichment activities." His tone was bitter enough to make me wonder what he had against elementary educational practices. "I might lose my home. Would that satisfy you?"

The crowd that had gathered around them began to clarify into supporters of each man. A ruddy man in work boots and a barn jacket tried to pull Vincent away from Mr. Wojinski, while a tall young woman with cropped red hair did the same to Mr. Wojinski.

"Dad, let's go. You're not going to fix this here, on the front steps," she said, leaning in close to him. "Things are going to change. The town voted."

Mr. Wojinski shook his head in disgust and turned to go.

"We're going to win, you know," Vincent said in a low voice as Mr. Wojinski retreated. The onlookers grew quiet.

"I wouldn't be so sure about that."

"We don't want anyone to get hurt." Vincent's tone was all the more menacing for its lack of volume. It pulled people near so they could hear.

As rain splattered the pavement, Vincent's friend pulled him in the opposite direction, and they disappeared into the darkness. The crowd dispersed. A crop of umbrellas and hoods headed for the parking lot.

Where had I heard similar words? I shivered as I remembered. It had been Charles Heard on the phone the day before he was murdered. Had he been killed because he was a Trustee?

Chapter Nine

I ended my run at the police station the next morning. I'd never gotten around to turning in the lighter yesterday. I asked for the chief through the thick glass in the police station lobby.

"He's not here. What can I help you with?" The disembodied voice of the officer at the desk was tinny.

I glanced at the round clock on the wall. 9:10. Should I hand over the lighter or wait to tell the chief himself? "Do you know when he'll be back?"

The young woman said he should be at the station in the afternoon.

"I'll come back then. Tell him Lauren Rousseau wants to speak with him, will you, please? I live on Upper Summer Street." I'd learned if you identified yourself by street name, everything ran more smoothly in Ashford. At the least, they understood that you lived in town.

I walked the few blocks home. The weight of the lighter in my shorts pocket comforted me. I didn't know why. When I put my hand in to touch it, the silver cooled my hand through the bag. I laid the bag on the kitchen table in a spot of sunlight. I filled a glass with water and drained it, my eyes on the lighter.

I pulled open the slim drawer at the top of the boxed double-volume set of the *Compact Edition of the Oxford English Dictionary* and drew out a heavy magnifying glass. Daddy had given each of his daughters the boxed set, twenty-four volumes compressed into two. The magnifying glass was to read the tiny print. Funny, now they seemed like an extinct species, these heavy blue books. These days people pulled up the pdf on their laptop or iPad and enlarged it to their heart's content. Heck, people probably even read it on their phones.

I sat and picked up the lighter. I could almost make out the lettering in the morning sun. I smoothed the plastic over the silver. I held the magnifying glass a few inches away from the lighter. And stared at the letters HLR. Elaborate engraved cursive carved the very initials of my grandmother's name: Helen Louise Rousseau. The same initials as my father's name: Harold Lawrence Rousseau.

• • •

After I cleaned up, walked Wulu, and slipped the lighter into my bag, I drove to the Agawam College campus two towns away in Millsbury. As I drove, I mused about the lighter. It had to be Daddy's. What were the chances of someone else engraving the same initials on the same antique lighter? But if it was his, why was my father's lighter at a murder scene? Or on the Holt Estate at all?

I arrived at my campus office without any answers. I tidied my desk, since I planned to work from home the rest of the summer. I filled the recycling bin with lecture notes, a draft of a paper I'd already completed and sent in, and a couple of assignments from a student who dropped the class instead of working to improve his grade.

I checked my college email account and made a note to think about ordering class books for the fall, then wandered the Internet for a few minutes. The memory of the sweet nutty taste of the fresh clams I'd sautéed for breakfast the day before lingered in my memory. My local Craigslist site showed two clamming forks for sale in the North Shore region. Why not? I could zip down to Town Hall tomorrow and pay for a license. So I'd lose the bet with Iris—we'd have a nice lunch out, and maybe I could find out what was up with her and Walter Colby.

I carefully carried my bonsai elm to my truck. Campus was quiet. Undergrads had moved out and gone home, and the intensive summer sessions hadn't started yet. This was the first summer since I'd come to the college that I wasn't teaching. Tenure had its perks.

Checking the map, I took a detour home through Rowley. According to an email that had showed up right before I left my office, the Craigslist clam fork was mine to pick up.

An elderly man answered the door of a Cape-style house with a *For Sale* sign on the lawn. A clam fork leaned against the porch railing. I introduced myself and told him what I was there for.

"Yes, there's the fork. I can't go out anymore, more's the pity." He shook his head. "You use it, young lady."

"I will, and thank you. How much do I owe you?" I had forgotten what the ad had stipulated for a price.

He waved a shaky hand. "You take it, now. My daughter's trying to sell off all my belongings. I'd rather just give this away." His eyes welled. "Betty and I, we spent many a low tide digging together. Now that she's gone, well . . ."

"Thank you so much, sir. You take care now." I hefted the tool and waved as I walked to my truck. The man waved back.

As I drove home, I wondered if I should reconsider Zac's proposal of marriage from a couple of months ago. I'd told him I wasn't ready. But this old man? He'd had a lifetime with his Betty. If I wanted to have a lifetime with anyone, I'd better get started. *If* that was what I wanted.

My stomach growled, but I pulled into the police station lot before going home. This time the chief was available. I waited in the lobby until he emerged from within.

"I've been meaning to give you this." I extended the bag with the lighter. "I was out at Holt a few days ago. I found this in a pile of leaves near where I found Mr. Heard's body."

Flaherty looked up sharply from the lighter in my hand. "What were you doing there? When was this? Didn't you see the police tape?"

I took a deep breath. "It was Saturday late afternoon. I wasn't going to go up there, but I met Mary Heard on the beach, and—"

"What was Mary up to?" The chief's voice rose so much that the officer behind the glass turned her head to watch us. "Come in. We need to talk about this. Follow me."

He set a fast pace to his office but I kept up, taking the same chair across from his desk I had occupied last time.

He clicked on his little recorder again and stated the date, time, and his name, then asked me to state mine.

"Why do you need to record this?"

"We have to document everything."

I sighed. "Lauren Rousseau, Eight Upper Summer Street."

"Please tell me about your recent intrusion on the crime scene of the death of Charles Heard."

I opened my mouth to object, then decided to simply tell my story. "It was late afternoon on Saturday, so May twenty-eighth. I met Mary Heard when she climbed off her boat at Steep Hill Beach. She said she wanted to see where her brother died. She wanted to take pictures. So I showed her."

Flaherty dangled the plastic bag in front of me. "For the record, Dr. Rousseau has relinquished a silver antique lighter in a resealable bag as evidence. Please tell me how and where you found this."

"For the record, I have not relinquished it." I kept my voice steady. "I wanted to show it to you. I think it's my—"

"Please relate how and where you found it." The chief frowned.

I rolled my eyes a little. "My dog Wulu stirred up a pile of leaves about two yards from your yellow tape. I saw something shiny. I picked it up with a tissue and put it in my pocket. At home I transferred it to that bag. So I didn't touch it. Correct procedure?"

He sighed and nodded. "Very nice." He frowned. "I wonder what else the Staties missed."

"Staties?"

"We're such a small town, the State Police detectives take charge of the investigation in case of murder. We work with them, of course."

"Of course." I also wondered what else they had missed.

"Now, if you would, please tell me about Mary Heard. What she did, what she said."

"As I said a minute ago, I met her on the beach. She motored up in a boat as I walked by. I had seen her at Iris's Bakery and she recognized my name. She was going to try to find her way to where her brother died anyway, so I offered to show her where it was."

"Did she take anything away from the scene?"

"Only pictures, as far as I know. I don't know if they were film or digital. I don't know much about cameras." I shrugged. "Wulu and I left. She said she wanted time alone there. I can understand that."

"You should not have taken her there, and you should not have left her alone there." The chief stood, gesturing.

"Excuse me." I stood, too. I had had enough of him ordering me around. "It's a public estate. If you don't want anyone going there, maybe you need to put up a guard or something. I came here because I wanted to talk to you about that lighter. Will you turn off that machine so we can do that?" At the look on his face, I added, "Please?"

Flaherty sat and complied. "Okay, go on. I don't have all day."

I retook my seat. "I thought that lighter looked a lot like my grandmother's. She gave it to my father. I never saw it again after he died. I took a close look with a magnifying glass this morning. That fancy engraving? It's HLR. My grandmother's name was Helen Louise Rousseau. She gave it to my father because he had the same initials. Harold Lawrence Rousseau."

"Ms.—that is, Dr. Rousseau, this is a vintage lighter that you found in a pile of leaves. What do you think the chances are that it belonged to your father? He died in an accident at sea, if I'm not mistaken."

Frustration mixed with sadness thickened in my throat. "What are the chances someone else had those same initials engraved on a silver lighter seventy years ago?"

The chief leaned back in his chair, looking suddenly satisfied. "My own grandfather's name was Henry Lotham Robbins."

"Did he live here? Did he smoke?"

"Well, no, on both counts. I'm simply saying it's a common type of lighter from an era when engraving was also common. And that other people can possibly have those initials."

I rose again. I'd had enough. "Do you need to keep that?" I nodded toward the lighter on his desk.

Flaherty nodded. "For now."

"Please make sure you return it to me. I'm leaving." I waited to see if he'd stop me, try to make me repeat anything further about meeting Mary.

He stood with a deep sigh and ushered me down the hall.

A door opened on my right. A man in a yellow shirt and a blue tie held it for James Wojinski. James frowned. He pulled his lips together like he wanted to keep himself from talking.

"Right in here, sir." The man pointed to the next door down.

Mr. Wojinski saw Chief Flaherty and stopped. "Come on, Dick. How long have you known me?" He spread his hands out in front of him. "I didn't agree with Charles Heard. But I didn't kill him!"

"We have a few questions for you, Jim." The chief glanced at me and then back at Mr. Wojinski.

Wojinski shook his head. "This is ridiculous." He stomped after the man in the tie.

Flaherty resumed walking, nudging my elbow with his hand to make sure I did, too.

At the exit, I turned toward the chief. "Is Mr. Wojinski a person of interest?"

Chief Flaherty rolled his eyes. "Have a nice day."

Schoolteacher Wojinski as a murder suspect? I wondered if this would end up being one of those news stories where a neighbor is quoted saying about a murderer, "But he was such a nice, quiet man."

I drove the few blocks to Town Hall, obtained my noncommercial resident's clamming license, and drove home. I stayed in the truck for a moment. The uneasy feeling about my father's death reared up again. I closed my eyes and pictured my father in a nimbus. I held him, and my worries, in the Light. I took a moment for James Wojinski, as well. Opening the truck door, I let them go. The concerns remained, but they felt less heavy after a moment of prayer.

I opened the passenger-side door and lifted the bonsai. Holding its stone tray with both hands, I kicked the truck door shut with my foot and started up the front steps. Wulu's black head appeared in the window, barking up a storm. Smiling up at him, I caught my toe on the lip of the granite step. The plant unbalanced me, and I started to fall. I held the plant out in front of me. I fell hard on one knee and then on my elbows.

I swore. I set the bonsai on the top step and turned to sit. My knee smarted, my elbows stung where the step had scraped the skin, and I felt shaky from the fall. But at least I'd saved the miniature elm.

• • •

The mats at the dojo were full almost to capacity that afternoon. Two dozen *karateka* vied for a clear spot in which to stretch without running a foot into a fellow student's leg. Dan ran them through the lesson with precision and encouragement. He didn't give me extra attention, but I caught his eye in the wall of mirrors once. The nature of his gaze brought the unavoidable blush to my skin. I turned away. I moved to the body bag to practice roundhouse kicks. My knee twinged but didn't seem to be seriously hurt from my crash onto it a couple of hours earlier.

After class was over, I swapped my *gi* top for a light jacket.

"Any interest in going clamming with me tomorrow morning?" Dan's deep voice came from behind me.

I turned. Dan, right next to me, leaned one arm on the wall and smiled at me.

"How'd you know?" I stepped back a pace and pushed hair off my forehead.

"Know what?"

"I picked up a clamming fork this morning, and my license, too. I went out with Iris the other day. It seemed like too much work. But fresh clams for breakfast? I guess I'm hooked. What time is low tide?"

"I didn't know." He shrugged. "Pick you up at five. What's your address?"

"Eight Upper Summer Street."

"I'll bring breakfast, too."

I groaned. "You'd better. Or at least coffee."

"See you then." He winked at me as he waved goodbye to two boys leaving with their fathers.

I strolled down Market Street. A beer or a glass of wine would taste good about now. I spied Iris locking up the bakery. Perfect. Some girl talk wouldn't hurt, either. I hailed my friend.

"How about a drink?" Iris called from across the street.

"I was about to propose the same thing," I called back. I laughed, crossing over. "That was easy. What and where? The bar at Ithaki?"

"Nah, too expensive for a drink. I know, let's grab a bottle of white and go up the hill in the cemetery."

The sun was still well up in the sky and the air felt mild. "Let's do it," I agreed.

Iris turned back into the shop for a couple of glasses, then we stopped into Marcorele's Liquor for a cold Chardonnay with a screw top. We chatted as we strolled down High Street to the town graveyard. We climbed stone steps set in the steep hillside to the new section on top that held rosy granite markers. Some featured a name followed by an empty space, still waiting for the second member of a couple to join the first in everlasting rest.

Iris found a stone bench in the sun. "I come up here sometimes just to think. Peaceful, you know?" She dug the glasses out of her bag and poured wine for each of us. "And it's the highest spot around."

I joined her on the bench. "Here's to us." The hills of town spread out in front of us, some wooded, one with houses following each other up to the top. Far to the right in a flash of white I glimpsed the town's new wind turbine turning lazily.

We sipped in silence. Iris broke it. "Any news on that murder?"

I shook my head. "What a mess." I told Iris the story of how I'd showed Mary the crime scene on Saturday and then had uncovered the lighter with Wulu's help.

"That sounds interesting. You think your papa left it there? Long time ago."

"I don't know what to think. Maybe somebody stole it from him and dropped it there. Then or now. Or maybe he gave it to someone. I'll probably never know. I do know the chief was pretty curious about me running into Mary up there."

"Chief Flaherty. Why he's so interested in Mary?"

"He didn't say. Maybe it was simply that we violated the crime scene. Or maybe she's a suspect. But as I told him, it's a public place. If they want to keep people away from it, they should guard it. Right?" I sipped my wine. "And then, as I was leaving, they brought Mr. Wojinski in for questioning. Chief wouldn't tell me if he was a person of interest, but I'll bet he is."

Iris whistled. "No way he killed anybody."

"You never know. He's in pretty good shape, and he had a big beef with the Trustees. How do we know what was going on in his head?"

"You're right, we don't." Iris nodded. "Anyway, lemme tell you about Mary. Lotsa gossip." She grinned. "Long time ago, Walter Colby was sweet on her. Ooh, Charlie didn't like that none. They fought, big-time."

"Really? Did they get in trouble for fighting?"

"Sure. Charlie broke Colby's nose. Sheesh. Then Walter's father— he was a banker, too—he did something with the Heard lease on the Bluffs that didn't go over so good with the Heard family. I never learned the details on that one."

I marveled at Iris's store of history. "Did Mary ever go out with Walter?"

"She did. Then she went away awhile. College, I guess. Or who knows, maybe she went away because she was pregnant."

"No, really?"

"Could have happened. Both those men are Trustees, you know. Or were. Now they gotta replace Charlie."

"Did Mary ever marry?" I sipped my wine again.

"Nope. I don't know why not. She and Charlie shared the family house on the Bluffs. She's still there, far as I know."

"And what about you and Mr. Colby? Walter? You seemed pretty friendly the other day at the clam flat." I nudged Iris with my elbow.

Iris blushed as she objected, "Hey, that's my wine arm!" She held the glass out in front of her to steady it.

"Well?"

"I can have a date, right? He's not married anymore."

"It's your life, sugar. Hope he treats you well. He's a Trustee, as you said. I hope you can, well, trust him. He could have killed Charles easily."

Iris opened her mouth to speak and then closed it. She pursed her lips as she gazed at me. "He could have. I don't think he did. I'm a pretty good judge of character, you know."

"Speaking of Trustees, what do you know about Dan Talbot's father?" I asked. "Why did he move away?"

"Swish swish." Iris sipped her wine and raised her eyebrows.

"Swish swish?"

101

"Why d'you think a man leaves his wife and kids and moves to San Francisco?"

I thought for a minute and shook my head. "Why?"

"Peter Talbot liked men, Lauren. Finally got honest with himself, way I see it, that he was gay. Good for him. Not so good for Danny."

I sat with that news. Dan hadn't seemed too pleased about his father's exodus west. Maybe I could ask him about it again in the morning. Maybe I could bring up my own father's sexual orientation. Or maybe not. That news still felt too fresh and raw to discuss with a stranger. Or even with Iris. I shifted on the bench.

"And his mom and grandma, they were really steamed. Did you know they are from Iran? And over there they really don't like gays."

"I heard him speaking Farsi in the dojo. But how did he get a name like Talbot?"

"That's his father's name. I can't even pronounce his grand-mother's name."

"So I'm going clamming with him tomorrow." I raised my eyebrows at my friend. "You got me hooked."

"I'm no matchmaker. But it sounds like a fun date." Iris's eyes sparkled.

"It's not a date! I meant you got me hooked on clamming. I even picked up a fork already."

"Since when isn't going out with a tall handsome man early in the morning a date?"

"Since now."

"And your Zac? What will he think about that?"

"Iris, it's not a date. I just keep thinking about the taste of those fresh clams. And Dan asked if I wanted to go. That's all."

Iris sipped her wine and whistled. The sky turned rosy. "You gonna have good weather for your date."

I rolled my eyes as I sipped my own drink.

"And, hey. You get tired of him, send him down the bakery. That guy's cute." She nodded in glee. "Maybe I cook him up some special buns."

I snorted and whacked my friend with my free hand. I felt myself relax with the wine, carefree girlfriend time, the summery weather. I set my drink down and leaned against the bench back, my eyes on the increasingly spectacular sunset.

A tinny *Zorba the Greek* tune emitted from Iris's belt. She unclipped her phone. "Probably Joey wondering where his dinner is." She smiled. "Hallo?" The smile disappeared in an instant, replaced by a furrowed brow and worried eyes. "Yeah? Yeah?"

"What's wrong?" I whispered.

Iris held up a forestalling hand. She bit out several more interrogatives, then said, "You sit tight, *manari mou*. I'll be right there." She disconnected the call and stared at me with a shadow clouding her eyes.

"What's up with Joey?" I knew Joey—Iris's "little lamb," her *manari mou*—must be in trouble. "Is he all right?"

"Them friends of his. One of them was driving, he'd been smoking weed. Joey, he don't do none of that. Lands in hot water anyway."

I patted Iris's hand. "Is he at the station?"

Iris nodded.

"Do you want me to come down there with you?"

"No. This happened once before. Last time they let the boys go with a warning. They know Joey's no troublemaker. Those friends, they're another story." Iris shook her head, then rolled her eyes. She lifted her empty wineglass. "Now Mama the wino shows up. At least I'm not driving, but I'm not gonna make a great impression. You got any breath mints on you?"

• • •

"I have a surprise for you in the van. I'll be back in a couple of minutes," Dan said the next morning. A smile played on his lips as he winked at me.

I had been digging clams with Dan for over an hour under a cool overcast sky, belying the previous evening's red sky. We'd chatted—"flirted" might have described it better—as we worked. My bucket was half full and my back was stiff, but the outing had been fun so far. I straightened and stretched my arms overhead.

"What kind of a surprise?"

"That wouldn't make it much of a surprise, would it?" He dusted off his hands and strode away. He called over his shoulder, "Bee are bee."

I stared after him, puzzled. Until I realized he was speaking text-talk. B-R-B: "Be right back." I shook my head and leaned on the handle of the clam fork as I surveyed the flats. We worked alone in this spot. Dan had said this area, Rum Cove, wasn't the premier flat, but it had a good yield and wasn't as crowded as the Bluffs flat. I checked out the walk to his van, which looked like a toy at this distance. We'd moved down the flat quite a ways.

I pulled my phone out of my pocket. 6:30. The tide would come in soon. As I wondered about this surprise Dan was after, I resumed my search for clams. I didn't want to go home with less than a full bucket. I mused about what Iris had told me about Dan's father while I dug and wondered how Dan had dealt with it at the time. The sun poked out from the sky's gray mask and spread over the flats.

The phone rang in my pocket, the ring tone a bad imitation of an old-style rotary telephone. I wiped my damp hand on my pants and retrieved the phone again. Iris's number appeared on the display.

"Yo." I had left Iris a message after I'd walked home last night but my friend had never returned the call.

"Lauren. It's bad news. Joey?" Iris sounded on the verge of tears.

"What is it, *fili mou*? Didn't they let him go?"

"No," Iris wailed. "They said he was high, too. And they found drugs in his pocket, in his backpack. I can't believe it. My baby."

"Oh crap, Iris. He's not locked up there, is he?"

"No, they let him go home with me. But we hadda pay some big money. He was actually arrested."

"Girlfriend, I am so sorry. Did you open this morning?" I knew how much Joey helped his mother in the summer and on weekends.

"Yeah. Joey's a wreck, though. Says somebody planted it on him. Says he never bought it, never woulda done that. What do I think, Lauren? What do I do?"

I spent a few minutes calming Iris down. I told her the name of a lawyer I'd heard was good, and assured Iris that her faith in her son was important whether he'd bought the drugs on his own or not. Iris hung up somewhat less agitated.

I picked up my fork and resumed digging. Why would Joey's friends have planted drugs on him? Well, who knew why teenagers did what they did, for that matter. Part of me yearned to have children, and another part was horrified at the thought. They did, after all, turn into teenagers one way or another.

Ruminating as I dug, I gasped when Dan touched my shoulder. "Oh! I didn't hear you come back."

A smiling Dan held out a white box tied with string in one hand. "Breakfast?" He held a thermos and a paper bag in the other.

The growl from my stomach was perfectly timed.

Dan spread a red-and-blue Red Sox beach towel on the ground and sat. He waved me over to join him.

I sat and selected a chocolate cruller, a treat I allowed myself rarely, and sipped the coffee he poured into a foam cup.

"I heard your father was one of the few Trustees to resign rather than stay on the job until he died." I gazed at the now incoming tide. "Why did he move to San Francisco?" Might as well play it innocent.

"He just decided he'd rather live out there." Dan threw what remained of his coffee onto the sand with a violent thrust. "He had no business leaving the family. Deserting us." He glared at me. "Why are you asking about my father, anyway?"

So that's how he was dealing with being abandoned. This temper was a side of Dan Talbot I hadn't seen before. It sounded like a lasting hurt was behind it. Rage was rage, though.

"It must be tough for you." I flashed on Jackie, and how upset she still was about our own father's absence, as was I. "There's been a lot of talk about the Trustees lately with the school funding issues. You know, at Town Meeting. I was curious."

Dan shook his head with force, as if to shake off the entire topic. "He's gone, okay? He's not part of this town anymore."

"I hear you." A cloud blew back over the sun and stayed there as if stuck with a cosmic magnet. "Hey, thanks for breakfast." I checked my watch. "I should get home. Did you dig enough clams?"

Dan nodded. "Tide's coming in, anyway." His voice lost its edge, but he avoided my eyes.

We picked up our buckets and forks and started the trudge back to the van. I spotted the driftwood tree we'd passed on our way in. Its dark wood made it look like an ancient metal obstacle thrown down to block an invading army.

I walked in silence next to Dan. The so-called date took on a bitter flavor. I never minded silence, but this felt like an unsettled quiet with conflict lurking only a pace behind.

As we neared the stranded behemoth of a tree, I spied a piece of wood sticking up behind the far end. Straight and smooth, it didn't look like a branch that belonged to the tree trunk. I didn't remember seeing a pole there before. I glanced at Dan, but he walked with his eyes on the sand in front of him.

I slowed my pace as we passed the end of the tree. I looked back at the pole. I stopped and stared. I felt as if spring had never come, as if the cold of winter were in my bones. The piece of wood wasn't a pole. It was the handle of a clam fork—and it looked like it was sticking out of Bobby Spirokis's back.

Chapter Ten

I froze. I had to move, call for help. I forced my head around. Dan was now yards ahead of me, striding toward his van.

"Dan!" I croaked. He didn't turn. He hadn't heard me. I looked at Bobby again. Maybe he was alive. Maybe I could help him. I dropped my fork and bucket and ran toward the still form that lay by the giant driftwood.

Arriving at his side, I halted, gasping both for breath and at the sight close-up. The clam fork pierced Bobby's left forearm. The sandy mud under it was a dark stain. Bobby lay facedown, his head turned toward the left. Blood dripped from a gash on his temple.

I thought I saw his nostrils move. I knelt next to his head to make sure. I laid my fingers gingerly on his neck. He was alive with shallow, quick breaths. At least he was alive. That left the more critical problem, the blood flowing from the wound on his arm. I didn't want to remove the clam fork—that would probably make it bleed even more—and searched my memories of long-ago Girl Scout first aid lessons, coming up with the word *tourniquet*. Yes.

I ripped off my jacket. I tied it as tightly as I could around his arm right above the elbow. I wished I had a blanket or had worn more coats so I could cover him with something warm until help came. I had to call for help, and fast. A glance back at Dan confirmed that he was already at his van and couldn't see me kneeling behind the driftwood. I felt in my pants pockets but didn't find my cell phone. The jacket!

I gently maneuvered into the right pocket of the now-tourniquet jacket and drew out my phone. I stabbed 911 and reported the situation.

"Yes, he's breathing, but it's really light and rapid." Would the ambulance arrive in time?

The dispatcher asked where I was.

"The Rum Cove clam flat. By a big piece of driftwood, a tree."

"Cover him if you can and stay right there. Put me on speaker and keep the call connected."

"I will. Please have them hurry."

I pressed the speaker button and set the phone on the driftwood. I looked back the way we'd come. Who would have done this? And why hadn't I noticed anyone else on the flats? Surely Bobby hadn't been lying here stabbed all this time. I squatted and felt the skin of his cheek. It felt cooler than his neck had a few moments earlier. Hang the cold. I drew my hooded sweatshirt off and smoothed it over Bobby's head and back. I rubbed his back in light gentle circles, repeating what Mom had murmured to me in decades previous: "You're going to be all right. Hang in there. Everything's going to be okay." In the distance, a siren started up the incline of its pitch.

This must have been some fight, I thought. But with whom? I glanced at the sand. It was scuffed, but I couldn't see any distinct footprints. I might have destroyed footprints with trying to help Bobby.

I'd seen him and Walter Colby argue downtown last week. Bobby had acted strangely the night of the murder and had been rude to me at the beach. Dan and Bobby had had some kind of run-in at the parade. A shudder ran through me, and not only because I wore only a T-shirt in the cool morning air. Dan had gone to the van for the pastries.

"What in hell?" Dan's voice boomed behind me.

I yelped. I had thought Dan was far down the flats at his van.

Dan knelt beside me. "What happened to him?"

"I don't know." I shuddered, trying to pull myself together. "I called to you, but you didn't hear me." My tone was urgent. "Bobby's alive. Just."

Dan's eyes scanned the fork, the blood, the motionless lobsterman on the sand. He shook his head. "Poor old Bobby. He had a tough life."

I bristled. "He still has one and it's getting tougher by the minute. Why don't you hurry yourself back out to the road and direct the EMTs?"

• • •

I pulled on my sweatshirt. The siren faded as the ambulance carrying Bobby to the hospital sped away. An Ashford PD officer interviewed Dan several yards distant. The officer had already questioned me, taking notes of my responses. He'd seemed skeptical that I hadn't seen Bobby or his attacker, but I told the truth about the morning. That was all I had.

I wrapped my arms around myself. I wished I were at home with my dog and a cup of hot chocolate. I couldn't roust the picture of those rusted tines piercing Bobby's arm out of my mind.

Another officer pushed stakes into the mud. He attached yellow crime scene tape to them and to the driftwood tree. He cast a glance at the tide that pushed its way ever closer and shrugged as he knelt and photographed the mud, the clam fork that now lay on the wet ground, the contours of the driftwood.

I jammed my chilled hands into my sweatshirt pockets. Watching the officer, I thought again of the hands that had wielded the wood handle of the fork. What had been their intention? Was the attack a sudden act, a welling up of violent passion, or had it been planned and executed to address a long-standing grievance? Had the person who lashed out at Bobby been intent on snuffing out his life, or did he or she mean to deliver a stern warning?

And then the practical questions took over. Would the police be able to identify the assaulter from some kind of evidence? Did fingerprints adhere to damp and splintery wood?

"Ready to go?" Dan's deep voice was gruff. He touched my elbow.

I nodded and headed toward the road carrying only my bucket, because the police had wanted to examine our clam forks. My earlier fantasies about Dan had vanished. His angry reaction to the discussion of his gay father and his actions on the clam flats made me feel uneasy. He seemed unpredictable. This was not a trait I was interested in, in anyone, let alone a romantic prospect. I'd had no business flirting with him, anyway. I couldn't wait to go home.

"Hey, wait up. I'm the one with the keys, remember?" His voice came from several paces behind me.

I sighed and slowed my pace.

"So what kind of questions did Officer Benny ask you?"

"Oh, you know." I raised an eyebrow. "What happened, where we were, what I saw. The usual."

"What did you tell him?" Dan gestured vaguely behind us.

I stopped short and turned my head sharply toward him. My tone was equally sharp. "I told him the truth. What did you tell him?"

Dan didn't meet my stare. "Same thing. Well, sort of. I said we were together the whole time." He stopped and twisted back toward me. "Aren't you coming?"

"Dan Talbot. Why would you tell him something like that? You know we weren't together the whole time." What kind of an idiot was he? "You went to fetch the breakfast. Remember?" I fixed fists on hips and didn't budge.

"Never mind. It doesn't matter." He resumed walking. "Neither of us did anything wrong."

I followed behind but kept my eyes on him. I knew I hadn't done anything to be suspected of. Dan, though? That story was not so clear.

• • •

At home, I showered off the salt air and the remnants of Dan's disturbing aura. I walked Wulu and enjoyed that cup of hot chocolate I'd been wanting. I spent several hours researching phonological changes in the northern Japanese vowel system.

But in the back of my mind lurked Iris's comments about Mary. My index finger hesitated above my phone, my eyes on the local phone book open to the H page. Mary was an Ashford native, and somewhere I had learned that she was on the board of directors for the Holt mansion. Maybe she'd have an insight into Bobby Spirokis.

I rose from my desk, slipping the phone into my pants pocket. The miniature elm seemed to call me from its spot by the window. I turned the bonsai pot ninety degrees and checked its growing tips. A spritz from a spray bottle gave a sheen to the tiny leaves. I knelt so my eyes were on a level with the tree.

"Any wisdom for me, *Sensei Kī*? Should I call Mary? I'll bet she could tell me a thing or two about the tensions in this town."

Teacher Tree kept its silence. I closed my eyes for a moment. I held the soul of Charles Heard in the Light. I pictured stabbed Bobby Spirokis surrounded by gentle, healing hands. Finally I held myself in the moment of quiet.

Rising, I took a deep breath. I returned to my desk and pressed Mary's phone number before I lost my nerve.

After exchanging greetings with Mary, I said, "I saw your bonsai downtown in your brother's office. I wondered if I could stop by and talk the art with you. I have an elm, but I'm sort of a beginner."

"I'm in my workroom. I'd be happy to show you around." She gave me directions to her house on the Bluffs.

I thanked her, said I'd be there in twenty minutes, and pressed End. I snapped pictures of the elm from several angles and tucked the camera into my bag. I really did want to talk bonsai with Mary. And if a few other tidbits of information emerged, too, what was wrong with that?

My stomach rumbled when I was almost out the door. Glancing at the clock, I wondered how it had arrived at one thirty already. Well, too bad. I grabbed a handful of roasted almonds from the tin on the kitchen counter and headed for my truck.

As I drove by the Rum Cove clam flat on my way to the Bluffs, I pulled to the side of the road at the same spot where Dan had parked that morning. Neck Road bisected a narrow spit of land, almost a causeway, connecting the mainland to the quasi-islands of Great Neck and then the Bluffs.

The clam flat was now just a calm bay that sparkled in the sunlight. Tiny waves lapped at the scrubby Rosa rugosa and beach plum bushes alongside the road. It made me feel as if the morning had been a bad dream. Digging for clams. Hearing the scorn in Dan's voice. Seeing Bobby's blood.

A few high clouds scudded by in a breeze that propelled a sailboat toward Plum Island Sound, the boat's sail full with wind. I watched it lean as it raced along. I remembered the exhilarating sensation of speeding along in the salt spray with Daddy. I frowned as something pinged in my consciousness. My mother had said Daddy told her he was gay right before he left. Dan Talbot's father was apparently gay. Had they known each other? Could there have been some connection? The Talbots lived in Ashford. I had grown up in Newburyport fifteen miles away. Maybe the fathers had met somewhere.

I restarted the engine. Mary lived at 4 Neck Road. I glanced at an address to my left as I entered Great Neck: 923. Mary must be all the way at the end. I traversed the hills and curves of the narrow road with caution. Residents and their guests were usually the only people who drove here, although they were public byways. Right after the narrowing that split Great Neck from the Bluffs sat the small Pavilion Beach. It allowed public access, but otherwise the Bluffs harbored no commerce, no chic little bistro, nothing to draw mainlanders into the enclave.

The last downhill of the road presented a striking view of the Holt mansion in the distance. The Grand Allée stretched unbroken up to the mansion atop the wooded hill right across the outlet of the Ashford River into the Atlantic.

I spied a mailbox labeled *4* and pulled sharply right into the steep driveway of a house built into the slope. As I exited the truck, I stared up at the house. It was both simple and stunning. A bank of tall windows faced east to the ocean. The turquoise trim set off silvered cedar shingles and matched the garage door. A mass of magenta and white impatiens blanketed either side of stone steps that led up to the door. A Japanese gate invited entrance to the back garden, beyond which I could see lush plantings. A wind chime tinkled its welcome.

I trudged up the steps to the porch. A gnarled cedar bonsai sat on a round stand next to the door. After I examined it, I knocked and then jangled a thick metal bell that hung next to it. No one responded, so I strolled around to the wooden torii-style gate.

"Hello? Mary?" Maybe her bonsai workroom was outdoors or in a shed. I leaned inside the gateway. "Yoo-hoo. It's me, Lauren." Still no answer. Mary had said to come right over. Where was she? The path beyond the gate curved around behind the house. I didn't want to appear to be trespassing. On the other hand, I felt drawn to learn what I could from this woman. Sister of the murder victim. Photographer. Bonsai devotee. Lifelong resident. Former flame of a local banker. And who knew what else. And if she'd been fine on the phone twenty minutes earlier, where was she now?

I strolled in along the path. The trees overhead dappled the plantings with bits of light. It was a magnificent shade garden. I didn't know the names of most of the plants, although I recognized several kinds of variegated hostas splaying huge leaves in layered circles. Tiny rose-colored sprays of blossoms poked out of another plant. Impatiens were tucked in everywhere.

Around the bend I came to a flagstone patio. A trellis above it supported a well-established wisteria. This woman was a gardener, all right, and not only of bonsai. But where was she?

"Mary?" I called again. I turned my head sharply toward a scraping noise, then sighed with relief when I saw branches of a bent-over cypress rub in the wind. Beyond the tree I saw a building tucked in the back corner of the property and headed toward it.

"Lauren?"

I turned. "There you are. I was looking for you."

Mary stood behind me on the path. Her hands were gloved and she carried a six-inch knife in her left hand.

Chapter Eleven

I tried to smile and calm my thudding heart at the same time. "Hi."

Mary returned a faint smile. She pointed her chin toward the back. "Workroom's over there. I was dividing a stubborn iris." She held up the knife. "They grow too big and the only solution is to slice the root ball."

"Right." I nodded, trying to look interested. I'd never divided a perennial in my life and wasn't too interested in finding out how from a woman with a big knife.

Mary led the way. Her long legs moved with confidence in khaki work shorts stained with dirt and rust. Her feet in heavy sandals were grimy with garden soil. A faded work shirt flapped behind her. The contrast was striking from the elegant attire I had seen her in on previous occasions.

Holding open the door to a low structure, Mary gestured me in. A hint of pleasure lifted the left side of her mouth. Her eyes softened as her gaze swept the room.

I entered and stopped. The building, large enough to house several families, was more of a bonsai design center than a workroom. Large windows facing north onto a sunny wildflower garden provided plenty of indirect light, with additional illumination cast by a roof window. Waist-high benches lined the walls, and two tables filled the center of the room.

Every bench displayed a half dozen bonsai trees. I stared in wonder at the specimens. I couldn't even start to name all the tree varieties. I spied an elm similar to my own next to a spruce like the one in the Heard Insurance office. A tiny peach tree sported miniature pink blossoms. I shook my head, amazed, then glanced at Mary.

"This is incredible. All yours?"

Mary nodded. She picked up a pair of fine clippers. She carried what looked like a Joshua tree, its gnarled limbs reaching into untree-like shapes, to a slatted shelf next to the large utility sink in the corner and began to prune.

I folded my arms, watching. "I'm impressed. How long have you been doing bonsai?"

"Oh, you know. Awhile." Mary's brusque tone brushed off my question.

As I strolled along the benches, I wondered why Mary seemed annoyed at my presence. Just under an hour ago she'd sounded welcoming and had told me to come by. I wasn't going to extract any juicy details from her if Mary didn't even want to talk bonsai. But it couldn't hurt to try. I approached the table where the dark green desert tree perched.

"Ever seen these in the wild? They're something." I stroked a bayonet-shaped leaf, careful to avoid the point. "There's a whole national park of them out in California."

Mary nodded.

"Is the way you prune them any different than how you'd treat a tree that grows around here?"

"A bit. Normal Joshua trees have a slow growth pattern as it is. As bonsai they are even slower. You know, it's not really a tree."

"Oh?" I had visited the searing-hot desert refuge years ago and had seen trees similar to these in my travels through Mali and Niger, but I'd never bothered to learn much about them.

"Right. It's actually a *Yucca brevifolia*, a giant yucca plant. They can live longer than seven hundred years."

"I had no idea." I watched Mary take tiny snips of the spiky bursts that adorned the ends of stubby branches. "Do you sell any of these?"

Mary shook her head in silence. She stopped pruning and turned the Joshua tree's tray all the way around once. She bent over to examine it, then straightened with a satisfied, "Good." She looked at me. "What did you want to know about your tree?"

I pulled out my camera. I brought up the views I'd snapped before I left home and extended the slim device to Mary. "What do you think? It's my first one, and—"

A thud like a door slam sounded from the direction of the house. Mary jerked her head toward the path. Her eyes widened. She glanced back at me. A minute passed. Mary exhaled as if releasing a burden and put her attention on the camera images. The camera shook slightly in her hand.

"This looks like a good specimen. When's the last time you repotted and fed her?"

I smiled at the feminine pronoun. I, too, thought of the elm as a female.

"A year ago, May. I should do that every two years, isn't that right?"

"Well, the repotting, yes. Feed her only in the spring and summer." Mary clicked to the next picture and then the next. "Make sure you don't overdo it. But I like your pruning technique." She thrust the camera back at me with a sudden move. She turned to a delicate red-leafed maple. "You really need more sun, dear."

I cocked my head, then realized Mary had addressed the tree, not me. I watched as Mary repositioned the tree to a table under the skylight in the southwest corner of the room, where it would receive direct light. Mary brought the Joshua tree to sit next to the Japanese maple. Almost under her breath, Mary said, "*Acer palmatum* loses its red color in the shade."

I decided to give digging for dirt, so to speak, one more try. "So, have you lived here your whole life, Mary?" I kept my tone casual as I stroked an ungainly beech, one of the only trees in the room that looked like it needed a pruning session.

"Yes, I have." Mary looked up with a frown. "What's your last name, again?"

"Rousseau. I grew up in Newburyport."

Mary set her hands on her hips. She cocked her head. "Mr. Rousseau. He taught sailing when I was a teenager. Related?"

I felt a chill, like this fishing expedition had taken a deep-sea dive by bringing Daddy into it. "He was my father. Harold Rousseau. But I didn't know he was a sailing instructor." I fixed my eyes on the tall woman opposite, who smiled toward the window as if at a fond memory. "I mean, I know he was a sailor. He took me out on the boat plenty of times."

"Sure. Walter and I used to take lessons together. We thought we'd sail around the world together one day."

I didn't remember my father giving lessons. Mary had to be at least ten years older than me, though. If Mary had taken lessons as a teen, I might have been too young to know about it. Walter. Maybe Iris's tale was true, then.

"Walter? Would that be Walter Colby?"

Mary nodded.

"Are you two still friends?"

Mary froze in front of the window. She whirled and stared at me with eyes flashing. "Listen, what do you want to know? What are you doing poking around here?"

"Nothing." I opened my eyes wide. I hoped I looked more innocent of ulterior motives than I was. "I simply wanted to talk about bonsai."

Mary shook her head hard, fast. "No, you didn't *simply* want to talk about bonsai."

I inhaled deeply. "Mary, I am so impressed with your expertise here. And I also wanted to get to know you better. I've only been in town a few years, and I'm still finding my way into friendships. You're interesting. I thought it'd be nice to see if we could be, well, friends." I spread my hands, palms up. I shrugged. I hoped Mary would believe me. All that was true, in fact. And if Mary was exceptionally good at reading subconscious signals, I couldn't do anything about it.

Mary gazed at me. Her luminous eyes appeared to grow moist for a moment. Then she shook her head, and a stern look replaced the wistfulness. "That's very nice. I'm pretty busy, though, you know. With this." She gestured around herself. "And my photography, and now Charles's business—" She turned back to the window.

Got it, I thought. Too busy to be friends. Well, okay.

A shape loomed backlit in the workshop's open doorway.

"Why didn't you tell me?" Walter Colby's voice was both plaintive and furious. His face glistened, and he breathed like an out-of-shape athlete. He wore a banker's black dress shoes, though, with pressed slacks that strained at the waistband and a pale green button-down shirt open at the collar. Surely he hadn't run here.

Mary snapped her head toward him. She folded her arms and turned slowly.

"Tell you what?" Mary spat out the words.

Walter opened his mouth. He glanced at me and shut it again.

I waited. I averted my eyes to the nearest miniature tree, hoping he would continue.

"That they think James Wojinski committed Charles's murder?" Mary asked.

My eyes widened. "Did the police arrest Mr. Wojinski?" I asked. "I saw them questioning him yesterday."

"I heard they're about to," Mary said.

Walter muttered something. It sounded like "mark." Mark what?

"Speak up, Walter." Mary glared at him.

"James didn't do it."

"Do you know who did?" I couldn't help myself from asking.

Walter looked over at me. He blinked. He cleared his throat. Suddenly the successful banker again, he said, "Of course not. That's for the police detectives," he said with confidence.

• • •

I left after a quick goodbye. The vibe that Mary and Walter needed some time alone was unmistakable.

As I climbed into my truck, I realized I'd never asked Mary about Bobby. When I arrived home, I found a message on my phone to call the police. I groaned but dutifully dialed. The dispatcher put me through to Chief Flaherty. We exchanged minimal greetings.

"I need you to tell me exactly what happened when you found Bobby Spirokis on the clam flat," he said.

"I already told the officer."

"Now tell me."

I rolled my eyes but repeated the sequence of events. Clamming with Dan. Dan going off to fetch breakfast. Dan returning. Me lagging behind him as we left and finding Bobby lying on the sand with a clam fork in his arm.

"Are you sure? Dan Talbot told us a different set of events."

"Of course I'm sure. It was only this morning."

The chief thanked me and rang off. I stared at the phone in my hand. I thought again about how Dan had reacted as we walked to the van. Why had he claimed we were together the entire time?

• • •

I awoke the next morning with a message in my mind and heart: *Go visit Bobby Spirokis.* I tried to ignore it during Wulu's quick walk in the rain. And hoped it might go away while I sipped my coffee. It stayed with me as I watched the drops fall from the graceful maple that shaded my front window. I knew from the past that when I felt a impulse like this I was better off doing it than avoiding it.

I hoped I wasn't making a habit of encountering people needing hospitalization but figured that was better than happening across people for whom a hospital would not be helpful, like Charles Heard.

The last time I'd stood in front of the hospital information desk had been in March, when my friend Elise was hospitalized. As the pink-jacketed, pink-cheeked elder behind the desk gazed up at me with bright eyes and an inquiring look, I also hoped Bobby Spirokis would feel kindly toward a near-stranger dropping in on him. I asked for his room and headed off to the designated elevator.

A few moments later I stood at Bobby's bedside. He slept, his head and injured arm both heavily bandaged. An IV dripped into his other arm from a bag hung on a tall pole, but he was otherwise untethered to monitoring machines.

I surveyed the private room. No flowers brightened the windowsill. No personal effects of any kind were in evidence. Did he have family? A wife and children to visit him and bring cheer to the sterile room? A mother to soothe his brow?

Closing my eyes, I held Bobby in the Light. A minute passed. My heart slowed, and calm seemed to float in the room like a healing cloud. A cart on wheels rattled by in the hall. A woman's voice nearby conversed in low tones.

"Hey," Bobby said.

I opened my eyes to see that Bobby had done the same. "Hi." I smiled, suddenly unsure about my motivation in being in his hospital room. "How are you feeling?"

"Not so good." His voice was low, his articulation slurred. "Hurts."

I nodded.

"Why're you here?" Bobby frowned under the bandages on his forehead.

"I found you. On the clam flats. So I wanted to make sure you were okay." I wanted to extend my hand, to squeeze the thick hand that lay on the white blanket. I didn't know Bobby. I kept my hand to myself.

Bobby's eyes widened. "Did you see?"

"See what?"

"Did you see?"

"I didn't see anything except you. You were lying on the mud. By a big driftwood log. What did happen? Do you remember?"

Bobby closed his eyes with a groan. He seemed to shrink into the bed. He opened them. "I need—"

A tall nurse strode into the room. "Good morning." He checked the IV bag and leaned in over Bobby. "Mr. Spirokis? I'm going to take your vitals now."

Bobby murmured acknowledgment.

"I'll get out of your way," I said. "Bobby?"

Bobby looked at me. His blue eyes were pale, as if faded from all his years on a sunny ocean.

I dug in my bag. I drew out my business card from the college, which included my cell phone number. I laid it on the bed tray. "I hope you feel better soon. If you need anything or would like me to stop by again, will you call me?"

Bobby closed his eyes again. The nurse, thermometer device in hand, gazed at me with what looked like an unspoken message to leave and let his patient rest.

I made my way to the Exit sign. I located the stairs and walked down the five floors slowly. Bobby had said, "Did you see?" He'd been about to tell me something. The nurse couldn't have had worse timing. I wondered if I should go to the cafeteria and then try to visit him again. But, no, he'd seemed so fragile. I'd better wait.

I wished Natalia wasn't on leave. In the spring, after my student had been murdered, it had been helpful to have a contact, a friend who was a police officer. Not that Natalia usually answered my questions during the investigation. More often she had chastised me for taking too much initiative in the search for the killer. But I knew if I asked Chief Flaherty about the attack, he would tell me exactly nothing.

I pulled up the hood on my rain jacket and dashed to my truck through rain now pouring down in earnest. I stopped short and stared in dismay. The front tire on the driver's side was flat. Then I looked again. The entire front of the truck tilted down. I made my way around to the passenger side.

The other front wheel also rested on the collapsed black rubber of the tire. I frowned, then swore. A dark object stuck out of the sidewall. I leaned down closer. My eyes widened. This was no slow leak. The object in my tire was the handle of a knife.

Chapter Twelve

I straightened. My hood fell back. I glanced, fast, left and right, ignoring the rain soaking my head. Who had done this? Were they still around? Anger rose up in my core. I felt my cheeks flush, despite the cool air. If some creep thought they could distract me by disabling my cherished old truck, they could think again. All I'd done was visit an injured man in the hospital.

Water dripped onto my neck. I examined the rear tires, but they were fine. I'd parked the small, weathered vehicle in the last row of the parking lot, the farthest away from the hospital entrance in one of the last spaces free when I'd arrived. Its hood faced shrubbery that bordered a strip of woods. Whoever did this had had good cover. I peered up at the nearest light post, wondering if there was a surveillance camera. Even so, that wasn't going to help me now.

Sighing, I pulled up my hood, drew my cell phone out of my bag, and punched in 911 since I had no idea what the Millsbury nonemergency number was. I described the crime to the dispatcher and then listened.

"What do you mean, do I know who did it? I just told you I was visiting someone in the hospital! Do you think the jerk who slashed my tires was standing here when I came out, ready with ID and an apology?" My pitch rose like a boiling teakettle's. "It must have been some vandal getting his kicks out of destroying other people's property."

I paced the parking lot in front of the truck as I listened again. No other cars had their tires slashed, though, so maybe the vandal idea was wrong.

"Yes, I understand." I took a deep breath and tried to calm down. "How long before someone shows up?"

The dispatcher explained that officer would be there shortly. I thanked her and hung up. I indulged myself in a minute of swearing at the dispatcher, the slasher, and the general state of my previously peaceful life. Then I took a deep breath. It didn't do me any good to fight the inevitable. I located my AAA card and arranged for them to come to the hospital lot.

After he asked me for the information on my tire, the man on the other end said, "Do you have a spare?"

I said I did.

"We'll bring a used tire of the same size on a rim for the second flat. It'll be a lot cheaper than a tow, ma'am."

I thought for a second. "Why don't you bring two? That way I'll still have a spare."

"Smart thinking. Will do."

I thanked him. I was about to climb into the cab to wait out of the ongoing drizzle when I had an idea.

"I can do something, at least," I said to myself. I tapped my phone's camera and made sure the time and date stamp was enabled. I snapped pictures of the tire with the knife handle, the other flat tire, and the sunken front end of the truck. I stood reviewing the pictures, but I kept my peripheral vision alert.

A car pulled up. A uniformed woman stuck her head out of the window of a small white hybrid. "Need some help?" The car sported an understated logo that read *All-Safe Security*.

Yeah, well, not exactly. Where had they been when my tires were being destroyed? I bit back a rude retort and gestured toward my pierced tire. "Someone slashed my tires." In your safe parking lot, honey.

The driver leaned back into the car. The orange light on the car roof lit up and rotated. She climbed out.

I gazed up at one of the tallest women I'd ever seen. This guard had to be several inches over six feet tall. Her navy jacket bore the same logo as the car, and her khaki pants seemed cut for a man's straight line rather than the guard's womanly curves. Her grizzled hair curled close to her head in a no-nonsense cut.

The guard nodded at me. "Name's Orlene Cobb. Tell me what happened, please." She looked at me with kind brown eyes.

I relayed finding my truck in its disabled condition.

"How long were you in the facility, ma'am?" Orlene circumnavigated the truck as she spoke.

"Oh, ten minutes. Maybe fifteen?"

"Might you have an idea about the perpetrator?"

Everybody's favorite question. "No. I go in, my tires are fine. I come out, they're cut. Do you have cameras out here?"

A phone on Orlene's belt beeped. She excused herself. Turning her back to me, she held it up and said something in reply to a voice that sounded garbled to me.

As Orlene turned back to me, a tow truck rounded into the parking lot, followed close behind by a Millsbury police car, blue lights flashing.

Amused, I smiled. A surfeit of riches, or at least of assistance. They might not find the person who attacked my car, but at a minimum I hoped I'd be able to leave for home before much longer.

Two officers piled out. One busied herself with the scene while the other introduced himself to me. He took my ID. Once again I described what had happened.

"Do you have any idea who might have cut your tires?"

I hesitated for a moment before offering that I didn't know, but that I'd been involved in a couple of incidents in Ashford recently. "But that can't be connected with this, can it?"

The officer, a trim man in his fifties, shrugged. He took another look at my ID and said, "Oh, yeah. I heard about you."

I raised my eyebrows.

"My buddy Dick is the chief over there. We're in the same wine-making cooperative."

I must have shown my surprise, because he went on. "We do everything but grow the grapes. Been doing it for years."

• • •

By noon, I had been sent home with two used tires. The knifed ones were in police custody. The police had finally finished their questioning, and Orlene had asked me to fill out several forms. The mechanic had been cheery and efficient. I was relieved to be home, and the rain had lightened, too.

Wulu was glad I was home, too. He ran to his purple leash and barked expectantly.

"One second, doggie. I'm hungry. We'll go out in a jiff." I poured a glass of skim milk and slapped some peanut butter on a piece of bread. Eating at the kitchen counter, I realized Orlene had never answered me about surveillance video. Zac could do wonders with otherwise blurry, dark footage. His expertise in video forensics had helped solve my student's murder in the spring. Except that Zac was out of town. Way out of town.

I scribbled a note to myself to call Orlene. Somebody else in the police department must be able to use the software Zac used, even if not as well. If the hospital had a camera on that part of the parking lot, that is.

I grabbed an umbrella and walked up the hill with Wulu. We proceeded to the turn and into the park. I put my hand out to feel the rain. It had turned to a misty fog, so I furled the umbrella as we strolled. My thoughts returned to the scene in the hospital parking lot. Why would a vandal have picked my rattly old truck to attack? I stopped.

What if I had been the target after all? My arms sprouted goose bumps. I drew my jacket around me. That would mean someone had followed me to Millsbury. Maybe he—or she—had even watched when I discovered the damage. I pulled Wulu close. We were alone in a wooded park. Maybe we were being watched right now. But by whom?

This was ridiculous. I shook my head to clear it. I didn't need to be afraid in the middle of the day in my own town. I checked my watch. I had several hours until karate class. I could work for a while and shove my worries to the back of my mind.

At three thirty, I pushed back my chair. I hurried into my karate gear, stuffed the *gi* top into my bag, and ran the few blocks into town. I'd forgotten to deposit a check at the bank and wanted to do it in person before they closed. I'd heard too many stories about ATM scams to trust a machine with my money.

When the bank door resisted opening, I swore. I checked the posted sign next to the door and swore again. The bank closed at three thirty on Fridays. So much for that errand. Now I was early for karate. And after my experience with Dan at the clam flats, I didn't want to arrive early for class and be alone with him.

Iris's was only a few doors down the street. I could at least pop in and say hi. It was after hours for the bakery, too, but I knew Iris would be there prepping for the next day, and she always kept the door unlocked while she was in the shop.

The bell on the door jangled as I opened it. No one was out front. I heard voices from the kitchen. Probably Joey helping out after school.

"Yoo-hoo," I called as I made my way to the back. "Iris, it's me." I inhaled the heady aroma of fresh bread.

I pushed open the swinging door and stopped.

Iris looked up from a wide table. Her cheeks pinkened. "You didn't tell me you were coming by." The apparent reason for the blush stood close enough to Iris to rub arms, clad in a long white apron with flour on his hands. Walter Colby was, in fact, rubbing arms with Iris.

"Am I interrupting something?" I croaked out. What was the banker doing baking?

Iris and Walter looked at each other. Iris winked at me. "Just giving Walter his Friday lesson. Working on Greek buns this week."

Walter let out a belly laugh. Sure enough, the marble-topped table held several large pans covered with small mounds of dough. He nudged Iris with his hip and smiled at me. "I'll never be as good as my teacher here, but I'm trying. I make a mean loaf of bread already."

What a different face than the one he had showed the day before at Mary's. I never had found out what Mary hadn't told him.

"What did you need, Lauren?" Iris gazed at me, fake innocence sparkling in her eyes.

"Nothing. I was on my way to karate. Well, I'll leave you two." I turned to go.

"Hey, want to go clamming again on Tuesday?" Iris asked.

I thought, picturing my calendar. "No, that's the one day I can't. I have a seminar in Boston that morning."

"Okay."

"Call me later sometime?" I let the question hang in the air as I pushed back through the swinging door. I felt a twinge of sadness. Or maybe it was envy. They looked so happy together. Walter. Greek buns. Right. Iris must see a side of Walter the public wasn't privy to. Well, good for her, although I wondered why he'd been at Mary's. I hoped Walter wasn't Charles's murderer. It didn't sound like they'd had a very peaceful past. And Iris dating a killer? That would be very bad news, indeed.

• • •

I sipped my second glass of wine that evening. Karate had worn me out. The class had been full, and I'd left promptly, not much up for quality time with Sensei Talbot. I'd opted for a turkey sandwich and wine for dinner and a night alone rather than trying to drum up some company. I was pretty sure Iris wouldn't be free.

I gazed out the window at the sunset. Good. The rainy spell was over. Maybe I'd go clamming in the morning. By myself, this time. Except I didn't have my fork. I could always just dig with my hands or bring a garden fork.

I strolled with my glass into the office and powered up the computer. One of my favorite bonsai blogs had a new post on repotting. I scanned it, taking a few notes. I noticed they had a Facebook link. I clicked it and then clicked the Like button so I would see their updates in the future.

It being Facebook, people I was already Friends with who had also "Liked" the bonsai site appeared at the top of the Fans list. And since I didn't have any Facebook or even actual friends who also worked with bonsai, I was surprised to see a familiar name.

Mary Heard was on Facebook? Well, why not? I wondered if Mary would accept a request to Friend her. I might as well try.

While I was there, I scrolled through the Facebook statuses of my friends. Smiling, I read my colleague Ralph Fourakis's update from his vacation in Greece: "Sun, salt water, Metaxa, grilled fish, talking politics. Life at home." I was going to have to schedule a trip to Greece the next time Ralph traveled to visit his family. There was nothing like visiting a new country with a native. You ate home-cooked food, were introduced to real people instead of tourist-oriented shopkeepers, discovered the back roads and hidden corners of a culture.

Of course, I had been invited to visit Haiti with native Zac and had refused. I wasn't quite ready for that yet, even though it would be another opportunity to understand a new place, in this case Haiti, from the locals' point of view. A pang of missing gave me a little stab when I realized Zac hadn't emailed back or messaged me. I checked the list of friends in the corner of the screen, but he wasn't logged in. He'd only been gone a week, though, and he was busy with family in the culture he'd grown up in. Hadn't I been glad to have a little time apart, anyway? I felt his absence a lot more here in my usual haunts.

Clicking over to the Bluffs community site I'd discovered earlier, I pondered the faces of the Trustees once more. Who would they choose to replace Charles Heard? I didn't think they'd ever had a female Trustee. Maybe they'd select Mary, keep it in the family. Maybe not.

I clicked the bookmark for Language Log, my favorite linguistics blog, where I could happily spend the rest of the evening reading entertaining posts about language by several well-respected professors in the field and comments by intelligent linguists and nonlinguists from all over the world. I had just settled into a post about wrong but ridiculously funny translations from Chinese to English on public signage—a menu featuring Fried Enema, a public sign that read *Tiny Grass Is Dreaming*, a restaurant named Meat Patty Explode—when my phone rang in the other room.

I dashed to the kitchen, where the cell sat charging, and picked it up in time. I said hello and raised my eyebrows at the voice on the other end.

It was Mary Heard. She asked if I wanted to meet her downtown for a drink.

"Um, sure," I answered. Looked like Mary wanted to be friends, after all. Or maybe she had something else up her sleeve. "In half an hour?"

Mary agreed. "The bar at Ithaki, all right?"

I said I'd see her there and disconnected. Maybe Mary had been at home alone on Facebook, too, and had seen my Friend request.

I glanced down. I still wore my karate clothes and hadn't

showered after I'd trudged home. Good thing I had time for a quick shower and a change of clothes.

Twenty minutes later I checked myself in the mirror. A black silk blouse tucked into newish jeans was stylish but casual. I pulled my thick hair back in a bun. It looked too severe, so I let the curls tumble down again. I rubbed a little tinted lip gloss on my lips and slipped on my new red ankle boots. They'd been a splurge on a trip west and were out of character for me. I usually wore comfortable shoes without a heel. But these boots made me feel stylish and sexy in a daring way. I grabbed a denim jacket and locked the door. As I trotted down the front steps, I thought about my reasons for wearing the boots for a meeting with Mary. I felt a bit silly. The Ithaki bar was a pretty happening place on Friday nights, though. Who knew who else I'd see?

• • •

Mary waved at me from the bar. She gestured next to her at the only unoccupied bar stool.

Several men stood with drinks in their hands talking to the bartender, a woman I had seen before. The bartender's leathery face and husky voice hinted at a lifetime of cigarettes smoked in the sun. She wiped the counter and let out a throaty laugh at something one of the men said.

I took the seat. As I removed my jacket, I saw that Mary also wore a black top, a snugly fitting sweater. "Guess you got the email about what color to wear tonight." I smiled at Mary.

Mary shrugged, ignoring the joke. She sipped from a snifter, then lifted it in my direction. "I'm drinking cognac. The Delord Armagnac. You?"

Armagnac sounded intriguing. I weighed my taste buds, the hour, and the possibility of learning something from Mary. "I think I'll have wine." I caught the eye of the bartender and ordered a glass of a dry Riesling instead of something stronger.

"Have you eaten?" Mary asked, fiddling with her glass. A place setting with a white cloth napkin sat on the bar in front of her.

"I'm all set." I thanked the bartender as she set a stemmed glass in front of me. I tasted the cool wine.

"I ordered dinner. Don't like cooking for myself." Mary gazed into the amber liquid in her glass. "I used to make meals for Charles." The volume of her voice dropped to almost a whisper.

I reached out an arm and laid it lightly across Mary's back. "I'm so sorry," I murmured. Mary had had a lot to deal with in a little over a week's time.

Mary straightened, brushing me off. I drew my hand back quickly. I knew Yankees did not take well to affection offered by virtual strangers. I was a Yankee myself, but my world travels had opened me to different measures of personal space and connection.

"Ms. Heard?" A male voice spoke. "Excuse me." A black-aproned Mark Pulcifer extended a large square plate toward Mary. It was a colorful meal that looked like salad greens topped with grilled scallops. Beet crescents, golden pepper slices, and feta cheese garnished the dish.

"Thank you, Mark." Mary was instantly back in form, all elegance and poise. She glanced at the plate. "That looks delicious."

"Would you like anything else?"

Mary looked up at Mark. She gazed at him with an expression that looked like she was lost. In time, in her thoughts, in the past.

Mark cleared his throat.

Mary shook her head, then smiled a little. "I'm fine, but thank you."

He looked at me. "Would you like to order, Ms. Rousseau?"

"You remember me from last week?"

Mark nodded. "It's part of my job, to remember clients' names." He frowned. "If I still have a job there. Ms. Heard, what's going to happen to the insurance agency now?"

"It's too early to say. But there's plenty of work for you for a while, even if I decide to close it down. Don't worry."

"Anyway, I'm not going to order food. But thanks." I smiled at the young man. "I didn't know you worked here." He must make good tips at a place like Ithaki.

Mark nodded his head. "I'm waitstaff now, but what I really want is to be in the kitchen. To cook with the chef here would be a dream come true."

"Good luck with that," I told him.

"Mark seems like a nice kid," I said to Mary as he disappeared into the kitchen.

Mary nodded. She gazed after Mark. "He is." She propped her elbow on the bar and rested her chin on her fist.

"How old is he, do you know? Has he already finished college?"

"He's twenty-four. His birthday is next month. He finished college." This information came out in a rush, as if Mary had been storing it up for a long time. "He's saving up for grad school. Law."

Okaay, I thought. What makes her think he wants to study law when he says he wants to be a cook?

"I know his great-uncles," I added. "Mark looks a lot like Phillip Pulcifer."

Mary raised an eyebrow. "Oh, I very much doubt that."

I sipped my wine as I watched Mary savor her food in silence. The conversations of other diners and drinkers flowed around us. A woman at the other end of the bar leaned in and said something in a low voice to the bartender, then both women laughed out loud.

"He looked like he was bitten by a rabid dog, *chéri*," the bartender said, nodding.

I stared. That *chéri*. The smoky voice. The bartender had been the woman behind the hedge at the funeral.

"Do you know her name, the bartender?" I leaned toward Mary and asked in a low voice.

"That's Gloria. Been here forever, since she moved down from Montreal, that is."

"Does she live on the Bluffs?"

Mary shot a puzzled look at me. "Yes. Why do you ask?"

"Oh, just wondering. I think I saw her there, you know, when I drove out to see you yesterday."

"She lives in a shack. It's an eyesore, but nobody seems to be able to make her fix it up."

I nodded. Interesting. "Does she live alone?"

Mary shrugged, clearly done with the topic of the life of the bartender.

I sipped my wine, then gestured toward Mary's plate. "Tasty?" I wondered why Mary had called me to meet her here. She hadn't been at all talkative. Well, maybe she simply needed company.

"Mmm," Mary said, nodding. "Dimitri grills the best scallops in the universe. Want to try one?" She cut one of the plump morsels in half and offered it to me on her fork.

I accepted the utensil. The sweet flesh of the perfectly seared scallop was flavored with a hint of lemon and olive oil, all it needed. "Mmm. Thanks. That's the best scallop I've ever had."

Mary nodded. "They know what they're doing here."

I sipped my wine, then said, "Can I ask you a question?"

Wary, she nodded again.

"You mentioned that you took sailing lessons with my father years ago. Would you mind talking to me about him?" The lump in my throat threatened to choke off further words. I blinked back suddenly full eyes and swallowed. "I have my own memories of him, of course, but I'd love to hear yours."

Mary gazed at me, then nodded again. "Why not? Let's see. Of course, I'd grown up sailing. But we wanted to compete, and Mr. Rousseau was known as one of the best sailing race instructors around. I convinced my father to talk with him and let Walter Colby and me take lessons, even though we were younger than he usually taught."

"I didn't know he knew anything about racing. That's amazing." I had never heard of my father sailing competitively. I realized there was probably more I didn't know about Harold Rousseau than what I did know, and wondered if this was true of all children about their parents. Or maybe it was only children whose parents hadn't survived long enough to see their offspring grow up past the age of nineteen. How I wished I could have had an adult relationship with my father.

"He was a good teacher. You need a certain kind of gift to work with teenagers, I think. And he had it. He could motivate us to work hard and still have fun."

"Did you end up racing?"

"Oh, yes. Walter and I ended up with a pile of trophies. But then . . ." Mary fell silent as Mark Pulcifer walked by, a laden tray held level at head height. "Then I went away."

"For school?"

"You could say that."

"Where did you study?" I wondered if she'd admit to what Iris had conjectured, that maybe she'd been pregnant.

Mary shook her head. "Too many questions."

Chapter Thirteen

At seven the next morning, I stopped short, equipped with a bucket, a garden fork, and rubber boots. Facing the Rum Cove flat, I stood in front of a sign on a post. Written in red was the message "Flat closed do to rain. Shellfish may be toxic." The telephone number of the shellfish inspector followed.

Apart from the typo, the message was clear. I looked around. The sun shone, the air was warm and mild, and the water out beyond the mud sparkled. "Due to rain? The rain stopped yesterday!" My shoulders slumped.

Sure enough, nobody dug on the flats. A Sunfish sailed around the point in the distance, and a gaggle of bicyclists in garish outfits powered past me on their way to the Bluffs. But no one bent over the sand, unearthing succulent shells full with sweet treat, plopping them into a bucket of salt water.

"I wonder how long they stay closed?" I mused aloud.

"Only a few days, usually."

I turned to see Dan Talbot astride a racing bike. He wore a helmet, a brightly colored biking shirt, and biking shorts. Had he followed me?

Dan waved down the road at the last cyclist in the group. The cyclist had paused and made a questioning gesture. Dan motioned for her to go on without him.

No, he must be with the group.

"Does everybody know about this rule but me?" I pointed to the sign. I was not happy about suiting up for digging and wasting gas money, not to mention looking ridiculous to the general public.

"It's on your license that you need to call before you come to make sure the flats are open. When it rains a lot, sewage can wash out onto the flats. Believe me, you don't want to eat a clam that's been sucking up, well, somebody else's waste."

I frowned. I certainly didn't. Next time I'd read the documentation more carefully. What was it that Mom always said? "RTFM." She was a retired technical writer. When she declared the acronym, my mother meant "Read the *fine* manual," as opposed to another possible f-word.

"Hey." Dan smiled at me. "I'm working the rest of the day at the Pineswamp Habitat House . . ."

At my look of confusion, Dan clarified. "Habitat for Humanity. We're building a low-cost house out on Pineswamp Road."

Did the dimensions of this man ever stop increasing? Now that I thought about it, I realized it wasn't much of a stretch for him to apply his carpentry skills to building affordable houses for people who needed them.

"But anyway," Dan went on, "at four o'clock today I have two reservations for a behind-the-scenes tour out at the Holt mansion. You know, the areas of the building where the maids and butlers worked. Should be fun, and my buddy can't go, after all. Would you like to join me?"

A tour of the usually hidden areas of a really intriguing hundred-year-old mansion? "I'd love to. Meet you there?"

"I'll pick you up at three forty," Dan called as he started to pedal, conveniently leaving no room for negotiation. "See you!"

I stared after him. So, my late afternoon was suddenly all planned out. Should I have accepted, given his behavior at the flats? Well, this was a public tour. It wasn't like I was going to be alone with him, except for ten minutes on the way to the mansion. I climbed in my truck and headed home, clam-free, for a run, a bit of work, and maybe an hour or two with a novel in the sun. I was on vacation, after all.

• • •

When I arrived at the bridge that crossed Toil-in-Vain Creek an hour later, I slowed my run to a walk. I stopped and wiped the sweat from my face with my T-shirt sleeve. I leaned against the heavy railing to stretch my calves. The water tower on the Bluffs rose up from the hill in the distance, although Holt Beach was out of sight around the bend of the Ashford River.

The events of the last week and a half felt like a storm cloud that swirled around me. Usually a hard hilly run cleared my thoughts and spirit. It wasn't working today, despite the sunny weather.

I thought of my father as I gazed at the roiling water. Who had been the man he had left my mother for? I had always thought my parents were in love. Perhaps they had been, or maybe it was the love of true friends, one of whom was caught in a situation society did not readily accept. I knew my sister Jackie's life as a lesbian hadn't been particularly easy, although the culture was more tolerant now than it had been when my father was a young man.

And what had happened to him a week later? Could this mystery man have been involved in Harold's death? I refused to believe it was an accident. Not for Daddy, not on a sailboat. It occurred to me for the first time to wonder if there had been an autopsy after his death. I'd have to ask my mother.

Too many questions, was right. I felt like my head was about to explode. And I hadn't even figured out who could have slashed my tires. Who had attacked Bobby Spirokis. And most important, since the police seemed to be without progress, who had killed Charles Heard.

• • •

Dan and I lagged behind the tour guide. The stocky woman seemed to know every fact about the Holt mansion, and the rest of the group clumped around her like a flock of ducklings. I lingered. I gazed, intrigued, at the inlaid wood of the floor. At the hidden heat registers. At an entire room Holt had imported from a European estate.

"Let's all keep together, shall we?" The guide waved us toward her. "Now this," she waved at a heavy metal door, "was what they called the Safe. The family owned a considerable silver collection and it was kept in here." The door opened into a small room completely lined in green felt.

I took my turn to peer in. Shelves, walls, everything except the floor and the ceiling were covered in the kind of cloth I'd only ever seen in the flat box that guarded my mother's silver flatware. A silver coffeepot and a stray serving tray sat orphaned on a shelf.

As if reading my mind, the guide said, "After Mr. Holt died, as specified in his will they auctioned off all the possessions that his children did not want. But this room had been full, believe me. One maid's position was to keep it all polished. That was her only job."

The group moved on. Dan leaned down to whisper in my ear, "I made out with Tracey DeJean in that room on prom night."

I laughed out loud. One of the matrons in the tour group looked back with a scowl.

"Yeah, we snuck past all the barriers to the places we weren't supposed to go." He winked and straightened, looking pleased with himself.

I glanced at him. I picked up none of the angry mood and strange behavior of the morning we'd gone clamming together. He seemed to be back to the genial, flirtatious man I'd experienced previously. Well, everybody had an off day now and then.

The gaggle of tourers had stopped in a cylindrical hallway. The guide pointed up at the domed ceiling and shone a small flashlight on a faded mural. She explained which family member each of the faces had been. She pointed out the Siamese cat, and then brought our attention to a section of wallpaper outlined by thin lines. It was a hidden door.

As she pulled on a ring-shaped handle recessed into the wall, the door opened onto a dark spiral staircase stretching up and down from the main floor. A thin woman who stood next to me gasped.

"It looks like something out of a murder mystery," she whispered.

The guide switched on a light that did little to illuminate the stairwell. She explained that it was one way the servants accessed the upstairs and downstairs, but that family members and guests would not have traversed those stairs.

Dan nudged me. He raised his eyebrows several times like Groucho Marx.

"Tracey?"

"Yup." Dan nodded, a fake-serious look on his face, a smile finally breaking through.

I poked my head in. The electric light was feeble, the wallpaper faded. I wondered how strong the staircase was, then remembered that a hundred years earlier things were built to last, especially by someone with as much money as Holt was reputed to have had.

The tour proceeded through the butler's pantry, an airy room lined with the same blue-and-white tiles used in one of the master bathrooms upstairs. A large metal table filled the middle of the room with wide metal cupboards beneath. The guide explained that steam had run through it to keep food and plates warm before serving. She then demonstrated a dumbwaiter in the wall, used to transport dishes and glassware from the room above.

The guide ushered the group down a stairwell without a handrail to the lower floor. It was dark, with only small dusty windows perched high in the walls. Pairs of pipes ran overhead along a rough ceiling reinforced with rusted girders.

"If anyone were walking upstairs right now, you wouldn't hear a creak. Holt specified almost obsessive overbuilding. He also included fire barriers between each floor, something rare for the times."

She paused in front of an elevator with a metal grid door. "This was how they brought the empty trunks down after they unpacked them."

"It looks like a jail cell to me," I whispered to Dan, who nodded. "Does it still work?" I asked the guide.

"I believe it does, although we don't allow the public on it." She laughed at the apparent ridiculousness of the thought.

"Maybe when they find whoever murdered Charles Heard, they'll lock him up in there," Dan said under his breath, his face suddenly grim. He stared at the archaic metal door.

I, in turn, stared at him. His eyes looked lost in another place. He was thinking about the murder. Because we were on the Holt Estate? I'd been the one to find the body, though, and I wasn't dwelling on thoughts of the murder. Or hadn't been up until now.

"Have you heard any news from the police about the investigation?" he asked me in a low voice.

"Me?" I shook my head. Why would he think I would have information? "Haven't seen squat in the *Chronicle*, either."

The tour guide again waved us over to where she had moved the group. "We need to stick together now." The guide flashed a polite but disciplinarian smile at us.

The group stood on a platform. It overlooked a pit that held two huge furnaces that flanked a small modern boiler in the middle. On the far side a concrete ramp sloped up away from the furnace area.

The guide pointed across the sunken area to the top of the ramp. "That's where they unloaded the coal. It slid down to where they could shovel it in."

I stared at the motes in the dusty light above the medieval-looking furnaces. The dungeon-like lower level had turned from a historical curiosity into the stuff of nightmares now that Dan had brought the memory of violent death into the experience. I expected to turn a corner and see Fortunato being bricked into his niche with the cask of Amontillado. Death by immurement. I wanted nothing more than to escape into the sunlight and fresh air above.

Chapter Fourteen

"Whoa!" I clung to the handle above my door as Dan sped his van around the curves winding down the hill from the estate. I made a note to avoid visiting the property in the deep freeze of winter.

"Sorry about that. I know these hairpins, forget that not everybody does." He laughed. "Know what we call that handle you're hanging on to?"

"The grab bar?"

"The 'Oh, shit!' handle." He grinned at me and then wrenched the steering wheel hard to make the next turn. He narrowly avoided a cypress tree.

"Good name for it."

"A beer and a burger at the pub?" Dan asked once we were on the road back to town.

A tour was one thing. Dinner out in the evening was quite another. "Thanks, but I can't tonight. Maybe another time."

Dan cast an odd look at me. He opened his mouth, then closed it without speaking.

After he dropped me at my condo, I took Wulu on a quick walk and then settled in with a cheese sandwich and a glass of Merlot. Ending the Holt tour in the basement, along with Dan's comment, had laid a creepy cast on my afternoon. I wasn't sure why. It was simply a museum tour of a grand old building. I was glad I'd avoided the afternoon turning into a date with Dan. I switched on the end of the afternoon's Red Sox game and worked on the crossword from the day's *Boston Globe*.

I poured my third glass of wine as the Sox lost. The tiny pesky voice of my inner nag reminded me that it might be wise to show a little restraint with respect to alcohol. I told it to shut up, took a sip, and turned the television off. I wandered about the condo carrying my glass, feeling aimless, until I ventured into my office.

I felt my pockets for my phone but came up empty. I strode into the kitchen that shone ghostly from the moonlight, and picked up my phone from the counter. I pressed my mother's number and walked to the front window as it rang. Mom must be out with Luke, I thought, when the message played. Luke was supposed to have returned from his trip today. Or maybe she was at his place for the night.

"Mom, can we meet for lunch tomorrow? I'm going to Meeting at ten, but I'd love to see you." I decided not to mention on the phone that I had more questions for my mother. "How about the Grog at noon? Love you."

My mother had steadfastly refused to acquire a cell phone. "I'm either not far from home or out of the country, dear," she had explained to me. "I'll be back home and check my messages soon enough. If people are so impatient for my company that they can't wait—well, patience is a virtue, isn't it?"

As I finished my message and disconnected, I saw a shape move in the shadows across the street. A person-sized shape. I leaned toward the window, careful to stay out of the bit of streetlight that shone in. The shape moved. My heart raced. Definitely a person, they seemed tall, but I couldn't make out other details. It could be a man or a woman. Whoever it was stayed in the shadow of the woods behind, and paced slowly back and forth.

I drew back into the depth of my condo, then moved to my front door, my hands and feet suddenly chilled. The lock and dead bolt were securely fastened. If this was someone casing my place, I needed to be sure I was safe. I checked the door from the kitchen to the back deck. It was my emergency exit in case of fire, with only a metal ladder that led down the two flights. The ladder ended a leap's distance from the ground. That door was also securely locked.

Maybe the person was stalking one of the other residents of my house. There were three other condos in it, after all. But with all that had gone on lately, I didn't want to take a chance.

Should I call the police? Call Iris? Call my sister? I took a moment to close my eyes and hold the situation in the Light. In a minute my heart calmed and my mind cleared. Without turning on any living room lamps, I strode to the front door and flipped on both the exterior porch light and the powerful light that illuminated the driveway. There was more than one way to hold a situation in the light, I thought with satisfaction. I crept back to the front window. Careful to keep back from the glass, I peered around the curtain.

A tall human shape now walked quickly down the hill. I decided to leave the lights on all night. It was well worth the price of electricity. I didn't know who had been stalking my house, but I felt safe with the person banished. For tonight, anyway.

• • •

I sat with my coffee the next morning and stared at the page I'd printed out from the Internet. It was from a   2004 edition of the *Newburyport Daily News*. My heart beat hard in my throat. Two tall men smiled in a grainy picture, arms slung casually over each other's shoulders, a sailboat behind. The caption read, "Harold Rousseau and Peter Talbot after their North Shore Regatta victory."

So they had known each other, Dan's father and mine. I couldn't remember ever hearing about a Peter Talbot from my parents. I checked the date on the story. July 23. Two weeks before my father's death on August 7. I had been at the Middlebury College intensive language school that summer studying Japanese. I had never heard of my father sailing competitively, but since he sailed so much, it hadn't seemed overly important to a college girl absorbed in her own life.

I glanced at the clock and swore. I was going to be late for Friends Meeting. I raced through my shower, threw on clothes, and drove to Millsbury as fast as was prudent, but it was already ten fifteen when I tiptoed into the Worship Room and took a seat on a back bench. The stillness of Friends in the rectangle of plain benches welcomed me. I closed my eyes and joined them.

After several minutes, the image of sitting in silence at the close of karate class rose up. So similar and so different from this. In karate, the discipline was formal. Much of it came originally from Japanese culture—bowing, the respect awarded a teacher—but the practice had evolved beyond that. The kata, a fluid, ritualized fight as beautiful as a dance. The class from beginners through black belts moving together in kicks and blocks. The *gi*, a loose, sturdy canvas uniform that both protected the body and set it free. As in any sport, one learned the rules in order to then let go and let the body operate on instinct. But in contrast to the end of, say, a tennis game or a long run, sinking into quiet meditation at the end of a physically exhausting karate workout let the mind be still and integrate with the body. Here in Friends Meeting, though? The stillness was all. There were no forms other than sitting, and occasionally standing to share a message. I found it almost harder to center and quiet my busy mind here than in the dojo.

"Friends, I am troubled this morning."

My eyes flew open. Dorothy stood directly across the room, gnarled hand on the silver handle of her cane.

"Our children are hungry. Our leaders are greedy. I grieve for nations at war. I pray for areas destroyed by climate upheaval. Let us strive for peace. Let us support our idealistic young people who work for change. May we go forth and take action as risky Quakers." Dorothy lowered herself to her seat.

It was a powerful message, and one typical from Dorothy. But I thought I could see the old woman wince as she sat. I mentally kicked myself for not being attentive to this cherished Friend, for not calling or visiting her midweek, not inquiring after her health or running a needed errand. I was young, healthy, and on vacation, after all. And not doing much to be a risky Quaker, either.

After Rise of Meeting and announcements, I sought Dorothy out. She sat with a cup of tea and a piece of coffee cake. She frowned as a little girl raced past her so close that she almost stepped on the old Friend's foot. I took the seat next to her. Up close I realized she was pale and looked thinner than she had even last week.

"Good morning, Friend," she said.

"Dorothy, how are you?"

"I don't complain, you know that. But I have been more well than now."

"Will you call me when you need help? I can drive you. I can pick something up for you, you know."

She nodded. "Yes, thank you. I will. The most help might be just to visit and sit with me."

Surprised at how forthcoming the usually curmudgeonly Friend was, I made a date for the following week. We chatted for a few minutes.

"Can I ask you a question?" I finally said.

At her nod, I went on. "Did you ever hear my father mention a Peter Talbot? Were they friends?"

"Oh, yes, they were quite close. In their college days, you understand. They met at Bowdoin and were roommates their last two years."

"I never heard Daddy mention him. Did they argue or something?"

"I don't really know, Lauren. Perhaps they became busy with work and raising families. I can't tell you more."

I thanked her and headed off to my lunch date with my mother. Maybe Mom would be able to fill out the picture.

• • •

The first swallow of IPA slid down my throat like I'd been thirsty all my life. My mother was late, so I had gone ahead and ordered. The Grog was a pub, so choosing pub fare was always the wiser choice. A black-aproned waitress set a cheeseburger platter on the weathered wooden plank table.

I thanked her and stared at the massive array of food, massive mostly in the number of French fries that crowded out the burger. I closed my eyes for a quick moment of prayer.

"Want to share a few of those?"

I opened my eyes to Mom sliding into the booth opposite me. "Hey, Mom. Help yourself."

She stretched her arm across the table to reach for a fry. "Perfect. Mind if I just munch? Luke and I ate breakfast late." The rosy tint of her cheeks hinted at why breakfast had been delayed.

"Sure. Too much for me," I mumbled around a mouthful of burger.

The waitress stopped by and took Mom's order for a glass of Chardonnay. "The house wine is fine," Mom said. She relayed details of Luke's trip to an estate sale in Maine, where she said he had acquired a treasure trove of antiques for his store.

"And how have you been, Laurie?"

My mother was the only person I let call me by my name's diminutive.

"I'm fine. No, I'm not fine. I'm really unsettled about Charles Heard's murder and about what happened to Daddy." I propped my chin on my fists, elbows on the table, and leaned toward her.

"Not that again." She frowned into her wineglass.

"Yes, that again. Mommy, I found a picture of Daddy and someone named Peter Talbot. They won the North Shore Regatta together. Only a couple of weeks before Daddy died."

My mom lifted her eyes to mine. "Yes, they did." The lines in her forehead deepened. She glanced at the wall behind the bar and then back at me.

"Did you know Peter Talbot? How did Daddy know him?" A pang stabbed me at the subterfuge of seeing if my mother would confirm what Dorothy had told me. I picked up my burger and took a bite.

She turned her glass. She stared at it. She ran a finger around the rim of the glass until it rang. She sighed, then gazed at me with a look I knew was her You-Asked-for-It look.

"I knew of Peter Talbot. He and Harold went to Bowdoin College together. Your father spoke about what good friends they had been. Peter lived here in Ashford, but they didn't spend time together." She sipped her wine. "That I knew of."

So that part of Dorothy's story was confirmed. I put down my burger and waited.

"I supposed it was because we were all busy raising families. But then, toward the end . . ." Her voice trailed off.

"Toward the end, what?" I leaned forward, my voice soft. "What happened?"

"Harold started being around less. He said he was sailing, preparing for a race. I was okay with that. Then the day after the race, I saw his picture in the paper."

"The *Daily News*?"

Mom nodded. "They looked so happy, arms around each other. I asked Harold about it. Why he hadn't told me he was racing with his old college buddy. He never really answered me."

"And then he disappeared."

She nodded again, her eyes full. She shook her head as if to shake off the memory, then she mustered a smile. "Now, tell me about that paper you're working on."

Topic closed. I had learned one new thing from my mother, that she hadn't known about Peter Talbot. I wished I could have had more to go on, but knew my mom well enough to know that further digging would get me exactly nowhere.

After we finished our drinks and my fries, she insisted on paying the tab. On our way out, I slowed as I passed the bar.

Gloria, the bartender from Ithaki, and Vincent Waters sat huddled at the ancient wooden bar. Their heads nearly touched. Vincent whispered. Gloria laughed.

I watched their faces in the mirror behind the bar. Newburyport wasn't that far from Ashford, but something seemed off about the two of them drinking here together. The fancy lawyer and the plainly working-class bartender. Being very chummy.

Vincent glanced up. As he caught sight of me, his eyes narrowed. He nodded almost imperceptibly, then looked back at Gloria.

I joined my mother in the bright sunshine outdoors. I blinked at the contrast with the pub's dark interior and wondered if the midday beer had been a wise choice, after all.

"Come up for dinner Friday? I'll cook something fun for Jackie's birthday."

I agreed. I hugged her and said goodbye. As I strolled to my truck, I couldn't erase the thought of Vincent and Gloria whispering and laughing together from my mind. And the look Vincent had given me—sort of friendly, sort of not.

• • •

I took Wulu on a walk around the block after I arrived home and relaxed on my back porch with the Sunday paper for an hour. Perusing an article on sailing in the Metro section, I realized I'd reread the same paragraph three times. I saw instead the picture of my father and Peter Talbot. I threw the paper to the floor.

"Time to clear some cobwebs," I muttered to myself. I changed into a T-shirt, running shorts with a pocket, and my running shoes. I tied my hair into a ponytail and rubbed some sunscreen on my face. I pocketed my phone, locked the door, and set off.

The afternoon sun was still strong. I wished I'd worn my sunglasses as I passed the town wharf. The town wharf? I laughed to myself. My feet had decided to take a different route without consulting my brain. That was all right. I was on a route that led out to the Bluffs instead of my usual Toil-in-Vain Road run. So I took a longer run. It was Sunday. Not a problem.

Cars whizzed by on the broad open section before the causeway. A silver pickup truck that towed a boat nearly sideswiped me as I ran on the right. I shook my head, waited for a vehicle-free moment, and switched to the left side, facing traffic. At least that way I'd know what hit me.

I crossed onto the spit of land that led to the Bluffs. The road split, forming the loop that circled the perimeter of the small peninsula. I chose the left fork onto Neck Road. At the yacht club, I was forced to stop and wait as more trucks with boats in tow entered and left the parking lot. The start of summer on a mild sunny day meant high activity at the club, which provided docks and fuel for boaters as well as a bar and restaurant. Waterside tables looked across the Sound to Plum Island. The water of the bay sparkled and buzzed with craft of all kinds. A Jet Ski like a snowmobile on water zoomed toward Holt Beach, and a couple of brightly colored kayaks navigated the passage. Small yachts motored by, and sailboats skimmed in the distance.

More reminders of my father. This must have been where he'd taught Mary Heard and Walter Colby how to sail. Why hadn't Charles taken lessons, too? Or maybe he had.

I ran on, inhaling the fresh salt air. I pistoned up the steep hill that led to the Bluffs. I slowed as I passed Mary's house. Should I see if Mary was home, try to find out more about those sailing lessons? I shook my head and ran on. I was out for a long run on a Sunday to clear my mind, not to clog it up with complicated interactions.

A sleek green sports car zoomed by. It almost clipped me. Its tires squealed as it took the sharp bend ahead way too fast. I swore under my breath. Crazy Sunday driver.

A minute later I heard the high-pitched sound of brakes applied in a hurry, then a loud crunch that made my stomach drop. I sped up. I sprinted around the curve. At the sight right in front of me, I put on my own brakes.

The green car sat crosswise. It blocked the narrow road. The crushed front of a white sedan looked inserted into the driver's-side door. The window in the door was shattered.

I ran up to the scene. No one emerged from either car. Steam rose up from the white car. I looked in the closed window. A woman with white hair sat between the seat and a deflated air bag that had blossomed out from the steering wheel. I knocked on the glass and exhaled with relief when the woman opened her eyes and looked sideways at me. At least she was alive. I tried the door but it seemed jammed.

I pulled my cell phone out, jabbed 911. I smiled and gestured to the woman in what I hoped was a reassuring way.

A cry from the green car made me turn my head, even as I relayed the location to the dispatcher on the phone and started to tell him what had happened. Gloria the bartender sat in the open door of the passenger seat, her feet on the ground, one hand gripping the top of the door.

"Help us! Please help us!" she wailed.

A man rushed out from the nearest house. Two cyclists rolled around the bend and, throwing their bikes to the ground, ran to the driver's-side door of the green car. A blue SUV pulled up behind the white car. Other neighbors emerged and surrounded the cars. A siren sounded in the distance.

"What?" I couldn't hear the dispatcher with all the noise. "Yes, two cars. Two people are alive. I don't know about the driver of the sports car. The white car looks like it went right into his door. Yes, I'll stay on the line. But what else should I do?"

The dispatcher told me to wait for the ambulance and the fire department, that their ETA was three minutes.

I watched as someone helped Gloria out, led her to sit on a patch of lawn, offered her a drink of water, handed her a blanket. A man who climbed out of the SUV tried to open the driver's-side door of the sports car without success. He went around to the passenger side and leaned in. When he stood up again, his face was a grim mask. He caught my eye and shook his head.

I felt sad to my core. It seemed the crazy Sunday driver had taken his last spin. I looked over at Gloria where she sat, a baby-blue fleece blanket draped over her shoulders despite the balmy weather. Could that be Vincent Waters in the driver's seat? He was a lawyer, he could certainly afford a sports car, which I now saw was a Porsche. And he had been drinking and snuggling with Gloria only a couple of hours earlier.

Several emergency vehicles roared up all at once. Lights flashed as professionals got to work. A police officer shooed the neighbors back to a safe distance and set out orange cones at the curve in the road. Paramedics tended to Gloria, while a firefighter pried open the sedan's door and helped the elderly driver out. Another EMT repeated the SUV driver's motions of leaning in toward the Porsche's driver's seat and also emerged alone.

As I disconnected from the call, Chief Flaherty strode toward me.

"Dr. Rousseau." He greeted me with a nod. "Are you okay?"

"Yes. They aren't," I said in a sad voice.

"Why is it you're always on the scene of the accident?"

I stared at him. I folded my arms. I wasn't going to stoop to answer that.

"I hear you were the one who called this in."

"Yes. I was running and the green car nearly clipped me speeding by." I turned and gestured toward the bend behind them. "Right around the curve there. Then I heard brakes and an awful noise. He must have fishtailed because he was driving so fast."

"Did you recognize the driver?" Flaherty squinted at me.

"No, I couldn't see in the window. But . . ." I glanced over at Gloria.

"But what?"

"I was up in Newburyport earlier at lunch with my mother. And I saw Gloria there having drinks with Vincent Waters."

"Oh? Where was that?"

"At the Grog. They looked pretty cozy. Is that Vincent Waters's car?" I felt sure it was.

The chief nodded. "I'm afraid he didn't make it. He should have known better than to drive so fast on the Bluffs." He shook his head. "They both live out here. Separately, I mean," he blurted with a grimace. "Vincent was going through a messy divorce from his wife."

That must have been the "plan" Vincent Waters had referred to in the conversation in the churchyard. I didn't care who lived with whom. I was just sad a life had been extinguished, and for such a senseless reason as driving too fast.

After I was dismissed, I resumed my run but felt jumpy and unsettled. I kept seeing Gloria shaking under the blanket. When a white sedan startled me by roaring up to a stop sign at a side street not far from home, I leapt to the edge of the road. My right foot landed in a depression in the pavement, and as my velocity propelled me forward, a wrenching pain shot up the outside of my lower leg.

I sprawled on someone's ground cover, cursing as I rubbed my ankle. It was definitely strained. I hoped I hadn't torn anything. Pushing myself up, I took a cautious step. It bore my weight, so I limped home. Not much of a *karateka*, letting myself be caught off guard. But there were extenuating circumstances. Now it was time for an ice pack, a stiff drink, and no more surprises.

• • •

"Police report a fatality in Ashford this afternoon. Well-regarded lawyer Vincent Waters died at the wheel in a two-car collision only yards from his home in the area known as the Bluffs. The authorities would not say if drugs or alcohol were involved. His passenger and the driver of the other car were not seriously injured."

I opened my eyes. The radio announcer moved on to another story. I lay on my couch. The ice pack fastened around my ankle was now a room-temperature pack. The dark room matched the sky outside. I must have fallen asleep. From his bed across the room, Wulu watched me with calm black eyes.

The radio felt like an intrusion. I sat and switched it off. I'd been part of the news today. I didn't need to hear any other tales of woe.

After turning on a lamp and the kitchen light and feeding Wulu, I emptied a can of lentil soup into a bowl and heated it in the microwave. I carried it and a glass of Merlot into my study, where I sat and opened my email.

Zac had written to me. That was sweet. He seemed so far away now. This was the longest we had been apart since we'd met a year earlier. Out of sight, out of mind? I guessed so. He wrote that he missed me, and filled me in on other news. He invited me again to visit, but said he knew he probably wouldn't see me until he returned in August.

Which was a long time from now. I sighed. I opened the digest from the Ashford Freecycle group, the local version of an organization founded to keep things out of landfills. Members either advertised items they wanted to give away or items they needed or wanted to own. I liked to check it regularly. Someone might be giving away an item I could use. I noticed a post from someone named Clammer4Ever that offered furniture. I clicked the link and smiled. "Offer: four-draw bureau. Quite electeric space heater." Someone with the local dialect who spelled words like they pronounced them, leaving off the final consonant of "drawer" and sticking an extra vowel in "electric." Hmm. Clammer4Ever. That name rang a bell. That had been the guy in the personals ad on the Bluffs page. At least he was consistent in how he misspelled "quiet."

On Facebook, I navigated to the Bluffs community page. I wondered if they'd have a news item about the crash, but I didn't see one. I checked the Trustees page. It didn't look like they'd appointed anyone new yet, and there was certainly no discussion of the controversy that raged in town. Maybe they only posted what they considered to be positive news.

A Bluffs resident and local lawyer was dead. That wasn't at all positive, for him or for them.

Chapter Fifteen

The morning sun already warmed the sidewalk when I locked my bike to a signpost in front of Iris's Bakery. My ankle still throbbed, but I'd wrapped it in a stretchy bandage and had stuck a couple of anti-inflammatory pills in my pocket to take with breakfast. Biking downhill had been easy. I wasn't so sure how returning home would go. Fortified with good Greek coffee, one of Iris's chocolate scones, and a dose of gossip, I ought to be able to make it back. Karate this afternoon would be out of the question, though.

The shop's door stood open. I inhaled a myriad of delectable aromas as I hobbled in. I took my usual table by the window. Not a minute later, Iris took the seat opposite. She wiped her hands on her apron.

"Did you hear?" She gazed into my face.

"Hear what?" I wasn't sure how Iris made her eyes broadcast serious and mischievous at the same time, but she did. "Did the lawyer get Joey off?"

"No, we don't know nothing about that yet." Iris looked around, then back at me. She said in a low voice, "In the Dodd Pub last night. Mary Heard attacked your Dan."

I opened my mouth to protest that he wasn't my Dan by any means. I stopped before I started. "Wait, what? Mary attacked Dan? What do you mean, attacked? And why?"

"Joey heard it from Katie Eames. You know her brother is bartender at the pub."

"I know. But what happened?"

"Katie said Dan was there having beers with some buddies of his. Mary stormed in, walked right to the bar, and whacked him with her pocketbook. She screamed that Dan killed her brother!" Iris looked almost pleased at this.

"Dan Talbot? Why would he kill Charles? Why did she think that?" I was totally confused. This didn't make sense. And Mary losing her temper? Whacking someone upside the head with her purse sounded completely out of character for the elegant, grieving bonsai artist. "Are you sure?"

Iris nodded. "It's what Katie told Joey. Dan had Mary on the floor in a lock before you could blink, Katie said. And a cop was there, too. He was off-duty, but he took over, calmed her down."

Stunned, I pictured the scene. I had considered going to the Dodd last night myself, and only hadn't because I didn't want to walk around on my sprained ankle. Getting somebody in a headlock? Why hadn't he just stepped back?

"Did the police take Mary in?"

"I doubt it. Your Dan probably didn't press the charges, and she could have done the same against him. Listen, time for working."

I nodded. "He's not my Dan," I added, without any hope of convincing Iris of that. Gazing out the window, I thought it might be a good day to ask Mary Heard over for lunch.

The bell on the door dinged as Walter pushed it open. He stood there for a few seconds, his eyes searching the place. He wore his usual banker clothes, but he looked like his concentration had been elsewhere when he got dressed. His tie was askew, his hair wasn't neatly gelled into place, and one shoe's laces flopped on the ground.

He saw Iris and beckoned to her with an urgent look on his face. She rose and joined him. He whispered in her ear.

She set her hands on her hips. "Then you have to go," she said in a normal voice.

He shook his head.

Iris put her hands on his arms and turned him around. She gave him a little push out the door. He complied. I saw him walk slowly down the sidewalk in the direction of the pub.

Iris sat down again, shaking her head.

"What was that all about?" I asked. "He's not going to the pub, is he? It's not even open until eleven thirty."

"Police want to question him."

"At the pub?"

"No, silly. At the station. They want to talk to him about the murder." The police station was two blocks beyond the pub.

"Do you know why?" I asked.

"He doesn't know. Something about him being a Trustee and his history with Charlie. It's a long history and not a very friendly one."

153

"Do you think Walter killed him?"

"I sure hope not. But there's stuff he isn't telling me. He's hiding something." Iris narrowed her eyes as she gazed out the front window. "And it's eating at him, Lauren. Making him crazy."

"Maybe you should stop spending time with him. You don't want to be alone with a murderer, Iris."

Iris slowly drummed her fingers on the table. "No. No, I don't."

• • •

At the peal of the doorbell, I glanced at the kitchen clock then hobbled to my condo's front door, an ice pack still strapped around my ankle. Bicycling home uphill from Iris's had aggravated the sprain, and this was the third time I'd iced it. One o'clock. Mary was right on time.

"Mary, come in." I gestured to my guest. "I'm so glad you could join me."

Mary preceded me into the room and set a good-sized Vuitton handbag on the couch. She turned and folded her arms. "What's this all about, Lauren?" She glared. "Suddenly we're pals or something?"

I stared at my guest. Face haggard and free of makeup, Mary looked ten years older than usual. She wore a faded blue *Sail* magazine sweatshirt of many years' vintage over a pair of jeans that looked like she'd dug a ditch in them.

I opened my mouth, then shut it. Mary was right, of course. I wanted to find out, from Mary's own mouth, what had happened at the pub.

"Let's sit. Lunch is all ready." I motioned toward the table. I had to think of what to say and figured there was nothing wrong with stalling. "I'm going to have a glass of white wine. You?" I held a bottle of Oregon Pinot Gris and a narrow-bowled glass by its stem.

Mary took a deep breath and let it out, although she didn't seem to exhale her anger with it. She perched on the edge of a chair at my round table and nodded, her face set in a grim look.

I handed her a full glass and poured myself one. I brought the plate of ham-and-cheese-on-sourdough sandwiches I'd made to the table, silently blessing the existence of the Coastal Greengrocer, purveyor of fine cheeses, meats, and breads only steps from Iris's Bakery. A bowl of mini-carrots and another of sour dill gherkins completed the table.

"Shall we?" I sat and sipped the wine. Should I come out and tell Mary the truth about why I asked her over? Or wait to see if my guest volunteered it?

Mary sipped her own, then set her glass down. "Very nice luncheon, Ms. Rousseau." The sarcasm was unmistakable. "Now, what gives?"

"After you called me to join you at Ithaki Friday night, I thought we were becoming friendlier. I'm on vacation, and—"

"Quit the crap, Lauren. You want to know what happened at the pub last night. Why didn't you simply ask me?"

Well, that cleared the air. I nodded. "You're right. I apologize. I should have asked." I gazed expectantly at Mary.

Mary stood with her wineglass. She took a step until she towered directly over me. Her hand shook. A splash of wine crested the lip of the glass and anointed my knee. She didn't seem to notice.

Ignoring the wet spot, I looked up at Mary's expression to see a mask of, what? Anger? Hurt? Plotting? I wished I were standing, too, but I couldn't push out of my chair without bumping into her. I hoped I wasn't going to have to employ some of my own karate moves, and on a busted ankle, no less.

In a raspy voice so low I could barely hear, Mary stared down at me and said, "Dan Talbot killed Charles."

I stared right back up at her. So Iris's story had been correct. Mary sounded convinced of the truth of her statement. Dan had acted a little odd since I'd known him, but kill someone? I didn't think so. Maybe Mary had created the scene in the pub because she herself had killed Charles.

"Mary, will you please sit down?" I wanted to add, "You have me trapped here," but decided against planting even the idea of being trapped. "And tell me why you think Dan killed Charles?"

Mary stalked to the front window, glass in hand. She peered out, then whirled. "I know he did."

"But how do you know? And why would Dan do something like that?"

"You're just like all the rest. Cool, handsome Mr. Carpenter can do no wrong." She sneered. "Sensei Trustee is regarded as some kind of god around here. I heard even you're under his magic spell."

"Me?" My voice came out in a croak. I cleared my throat. "I went clamming with him one time. And he's my karate instructor. No magic spell, believe me."

"Well, that's what the town gossip mill says. Including your little Greek friend. And speaking of gossip, I heard that Vincent Waters's brake lines were cut. That's why the crash killed him. Poor Vinnie."

"I wonder who would do something like that?"

"In Ashford, who wouldn't?" Mary turned back toward the window. "I am so completely sick of this town and all its petty issues and dramas."

It sounded like Mary was talking to herself more than to me. She went on, "If I didn't have to deal with Charles's business and so on, I'd clear out of here so fast you'd never even see my taillights. Move to France. Or Costa Rica. San Francisco. Anywhere but this ingrown bed of spite and malice."

San Francisco. Exactly where Dan's father had fled to, a fellow escapee from spite and malice, apparently. Also apparent was that Mary didn't seem willing to tell me why she thought Dan killed her brother.

"So what happened last night, Mary?" If I couldn't hear the reason, at least I might learn the story of the altercation firsthand. "Come and eat, too."

Mary walked back to the table but did not sit. "I went down to the pub for some dinner, and when I saw Dan, I just flipped. I called him a murderer." Her voice shook. "I started whacking him with my bag." She pointed her chin toward the bag on the couch. "And I carry some weight in that baby."

I restrained myself from saying, "You go, girl!" in time. Mary's account was both so honest and so out of character that it delighted me at the same time it made me uneasy. "Then what happened?"

"The jerk threw me to the floor in some fancy martial-arts move. Luckily Officer Stelios—Bud, to those of us who went to school with him—was there having a bite to eat. He hauled Dan off of me."

"Did the officer arrest you for assault?"

"I should have had Dan arrested instead." Mary waved a hand in dismissal. "Your honey declined to press charges."

I opened my mouth to object, but she held up a stalling hand.

"Honey, no honey, whatever. I told that Talbot boy if he tried to come after me next, no amount of martial arts would help him." She took two steps to the couch and pulled an object out of her handbag. She faced me, pointing a handgun.

"Hey! Put that thing down." I flung my arms in the air. "What are you doing?"

She laughed, sounding slightly crazed. "Don't worry, the safety's on, and I'm licensed to carry. I only wanted to show you why Dan Talbot better not mess around with me." She lowered the weapon and stuffed it back in her bag.

I lowered my arms, shaky with relief. "Did you have the gun in your bag when you swung it at Dan? That could have gone off, you know."

She shook her head. "Yeah, no. I mean, I had it, but it wasn't loaded. Sure gave the bag a little extra heft, though." Looking pleased with herself, she finally sat across from me and took a sandwich from the platter, biting into it. Her face relaxed as she chased the food with a generous swig of wine. Her demeanor was much calmer than how she'd appeared minutes earlier, although she wasn't quite back to the collected dignified persona I had seen her as until now.

"Nice sandwich. Greengrocer?" Mary looked over her wineglass at me. "He stocks fabulous ingredients. Now, I thought you wanted to talk with me more about your bonsai tree."

I was happy to engage in small talk for the rest of the hour. And not to see the gun again. Once Mary had let her fury out, it seemingly evaporated, and her customary personality reemerged. When the visit seemed to be over, I saw her to the door.

She said, "Stop by in a couple of days and we'll work on pruning technique. Wednesday, maybe?" She headed down the steps. "Oh, and thanks for lunch."

I waved, then stuck my hands in my pockets and leaned against the doorframe, watching her turn her Jaguar and head down the hill at a sedate pace. What a strange woman. I hadn't learned much new, except that she was licensed to carry a small handgun. And that she could explode out of character when it came to family loyalty and small-town rivalries.

I mused on what I knew. Mary was tall and strong. She could have easily killed Charles. And stuck Bobby with the clamming fork. But why? And was Dan now at risk of being shot? And why did Mary say Dan killed Charles, anyway? I shook my head at what I didn't know.

Behind me, Wulu barked twice and butted my leg with his head.

"Walk time?"

Wulu turned and ran for his leash.

I had locked the door from the outside when the house phone rang from inside. I tied Wulu's leash to the landing railing, unlocked, and dashed back in.

I said hello in a breathless voice.

Dan greeted me. "How's your ankle?"

How did he know about my ankle? "It's okay. I won't be in class this afternoon, though. Supposed to stay off it."

"No problem. Just thought I'd check in on you." Dan's resonant tones broadcast nothing but caring and concern.

"Thanks. Oops, have to go. My cell's ringing," I lied.

We said our goodbyes and I hung up. I stared at the phone. I started when Wulu yipped from the porch.

"Well, it's a small town. Iris probably blabbed to him," I told myself as I untied Wulu. "That must be it."

I strolled slowly up the hill. I let Wulu poke his nose everywhere in the border of the woods and wondered about Dan poking his nose too far into my life.

• • •

I gave a little knock on Bobby's hospital room door an hour later. I held a double bunch of yellow daffodils in a cellophane sleeve in one hand. With my other I cradled my purse, extra heavy because of the simple vase I'd added to it. I peered into the room. "Bobby?" I called.

A young woman with a cast on her arm looked up from the hospital bed.

"Oh! I'm so sorry. I thought, well, never mind. Wrong room, I guess." I backed out, then rechecked the number next to the door. This was definitely the room Bobby had been in on Friday. Today was Monday. Had he already gone home? I should have called first. I turned, nearly colliding with a nurse.

As I excused myself, I looked up into the face of the same man who had been caring for Bobby earlier.

"Can I help you?"

"I'm looking for Bobby Spirokis. He was in this room. He had a wound in his arm, and—"

"Rehab."

"Rehab? He's been transferred?"

The nurse nodded.

"Can you tell me where?"

"Next door. Emerson Skilled Nursing."

I thanked him and found the elevator. That had to be good, that he was well enough for rehabilitation, to receive some physical therapy, to be up and around with assistance.

I made my way to the low building that was, in fact, next door to the hospital. Once inside, I was directed by a goth-looking teen at the front desk to Room 107. I walked down a long hallway, checking room numbers. An elderly woman leaned on a walker. A burly man in scrubs hovered behind her as she placed one foot in front of the other in slow motion. Several rooms were empty. One held a man with waxen skin lying on his back in bed. His roommate was slumped over in a wheelchair near the window. The air smelled medicinal with overtones of urine.

I shook my head. Was this a rehabilitation center or the proverbial nursing home, where elders without family to care for them were housed until they died?

I arrived at 107, but it was empty. A small picture sat on one of the two nightstands. I walked over and leaned down to examine it. A man and a woman stood with Bobby on a dock. The man was a little taller than Bobby, and the woman several inches shorter, but they were clearly his siblings. They shared his sturdy build and ruddy complexion. The three, arms linked, looked windblown, happy. I didn't think I'd seen that picture in his hospital room. At least he had family, and someone had visited. A bit of white poked out from behind the frame. I shifted the frame. It was my business card. Bobby hadn't called me, but he'd kept the card.

I looked around the room. It looked clean, but the flowered wallpaper was slightly faded and some of the woodwork was chipped. A five-star hotel this was not. I shrugged. I dug the vase out of my bag and filled it with water at the bathroom sink. I had started to arrange the flowers in it when a male voice at the door made me turn.

"I don't need your damn help," Bobby said over his shoulder. He clumped into the room. He leaned on a cane with his right hand. The other one poked out from a blue sling supporting his left arm. The bandages had been replaced by a simple Band-Aid. He wore jeans with a navy Red Sox sweatshirt.

Why did he need a cane? Maybe he had another condition I didn't know about.

A curvy young nurse in deep pink scrubs followed close behind him. In a low, firm voice with a trace of accent, she said, "Mr. Spirokis, I need to make sure you stay safe. You're doing very well, but you're my patient. I am responsible for you." She cocked her head and smiled despite standing behind him.

Bobby stopped when he caught sight of me. "What are you doing here?" His voice was gruff as he drew his eyebrows together. He stared at me, then sank into the chair next to the bed, his face pale and glistening with sweat.

"I wanted to see how you were. I brought you these." I gestured at the flowers. Their bright buttery petals glowed in the utilitarian room.

"Those are beautiful." The nurse turned her thousand-watt smile on me. "Aren't they, Mr. Spirokis?" She winked at me as if we were caregiver coconspirators.

"I guess. Thanks." Bobby nodded at me. "Sorry, I'm beat. They're working me like a dog in that therapy room. And then Majgone here has to follow me around like I'm a kid or something."

I checked the nurse's nametag. Mojgan. Bobby hadn't pronounced the Iranian name quite right. *"Shoma chetur hastin?"* I'd now tried out my rusty Farsi twice in a week. I wondered if Dan knew Mojgan.

"Man khoobam, mamnoon! Khali khoob—that's very good," Mojgan said with a laugh. "Where did you learn to speak Farsi?"

"I studied it in college. But that was a long time ago," I said. "I'm Lauren Rousseau."

As we shook hands, Bobby looked back and forth between us with a look of confusion on his face, then he shook his head. "What, you're from Iran?" He pronounced it "eye-ran."

Mojgan said she was, but that she'd lived in this country for fifteen years. She poured a cup of water for Bobby and handed it to him. "I'll be back with your meds. Nice meeting you, Lauren."

"Likewise." I waved, then said to Bobby, "May I sit?"

Bobby gestured at the bed. He took a sip of the water. He closed his eyes.

I watched him. He didn't look well, but then the attack had been very recent. I really wanted to ask him about who had attacked him, but I couldn't with him not yet well.

"I'll leave you to your rest, then," I said. "I wanted to be sure you were all right."

He opened his eyes. He narrowed them and gazed at me. "Any gossip around town about who did this to me?"

I shook my head. "Not that I have heard. You didn't see who did it?"

Bobby closed his eyes again. He didn't answer. He opened them again.

"Hey, I'm sorry I almost ran you down last week."

I cocked my head. "Ran me down?"

"In my truck. On Upper Summer Street. I was late for work."

"So that was you. No problem. I walk my dog along there, though. You might try to be more careful. It's a small street." I smiled, hoping it would buffer my response.

Bobby nodded. "I will."

"Funny thing happened at the Dodd Pub last night," I said.

"Oh?" He seemed to perk up at that.

"Mary Heard attacked Dan Talbot. Said he killed her brother."

His eyes widened. He opened his mouth as if to speak, then closed it again.

I waited. Bobby had been on the estate the night of the murder. He might be the killer, himself. Or was he just surprised to hear that Mary Heard would attack anyone?

He began to sweat again and wiped his forehead with his free sleeve. His hand shook, and he breathed in and out too fast for a man sitting in a chair.

Mojgan bustled in wheeling a cart with a laptop computer open on top, a tiny white paper cup next to it, and several wire drawers holding supplies below. She lifted the cup but took one look at Bobby and set it back down. She pressed her fingers to his wrist to take his pulse, keeping her eyes on the analog clock on the wall, which read five thirty. A look of alarm came over her previously smooth, warm face.

"You're going to have to go, Lauren." Her tone was brisk. She handed Bobby the water and the pills, then tapped an intercom button. "I have a Code 23 in 107. Code 23 in 107." She grabbed a blood pressure cuff from the cart, pushed up his sleeve, and started to wrap it around his arm. Without looking up, she said, "Lauren. Out."

I rose and squeezed around them, and then flattened myself against the wall to avoid colliding with a second nurse who rushed into the room. I looked back at Bobby. He was in good hands, and it looked like he was going to need them. The mention of Mary's attack on Dan had shocked him into some kind of episode. I hoped it wasn't a heart attack. Had I brought it on by mentioning the murder? What did Bobby know? I closed my eyes and held him in the Light for a moment. I walked slowly down the hall. Why had the news shocked him so? I wished I knew what he knew.

I left the building and headed for the hospital lot. I'd had to park in the back of the lot again, where the only available spaces were when I'd arrived.

Someone stood next to my truck. The person was backlit by the slanting near-solstice sunlight. Who was that? If they thought they were going to stab my tires again, they were about to have a big surprise.

"Hey!" I called, striding toward the truck despite the pain in my ankle. "What are you doing?"

The person turned to face me.

I slowed, the light dawning. "Hi, Orlene. We meet again."

The woman put her hands on her hips. "I recognized your truck. Thought I should keep an eye on it."

"Thanks."

Orlene nodded. "How you doing, anyway? The police find who messed with your tires?"

I shook my head. "But I hope they will."

Orlene shrugged. "Ought to try to find a place closer to the front next time."

Chapter Sixteen

Favoring my ankle as I trudged up the steps to my condo, I raised my eyes to the top step. A fishbowl-shaped vase filled with flowers and greenery greeted me. Sitting down next to the vase, I plucked the little envelope out of its plastic florist's holder and opened it.

Missed you in class. Feel better soon. From your secret admirer, Carpenter Dan

I examined the arrangement. It was a lovely spray of white rosebuds and miniature pink carnations with tiny purple flowers tucked into the fernlike greens. I sighed. My not-so-secret admirer. I brought it into the house. I had to admit it was a sweet gesture, sending me flowers. I didn't think I'd been encouraging him. On the contrary, I'd done my best not to let this thing turn romantic. He obviously wasn't hearing the message. Although, I mused, I *had* gone with him on the mansion tour just a couple days earlier. Which felt like half a lifetime ago.

I opened the refrigerator and stared. Slim pickings. Stomach growling, I sighed and closed it again. Wulu gave a little bark.

"You have dinner fixings, anyway. Here you go, buddy." I filled his dinner dish with kibble and freshened his water dish, then grabbed my purse and keys again. "We'll walk when I get back from the pub, Wu." I locked the door and headed slowly down the hill.

A Prius honked as it turned up my street.

"Jackie," I called. The Prius backed down, and Jackie leaned her head out the window.

"How about dinner at the pub? Wanted to kind of make amends after Saturday," Jackie said with a sheepish smile.

"This sister reads my mind. That's right where I was headed."

Jackie slid out of her seat and locked the car. We headed for the river.

"Are you limping?" Jackie asked. "What happened?"

I nodded. "Twisted it running."

"Want to drive down?"

"No, it's getting better. And I need some fresh air. But that's not all that's happened." As we strolled, I filled Jackie in on the recent events. I didn't leave anything out, not even the bits with Mary, Dan's flirting, how Bobby reacted in his rehab room.

"How do you get involved in this crazy stuff?" Jackie said. She gently elbowed me.

"I have no idea. And it's not my idea of a good time, believe me."

We wandered down Town Hill and made it across the insanely dangerous main intersection of town. Drivers going up and down the hill and coming into and out of town had to stop and then cross or turn onto the state route, whose drivers did not have to stop. Small town not withstanding, it was a crazy crossroads. Every time I made it across safely I counted my blessings. And after witnessing the car crash, I was even more nervous.

"Bar or dining room?" I asked.

"Dining room, I think. It's quieter. Listen to me. I sound like an old fart."

"Hey, I'm good with quiet at any age." I returned Jackie's elbowing. "Besides, aren't you almost forty? That's totally old fart territory."

"Not until Friday, I'm not."

I was about to reach for the door to the dining area of the pub when it swung open. Mark Pulcifer held the door for a young woman about his age. She laughed. His face reflected her joy.

"Hi, Ms. Rousseau," he said when he caught sight of me.

"Hi, Mark. Nice to see you again. Hey, did you hear yet what's going to happen to the agency?"

He shook his head. "I decided I don't care. I want to be a chef, not an insurance salesman."

"How are your uncles, by the way? I mean your great-uncles, of course."

"They're fine. Samuel is doing better."

"Good. You know, I think you take after Phillip. You look so much like him, or what he must have looked like at your age."

"No way, Ms. Rousseau." Mark laughed. "I'm adopted." The girl pulled at his elbow, and he said goodbye.

"Who's that kid?" Jackie said as we slid into opposite sides of a straight-backed wooden booth that was surely older than both of us. Probably even older than our parents, I reflected. The Dodd Bridge Pub wasn't one to update itself with the times.

"Mark Pulcifer. He worked for Charles Heard."

"Pulcifer. Isn't that the name of the boat shop that burned down a few months ago?"

I nodded. "It's interesting that Mark is adopted."

"Why? Lots of people are adopted."

"Never mind. It's a long story." Could Mark be Mary's birth son? Mary had been giving him such a look on Friday night. And she knew exactly how old he was. Something to talk with Iris about, for sure.

James Wojinski, his wife, and their daughter sat across the aisle. Their table was filled with half-eaten plates of fried clams, onion rings, and French fries, plus wineglasses. Fiona's plate was still nearly full, as was her glass. Her fingers tapped the table. I smiled at them and said hello.

A little girl approached our booth. She pulled at her mother's hand.

"See, Mommy? I told you, it's the new student at karate."

"Hey, Maddie," I said, smiling at my fellow *karateka*. "How are you?"

"Good." Maddie bounced on tiny yellow sandals. She wore a yellow and green striped dress over green stretchy shorts. "You didn't come to class."

"I know, I couldn't make it."

"How are you liking it?" she asked.

I laughed. "I like it. It's hard work. I studied karate in Japan, but that was a long time ago. My muscles get sore."

"Just keep practicing. It'll get easier." Maddie nodded with the wisdom of an elder. "Oh, this is my mom. Mommy, this is Lauren."

Maddie's mother introduced herself and then said, "Come on, honey. Your fries are getting cold." To me she murmured, "She's running for mayor," and rolled her eyes.

"See you in the dojo!" Maddie skipped back to her table followed by her mother.

"Wow. I wouldn't talk to anybody in public when I was that age," I said with a smile.

"She's cute, all right."

Katie came by and took our orders. As she left, Jackie leaned across the table.

"I know this is going to sound like preaching, Lauren. But one of these days you might want to look at how much you drink."

I cleared my throat. "I'm having a tall IPA with my dinner. I don't have vodka for breakfast. What exactly do you want me to look at?" Of course, I'd had the same thoughts. But wasn't quite ready to look at the issue, as Jackie put it.

"All right. I had to say it. So, you talked to Mom lately?"

"Stuff going on there, too." I exhaled. "But you already know it."

At Jackie's nod, I began in a low voice. "It's hard for me to believe that Daddy didn't disappear. He left us because he was gay."

"I know he was gay."

I nodded. "Yeah, Mom told me you knew. Thanks loads for keeping it from me. Anyway, I wonder if some of the crazy stuff that's going on around here is related to what happened to him all those years ago."

Katie brought my beer and Jackie's white wine.

Jackie tilted her head and narrowed her eyes at me but waited for me to speak.

I opened my mouth to continue. And kept it open as a man in a sport coat and tie flung open the outside door. He was closely followed by Chief Flaherty and several more uniformed Ashford police officers. The man in the suit strode to Mr. Wojinski's table.

"James Wojinski?" he asked.

Mr. Wojinski nodded with a bewildered look.

"Yes, his name is James," his wife said with a scowl. "You're the police."

"I'm Detective George Smithson with the State Police. Mr. Wojinksi—"

Fiona stood. "I did it. I wished for him to die, and he did." She held both wrists out in front of her.

"You did what?" the detective asked. He frowned at her.

At the same time, Mr. Wojinski said, "You didn't do anything, Fiona. Sit down, honey." To the detective he added, "She's not well mentally. I'm sorry." He tugged on his wife's sleeve.

"No, I'm guilty." Fiona's voice was strong. "They're here because I caused that lawyer's death. Vincent Waters deserved to die. Arrest me."

A gasp echoed around the room. Mr. Wojinski stood, his face a mask of disbelief mixing with fear. The detective shook his head as if to clear it, looked at Fiona, switched over to Mr. Wojinski, and then back to Fiona.

I remembered noticing Fiona's strong hands and wrists in Iris's Bakery that morning. Could Fiona have been the cause of the lawyer's fatal car crash instead of his own speeding? But how?

"But why?" Mr. Wojinski's anguish ripped from his lips. But he didn't sound surprised.

Fiona turned to face him with a calm expression. "You said he was evil and dangerous. Evil needs to be removed from God's world. Evil is the Devil moving among us." She stood straight: fulfilled, triumphant. "Take me," she said to the detective.

"Actually—" the detective began, then halted. He wiped his forehead with a hand. "Chief?" he said to Flaherty.

"Come with me, Mrs. Wojinski. We'll straighten this out." Flaherty took her elbow and began to escort her toward the door.

"No! You can't do that," the daughter protested. "She's not well. She's under care of a psychiatrist."

"Yes, we can. Sorry, Tina." Flaherty looked apologetic but continued out the door with Fiona.

The detective cleared his throat. "James Wojinski, you are under arrest for the murder of Charles Heard."

Chapter Seventeen

Jackie and I looked at each other, and then at Mr. Wojinski.

"I didn't kill Charles!" His normally tanned face went pale. He stood. "I wouldn't kill anyone. This is a mistake." He kept one hand on the table. The other fluttered at his side as if it had lost its way.

"What are you doing?" Tina stood. "My father doesn't even kill cockroaches."

One of the uniformed officers read Wojinski his Miranda rights and then stood behind him in the aisle, blocking the way farther into the restaurant. The room was quiet, all heads turned toward Wojinski and the detective.

"Please come with us." The detective extended his right arm behind Wojinski and gestured with his left toward the exit. "Don't make us handcuff you, sir," he murmured.

"Wait." Wojinski slipped his hand into his pocket.

Instantly the detective locked his hand onto Wojinski's arm. "Sir, take your hand out of your pocket. Now."

"I have to give Tina my keys! I drove here. And my money. For the dinner." He squeezed his eyes shut and looked like he might pass out.

"Officer?" The detective motioned an officer over. "Pat him down, make sure his pockets hold only keys and wallet."

The officer did so and nodded at the detective.

"All right, proceed. Take out your keys and wallet and lay them on the table."

Wojinski complied with a trembling hand.

"Dad—" Tina stretched out her hand.

Mr. Wojinski looked back at his daughter, his eyes torn with anguish. "Honey, call my lawyer," he said. "This is all a big mistake. And your mother—"

The officers led him out the door. Wojinski's daughter looked stunned. She shook herself and motioned to the waitress, who brought the check. Tina handed her a wad of money and dashed to the exit.

"Wow." I turned to gaze after her and then back at Jackie. Beyond the booth at the entrance to the bar area, a clump of people spoke in low voices.

"Shouldn't've argued with Heard in public all the time like he did. Just gets you in trouble." A man's voice rose above the others.

"Oh, shut up, Bill. Arguing can't land you in trouble. They wouldn't have arrested him without real evidence." The speaker was a trim young man with a military-style haircut. "That's the first thing we learned in the academy."

"Come on, everybody. Party's over." The head waitress shooed the onlookers back into the bar.

"He's right." I rested my chin on my hand.

"About what?"

"They can't arrest somebody without evidence. I wonder what they have?"

"Not really your business, is it?" Jackie asked. "What's up with his wife, anyway?"

"Seems like schizophrenia or something. She acts very out of the norm." I frowned. "But thinking she killed someone by wishing it? That's really crazy."

"Listen, let's change the subject and enjoy our dinner. Like, how about them Red Sox?"

• • •

An hour later, we said goodbye at Jackie's car, and I trod slowly up my front steps. I took Wulu out for a quick walk and locked up. I poured a couple of fingers of Scotch, with a quick pang related to Jackie's comment about my drinking, and sat on the couch with my feet up. As I sipped, I saw Fiona's defiant expression as she confessed to causing the car crash and the anguish on James Wojinski's face as he was arrested.

Fiona's crime I could understand, at least in the context of mental illness. But was James's the face of a murderer? Sure, he'd had very public disagreements with Charles Heard, but who hadn't? If the accusation of murder proved true, then Bobby Spirokis, Walter

Colby, Mary Heard, and Dan Talbot were all innocent, along with everybody else in town. So why had Mary accused Dan of killing her brother?

I wandered into my office. I smiled at the picture of Elise and myself taken at the top of Mount Fuji all those years before. Our cheeks were ruddy from the climb, and we looked happy. Elise was currently still in rehab. I hoped she was on the mend and that it would stick. I sank into my desk chair and turned on the computer. Wulu wandered in after me and sat on my left foot as he often did. He never sat on my right foot.

I had a new Facebook instant message from Dan. I didn't think I'd encouraged him romantically, but he kept coming around. I sighed and opened the message, noticing the little green dot indicating that he was currently logged in.

"How are you, Lauren?" he had written.

"Fine," I typed in return. "What's up?"

"Nothing. Just having a quite evening. But there's another tour at the Holt mansion tomorrow. Want to go? I have tickets."

"I'm not sure. It's different from the other one?"

"Yes. This one focuses on how the Holts themselves lived."

"I have a lot of work to do here." And I wasn't sure I wanted to be hanging around with Dan in an extracurricular way, so to speak.

"It'll be fun. Four o'clock again."

There couldn't be any harm in going on a guided group tour. "Okay. I think my ankle is better enough for a stroll through the luxurious parts of the mansion."

"Good. Want me to pick you up, say three thirty?"

I thought quickly. "No, I'll meet you there. I have to be in Boston for a seminar in the morning. If I catch the two thirty train home, I should make it in time." It felt safer to arrive there under my own steam and be able to leave when I needed to. This wasn't our first date—well, it wasn't a date at all—but that was what Match.com recommended for the first date with someone you met online: always handle your own transportation there and back.

"Thanks for the flowers, by the way," I typed.

"Anytime."

We wrote goodbye to each other, and his name disappeared off the list of logged-in friends.

I sipped my Scotch and gazed at the screen. He'd had a "quite" evening. Maybe he was Clammer4Ever. So what? A carpenter and sensei didn't have to be a perfect speller. But was he telling the truth? That was the more important question.

I clicked over to the Holt Estate website, curious about what other kinds of tours they held. If they offered tours of the grounds, I could bring Gardener Jackie. She'd love it.

I pulled up the schedule of tours. Funny, it looked like the estate was closed on Tuesdays. It must be an old list. I checked the date the website had last been updated. Sure enough, it was two years ago. Some nonprofits didn't realize that if you have a website, you have to keep it current. The site did list a tour of the landscaping. I read that it was a two-hour walk that included a discussion of the extensive plantings and architectural details of the estate. I made a note to reserve slots for Jackie and myself sometime soon.

A gust of wind rattled the window. I stared into the dark night. I pictured James Wojinski in a jail cell. Something was just not right.

• • •

After my early run the next morning, I showered and ate a piece of toast as I stood at the counter. "How about a walk before I leave for Boston?" I asked the dog at my feet.

Wulu jumped up and ran for his leash. As we strolled, I thought. The urge to find out more about my father and his death tugged at me until yielding to it was easier than suppressing it. With any luck, the seminar would end on time and I could dash over to the Boston Public Library. They'd have sixteen-year-old news articles on microfiche, files not available either in the Ashford Library or online. I'd gotten lucky with that one *Daily News* article online and hadn't been able to locate anything else.

I walked into downtown Ashford and caught the eighty thirty train into town. I took notes on everything I knew so far on the hour ride into the city, but the notebook page was barely half full by the time the train pulled into North Station.

By the afternoon, I had found several news stories on my father's death in the library and had made copies. Then I'd seen the time and rushed back across downtown to catch the train north.

• • •

Early commuters in sensible shoes and backpacks designed for laptops enveloped me as I hurried down the platform toward the northbound two thirty train. The crowd parted around a dozen excited fans coming toward them in Bruins jerseys, who rushed toward the hockey arena that shared the building with the train station.

I shifted my African bag to my right shoulder, the all-purpose bag that accommodated wallet, hairbrush, books, lunch, water bottle, and anything else I stuffed into it. The train north idled down the platform, but it wouldn't wait for long. I wondered why they hadn't pulled it all the way in as they usually did.

I passed to the right of two ear-budded boys who slouched along with skateboards tucked under their arms. I felt a sudden pressure on my back. A shove. A push toward the edge of the platform. I tripped and started to fall into the empty air above the tracks six feet below. I cried out. My handbag dragged me downward.

"Dude!" One of the boys grabbed my arm and pulled.

As fast as it had happened, it was over. I gazed up into the face of a worried-looking teenager. My legs shook and my heart would have maxed out my running monitor if I'd had it on.

"Lady, you okay? What, like, happened?"

"Somebody pushed me. Hard." I looked both boys in the face. It couldn't have been either of these kids. Could it? One was freckled and red-haired. The other one, who had rescued me from my fall, was darker with jelled spikes of black hair. Who, then?

"Yeah," Redhead said. "Some guy was there, then he wasn't."

My voice shook as I asked, "What did he look like? How tall was he?"

The boy shook his head. "I didn't really, you know, see him very well. Taller than me."

I felt a tap on my shoulder.

173

"Ma'am? Is everything all right?" asked a concerned black-uniformed MBTA official.

"I think I was shoved toward the tracks. I almost fell in."

The woman fixed a stern gaze on the boys and opened her mouth.

"No! Not them. He rescued me from falling." I gestured at the dark-haired boy. "It was somebody else."

"Do you want to file a report with the T police?" The officer raised her eyebrows.

I turned toward the boys as the loudspeaker announced that the train to Newburyport would leave in one minute.

The boys glanced down the track. Darkhair started to jitter.

"Shoot," I said. "Can I do it later?"

The woman nodded, hands on hips. "We have security cameras."

"Thank you," I called back. "Let's go, guys," I said to my new young friends. We ran to the last car and eased in. The train began to move. I laid a hand on Redhead's arm.

"Are you sure you can't remember anything else about the man you saw?" I looked from one to the other, imploring them silently: Please help me find this guy.

They looked at each other. Redhead shook his head.

Darkhair gazed up at the corner of the car, as if thinking, then back at me. "Sorry."

"Can I at least write down your numbers, then? Please? Maybe you'll think of something else you saw or heard."

The two exchanged a look. Darkhair shrugged. "Okay."

"Thanks." I braced myself on the back of a seat. I rooted around in my bag for a pen and a scrap of paper.

"Uh, ma'am? Doncha want to put it, like, in your phone? I mean, you have a phone, right?"

I looked up and laughed. He probably thought I was old enough to be the kind of antique person who was incompetent with cell phones, computers, and television remotes.

"Great idea. Hang on." I located my phone and clicked the address book function. "Ready."

Darkhair turned out to be Ernie Aguirre and Redhead was Rob

Connolly, both of Hamilton. I gave them my contact information, too.

"I really appreciate it, you guys."

Rob nodded. Ernie said, "No problem. Glad you didn't, like, get the third rail." They waved and headed down the aisle toward the front of the train.

I apologized to a man on the aisle as I squeezed past him into an empty middle seat of three. I closed my eyes. I felt the shove again. The awful feeling of losing my balance. The prospect of falling, of hitting my head on the tracks or the gravel. I wasn't sure the commuter train had an electrified third track, and I was infinitely glad I hadn't had to find out. And hoped I could discover who had done it.

• • •

As the train clattered northward, I leafed through the copies I'd made. I didn't learn anything new. There was no mention of an autopsy after Daddy's death. I read a brief death notice, which invited the public to a Memorial Meeting for Worship. I remembered sitting in the Meetinghouse with my family, Friends, and friends, weeping quietly as others shared memories of my father. I had no recollection if Peter Talbot had attended or not, but why would I? I hadn't even known him or been told of his connection with my father.

I descended from the train in Ashford and climbed into my truck. I was halfway to the Holt Estate and absorbed in thoughts about what I'd read on the train when I heard a rhythmic bumping sound from the back of the truck. My heart sank. Another flat. I pulled over onto a wide spot on Argilla Road and climbed out. Sure enough, the rear right tire was flat. At least this one didn't have a knife in it. Although it reminded me that the police had never gotten back to me on who had slashed my tires the week before.

I sighed. At least I had the spare. I grabbed the jack and lug nut wrench from behind the seat and set to work. The tire was almost rusted onto the lug nuts, but I managed to wrestle it off. I took a break for a minute and called Dan from my cell, but he didn't answer. I left a message that I was running late and then finished the job. As I hoisted the flat into the bed of the truck, my sleeve caught on a nail that poked out from the treads. It was a simple flat from the kind of sharp object anyone could run over. Relief washed through me.

I dusted off my hands and climbed back in the cab. It seemed odd that Dan hadn't answered my call. Maybe he'd left his phone in his van and strolled the grounds waiting for me.

When I finally pulled into the lot in front of the mansion, the only vehicle there was Dan's. *Where was everybody?* I climbed out and walked around the right side of the building to the entrance. Pulling open the wide door to the foyer with some effort, I spied Dan. He stood in front of a portrait, hands clasped behind him. The heavy door closed behind me with a loud click.

He turned with a big smile. "There you are!" He walked toward me, arms open.

"Where is everybody?" I backed up a step and turned halfway toward the door. Those arms looked like they wanted to come in for a hug. Not what I felt like right now. "I thought you said there would be another tour today."

"There was. But you were late, and nobody else had signed up. So my cousin gave me a spare key and said I could show you around."

"Your cousin?"

"Sheila Lopes. She's the admin here."

"Lopes." I nodded. "I borrowed her sweater. The night I found Charles."

"So it's just us two." He waggled his eyebrows like he had on the previous tour when he mentioned his high school girlfriend. "But I know the whole routine. I used to lead tours here when I was in college." He walked to the door, extracted a key from his pocket, and locked it.

"You're locking us in?"

"No," he scoffed with a smile. "I mean, yes, but it's only to keep errant tourists out while we're upstairs. Shall we?" He gestured toward the wide hall that led into the heart of the mansion and started in that direction.

"If you're sure it's all right." I hung back.

He glanced back at me with a scowl that changed to a grin so quickly I wondered if I'd imagined it.

"It's fine. I'm going to tell you all the inside secrets of the Holt family. Ready?"

I nodded and fell in next to him. I slung my bag across my chest. Motes danced on a beam of sunlight that slanted through high arched windows. As we climbed the wide graceful staircase in the center of the house, I told myself I was lucky to have a personal guide to the estate.

"How was your trip to Boston?" Dan asked.

"The seminar was interesting, a joint event put on by MIT and BU on theories of phonological variation."

"Like I'll ever know what that means." He chuckled. "I was in the city myself today. Had a Habitat regional board meeting in the North End."

He walked me through the suite that had been the Holt son's rooms. "Check out Clayton's bathroom," he said.

Although the mansion was built in the early 1900s, the bathroom could have passed for current state of the art. Turquoise glass tiles lined the shower stall, which featured gold fixtures, two showerheads with separate controls, and a marble floor. A heated towel rack and an ornate sink filled out the room, with the toilet in an adjacent water closet.

"Wow. What year was this built?" I asked. "That bathroom is a lot fancier than mine."

"Mine, too. The house was finished in 1928." He beckoned me into the bedroom. "Check this out." He pointed to a wind indicator mounted on the wall. "Both father and son loved to sail, so there are five of these throughout the house."

The bedroom had graceful proportions, with an airy feel and a manly décor. Turquoise accents lightened the browns and tans of the upholstery and bedspread. A door opened out onto a screened porch. I peered through the glass of the upper door.

"That was his private entrance from the outside."

Dan's voice sounded from right over my left shoulder and the heat of his body warmed my back. I had a sudden impulse to lean back against him but restrained myself. Instead I turned and moved a step to the side.

"Was he a party boy?" I asked.

"Let's just say he valued his independence. Strange, since he was completely dependent financially on his father." He tilted his head toward the way we had come in. "Let me show you Cornelia's suite."

Befitting the daughter's gender and the era, Cornelia's suite was decorated in rose and cream, with floral wallpaper and white wicker. But the room was as airy and open as her brother's.

"Looks like girls didn't merit a separate entrance."

Dan tsk-tsked with a smile as he shook his head.

The larger glass tiles in that bathroom were painted with silver sailboats. I leaned in to examine them.

"Look!" I laughed, pointing. "This sail has a face in it. And this one has a horse."

"There are touches like that all over the house. Do you remember the painting in the domed entryway? Even the cat's portrait was included."

"That's right." I smiled and continued to look around the bathroom. "But no shower for the ladies?"

"No, they took scented baths, instead." He walked out of the bathroom and back into the bedroom.

I felt at ease. I was enjoying this relaxed visit with Dan, and he did seem to know all about the mansion. I didn't remember why I'd been at all worried in the first place. I could honor my commitment to Zac and enjoy Dan's company. Nothing wrong with that. Especially since Mary's accusation against him had been disproved with Mr. Wojinski's arrest.

My phone vibrated twice, then twice again. A text message. I dug it out of my back pocket and opened my messages. It was from Ernie, and the message began, "The guy on the train." I opened the message.

"When we got off train in hmltn, I think dude who pushed you did, too. I'm not sure becuz I didn't get that good a look. Ernie."

I squinted at the message. Hmltn must be Hamilton. A photo was attached. I stared at a photo of Dan. Maybe. It was fuzzy and taken from a distance. I glanced over at him, but he hadn't noticed.

But it couldn't be Dan in the picture. For one thing, what would he be doing in Boston? Oh, he just said he was at a meeting in the North End. Which was where North Station was. But why would he push me? This seemed crazy. And even if Ernie had seen Dan down there, he wouldn't have pushed me. Plus, the boys said they lived in Hamilton. Why would Dan get off the train in Hamilton, one station south of here, instead of in Ashford, where he lived?

I shoved the phone into my purse as we proceeded down the hall to what looked like the master suite.

"The conjugal bedroom?" I asked.

He shook his head. "Richard had his own bed in his set of rooms. This was strictly Florence's territory."

I wondered, when the couple did have "relations," how they decided which bed to use. Separate beds in a marriage seemed like a crazy notion, even though I had friends in their thirties who kept separate bedrooms despite being apparently very happily married. With children.

My phone vibrated with the text signal again. I extracted it from my bag and checked the display. Bobby Spirokis. I glanced swiftly at Dan. He stood with his back toward me, hands in pockets, absorbed in a book that lay open on a round table in front of one of the windows. I looked back at the phone and brought up the message.

"Saw Talbt leve Allay rite befor you fond body. Blood on hs hand."

I found myself staring at my phone again. Either he really couldn't spell or he couldn't text very well. Or both. But the message was clear. Dan had been on the Grand Allée. After Charles was murdered. With blood on his hand. Dan had said he hadn't been anywhere near the estate or the beach. My heart thudded in my ears. Why would he lie about being at Holt the afternoon of the killing? I could think of only one reason. And I'd asked him too many questions about the murder. Maybe he *was* the one who tried to push me off the platform, after all.

Chapter Eighteen

How would I keep my cool? More important, how soon could I cut this tour short and escape him? I took a quick look up at Dan, and my heart sank. He watched me with narrowed eyes. What had my face looked like? Terrified? Suspicious? I forced a smile.

"My sister's bugging me to go bird-watching with her." I raised my eyebrows as I waved the phone in the air. "Like that's my idea of a good time." I shoved the phone back into my bag.

"I'd go with her. My annual list is a bit thin yet."

This time I laughed for real, although more nervously than usual. "You do that stuff? I mean, keep a life list and a year list of all the birds you've seen?"

"Sure. Doesn't any self-respecting Yankee?" He also laughed, and like he meant it.

I felt my tension dissipate to a level where I could pretend things were normal. Maybe there was an explanation for Dan being on the Allée right after Charles died. Maybe someone else was the killer. As long as I could pretend, I could project normalcy. I hoped.

"Is Mr. Holt's room next? I need to be getting home soon. Wulu, you know." This was the first time I'd really appreciated the needs of my furry friend pulling me homeward.

"Follow me." He strode out the door and down the hall.

I hurried to keep up. Richard Holt's suite was uninteresting to me, especially now, and after a few minutes we made our way toward the stairs. Dan cocked his head to look at me.

"Have you heard how Bobby Spirokis is doing? I've been worried about him since you found him that day on the flats."

Why the sudden interest in Bobby? He couldn't have seen the text. "Actually, I visited him in the rehab yesterday. He was sleeping, so I left," I lied. "How about you?"

"I don't think he'd appreciate seeing me." Dan returned his eyes to the Oriental runner underfoot.

"Why not?"

"We haven't always seen eye to eye. Speaking of that, did you hear that Mary Heard accused me of killing her brother? The woman is nuts."

I stepped onto the top stair. The direct sunlight had dipped below the level of the high windows behind them. In front through a large window I could see the trees on the Allée bent over in a stiff wind. The shadows on the stairwell fluttered.

"Yes, Iris told me."

Dan wrapped his hand around my elbow. "Mary's crazy." He squeezed.

I took in a breath and exhaled. I tried unsuccessfully to extract my elbow from his grasp. He was the black belt, I reminded myself. I didn't have a chance with self-defense moves.

"You need to be careful, you know." He kept his hand tight on my arm as we descended.

The stairs ended not far from the silver storage room we'd seen on the first tour.

"Let's check out the Safe again." He steered me toward the silver room.

I thought at warp speed. I had to figure out my exit, and fast. "That's where you made out with Susie."

"Her name wasn't Susie, but you're right." He pulled open the heavy door. "I've showed a couple of my karate students some of my moves here, too."

I turned so we faced each other. "I wonder what new moves you could teach me." I lifted my chin. "I've never done it in a mansion." I had to make him think I didn't suspect him.

Dan nodded slowly. "Sounds like a plan." A smile spread across his face.

I lowered my head. "But I have to visit the facilities. Why don't you get comfortable in there and I'll be right back."

Dan snorted with pleasure. "Don't be long."

I strode down the main hall to the restroom sign, no doubt provided for the tour guests. Before I turned the corner, I checked over my shoulder. Dan stood in the green-felt-lined room, his now shirtless back to me, his hands on his belt.

My heart pounded. How could I have been such a bad judge of

character? How could I have come on a tour alone with this maniac? I let the door to the restroom slap behind me. No fancy tiles in this utilitarian room. I flushed one of the toilets while I looked at my phone and swore to myself. No bars down here. If I ran for the door now, he'd see me and come after me. I had to come up with a plan. I wracked my brain, ran some water, and walked slowly back to the Safe.

Dan stepped out from the corner of the room into the middle. He wore only a pair of black briefs. He narrowed his eyes.

"Aren't you a little overdressed?"

I held up a finger. "Patience, Sensei. Patience." I slid behind the door. Taking a deep breath, I slammed it shut. He yelled from within. I tried to turn the big disk of a lock. It stuck. The door vibrated. *He must be pushing it from the inside.* I set my feet and threw the best forward-kick-with-heel-strike I'd ever executed. I followed through with my body. I visualized my foot slamming right through the heavy metal door. I grabbed at the disk. It turned. I had no idea if he could open it from the inside. I looked around frantically. A metal letter opener lay on an ornate little table. I snatched the opener and stabbed it between the disk and the door, hoping it would somehow jam the opening mechanism long enough for me to flee.

I dashed for the exit. But when I arrived, I remembered he had locked the outer door with a key. It wasn't in the lock, either. Why didn't this place have a fire-release bar on the door? I cursed and whirled. All the windows were too high. I heard a mighty rattling from down the hall. Where could I go? I sprinted the few yards across the foyer and back to the start of the central hallway. There had to be a red Exit sign somewhere, but I couldn't see one.

That service staircase—where was it? There. The faint line in the wallpaper. I scrabbled my fingers under the recessed ring, tore the door open, entered, shut it firmly and quietly. Then gasped at the darkness. No time to find the light switch.

I felt my way down, around the spiral, hands in front of me, until my foot hit the door at the bottom. I fumbled for the latch. The door opened into the vast cellar. I closed it behind me. But now where?

A faint yell erupted from upstairs. Had he found his way out? I had to move fast. I looked across the murky air of the cellar. A glint of light shone around the coal door on the other side. I headed for the ladder that led to that level and then stopped. I had to block the door to the spiral staircase. A heavy moving dolly stood nearby. I dragged it over, locked its wheels, and tried to jam the top up against the door latch so it couldn't move.

I ran back and clambered down the ladder, then sprinted for the coal door. The light was so dim down here it was like swimming in a silty pond. I felt around for a knob, latch, anything to grasp the door with. My hand fell on a rough wooden handle. I pulled. It didn't move. I pulled harder, rattled it. The door felt loose but wouldn't open. I heard nothing from upstairs. But if Dan caught me, I was dead.

Maybe the door opened outward. I shoved my shoulder again and again into the door. It budged, but only a little. I took a deep breath, assumed an anchored stance, and gave it another front kick. I followed through with my body. The door gave way.

My momentum propelled me through the opening. I'd never been so glad to see daylight. My toe caught on the threshold. I fell, wincing at the blow to my knee and my scraped palms. I scrambled to my feet, slammed the door shut, glanced up. I was in the parking lot. I sprinted for my truck. I tripped on a rock and sprawled on the ground. At another muffled sound, I looked around. He wasn't out of the building yet. It must have come from inside. I pulled my shaking self up and ran.

As I passed Dan's van, I had a brainstorm. I wrenched open his driver's side door. Yes! I grabbed his keys out of the ignition and covered the few yards to my own vehicle in record time. My hand shook so badly I was barely able to stick my own key into the ignition. As I started up, I heard a yell. I shot a glance over my shoulder. Dan, still in his underwear, anger boiling off him, dashed toward me. I sped away, my heart in my throat. Gravel spun.

I drove faster than was safe but not as fast as I wanted on the hairpin turns that wound down the hill. As I exited the estate, I swore. The road was clogged with people leaving the beach at the end of the day. The traffic crept along the single lane toward town. Dan could run down the hill and catch up with me on foot in this traffic. Thank God he wasn't dressed. He wouldn't chase me in public in his underwear. Would he?

A kind driver let me into the line, and I waved thanks. My heart rate still raced. I left the salt marsh behind and entered the wooded section.

I spied the Russell Farm parking lot. I needed to be near people. I had to calm down and think for a minute. Slowing, I pulled into the lot near the road. Families munching cider doughnuts and children licking ice cream cones strolled out of the busy barn where the farm sold produce and other delicacies. I sat in silence, eyes closed. I held this moment in the Light. I willed my heart to slow, my mind to gain control.

I pulled my phone out. Bars again. I exhaled with relief. I was about to press 911 when I paused. Would the police think I was crazy? I knew in my gut Dan was the murderer. But I had no real evidence that he had killed Charles. And they'd laugh at me if I said so. They'd have to question Bobby about what he had seen.

A new terror flashed into my brain. Maybe Dan had a hidden key in his van. He could be on his way now. Where would I be safe from him if he came after me? I looked around in panic. I started the truck and pulled to the far side of the parking lot, where I would be one vehicle among a hundred. I backed into a spot that bordered the woods, where I could keep an eye on the road.

I thought of who I could call. Jackie didn't pick up. I disconnected. I didn't leave a message.

Iris. Iris was like a rock to me. A steady levelheaded presence. I pressed Iris's cell number. She'd be done at the bakery by now. Unless she was giving another pastry lesson to Walter. The phone rang. And rang.

"Pick up, please pick up," I whispered. My eyes widened. I swore. Dan's van rolled into view on the road. He must have had a spare key. I held my breath. Would he turn in here? Then I let it out. He continued toward town.

"Lauren?" Iris sounded breathless.

"Iris! I'm so glad you're there. You have to help me."

"Are you in trouble? Where are you?"

"I'm at Russell Farm. I think Dan Talbot killed Charles. The police need to talk to Bobby Spirokis in the hospital before Dan goes there. He——"

"Wait a minute. Slow down. What are you talking about?"

"I was just at the Holt Estate. Dan was giving me a private tour. Bobby texted me that he saw Dan on the estate right after Charles was killed and that he had blood on him. I think Dan was suspicious. I shut him in the Safe and escaped, but he found his way out. And a minute ago he drove past me toward town. He must be a psychopath or something. I think he's going to try to get at Bobby." I heard my own anxiety as my voice rose.

"Listen. I'm gonna call my cousin Stelios. You know, Officer Papadopoulos. Same name as me."

"What if the police think I'm crazy?"

"Don't worry. Stelios will listen to me. You come to my house. Walter is here. We'll keep you safe. Okay?"

"Tell your cousin to put a guard on Bobby Spirokis at Emerson Rehab in Millsbury. They can't let Dan Talbot anywhere near him."

"Got it. Now get your fanny over here."

I thanked her and disconnected. A father loaded a small crying boy into a car seat in the van parked next to me, and a couple in beachwear walked hand in hand toward their car. A west wind whipped the leaves on the nearby trees and ushered dark clouds overhead. I pulled on the jacket I kept in the truck.

I checked the time on my phone. Five thirty. The farm stand probably closed at six. I felt drained, as if I'd run a half marathon or swum a mile. I couldn't sit here all night, though. I slipped the phone into my pocket and started the engine.

As I drove toward town, I kept an eye out for Dan's van. My hands, damp with nerves, slipped on the steering wheel on one of the Argilla Road curves and I crossed the center line. I swore and gripped it more tightly as I steered back into my own lane. At least there were no oncoming cars. The sky darkened and fat raindrops started to hit the windshield.

I cruised slowly through Ashford's center. I kept checking in all directions for Dan's van but didn't see it. I headed for Iris's house in the old mill neighborhood. The small pink two-story house had never looked so comforting. I parked in front, grabbed my bag, and strode up the walk. Iris swung the screen door open for me. Walter Colby stood behind her.

Iris put her arm around me. She bustled me inside and sat on the couch next to me. Walter took a long look up and down the street before he closed and locked the door. The house smelled of tomato sauce, fresh basil, and safety. The television was tuned to local news but the sound was muted.

"What do you want?" Iris asked. "Tonic? Tea? Wine?"

At the last, I nodded my head. Iris raised an eyebrow at Walter, who headed for the kitchen.

Iris called out, "Check the back door, will you?"

"For what it's worth," Walter called back. He emerged a minute later bearing three glasses of red wine.

I took a sip. I shut my eyes for a second and then looked from Walter to Iris.

"Thank you," I said. "Thank you both."

"Forget about it," Iris said. "So I called Stelios. He said he'd put a guard on Bobby. If he's still in the rehab place."

I stared at her. "I didn't even think that he might have been discharged. I saw him yesterday, and he was in pretty bad shape. I hope he's still there."

"Tell me. Did Dan admit he'd killed Charles?" Iris squeezed my hand.

"No." I shook my head. "But he kept looking at me like he thought something was up. I didn't feel safe. Plus, nobody was around. He'd said there was a tour, but then it was only the two of us."

"How did he swing that? Does he have a key to the mansion?"

"He said his cousin is Sheila Lopes and that she gave him the key to lock up when no one else arrived for the tour. I was late because my truck had a flat and I had to change it."

Walter had remained near the front window, where rain now tapped sideways directly onto the glass. He snapped his head toward me. "Sheila isn't his cousin. And she's out on medical leave, had a knee replacement."

"How do you know?" Iris asked.

"She's the aunt of one of my tellers at the bank."

"That's creepy. He wanted you in there alone with him." Iris frowned. Her left hand idly stroked the bronze statuette of an armless Aphrodite on the end table.

"I wonder what else he lied about," I said. "I used to think I was a good judge of character. But Dan, he——" My hand shook. It set up waves in my wine.

"I always thought he was kind of funny," Iris said.

"He was an odd Trustee, I can tell you that." Walter glanced out the front window and then drew the drapes. "He agreed with the rest of us on important matters, but it was like he was always hiding something, not being open."

"Wait. If this Sheila isn't his cousin, where did Dan get a key?" I gazed into my wine and thought. I looked up with alarm at Walter and then at Iris. "I bet I know. Who else has a key? Bobby, that's who. He does maintenance at the estate. Dan must know Bobby saw him emerge from the woods after he killed Charles. Dan had to be the one who stabbed him with the clam fork on the flats that morning. He could have stolen the key then." I set down my glass and shoved my hands into my jacket pockets.

"We gotta tell the police." Iris reached for her phone on the coffee table in front of the couch.

"I don't think so," a deep voice said from behind them. "Drop that phone, Iris."

I snapped my head in that direction.

A fully clothed Dan stood in the kitchen doorway, his hair flattened with rain. And the gun he brandished looked very persuasive.

Chapter Nineteen

Dan crossed the room in two quick strides. He grasped my neck with his left hand and pulled me to my feet, forcing me to move away from the couch. Iris set the phone down in plain view.

"Didn't see me following you, huh?" Dan snarled.

"Let go of me." I tried to twist away. But when I felt the barrel of the gun on my ear, I stood very still.

"Nobody locks me in a room and gets away with it. You know something you're not saying, Professor." Dan's laugh held no pleasure. "By the way, the lousy lock on your back door was very helpful, Iris."

"Danny, don't be stupid." Iris stood. "Put that thing down."

"It's a little late for that. Sit down."

Iris complied, but she added, "You can't kill all of us."

"Talbot, don't be a fool." Walter took a step toward Dan and me.

Dan pressed the gun more firmly into my ear. "Stay where you are, Colby, or say sayonara to Lauren."

Walter stepped back to the other end of the coffee table.

I wondered how long I had left on this earth. My legs shook, my face seemed numb, and I couldn't feel my toes.

"When the detective interviewed me, I should have told him the truth about that afternoon on the beach," Walter spat out.

Dan barked a mirthless laugh. "That piece of crap Heard was blackmailing me. He found out I'd killed Rousseau all those years ago—"

I gasped and my eyes widened.

"Yes. I killed your daddy. He was the one who turned my father into a homosexual. He ruined my life. They were both disgusting."

So my father's death hadn't been an accident. "His lighter," I murmured in sadness. I pictured again the beautifully engraved initials my father and grandmother shared.

"Nice piece of silver. Lost it recently, though."

I knew exactly where he'd lost it. "Why did you kill him? You didn't kill your own father. Why mine?" I failed to keep my voice from trembling.

"Your father was to blame. My father split. Went to live with all the homos in San Francisco. Far as I know, he's still there."

"What kind of Neanderthal are you, Dan?" Iris stared at him.

"Oh, shut your trap, Iris. Not everyone behaves like you Western whores. I don't put up with that perversion."

Walter shook his head. "I should have told the detective about our little Trustees picnic on the beach with Wojinski," Walter said. "When we thought we could convince him to change his mind about the Bluffs. And I should have told the cop about how I left with him and you stayed with Charles. I wondered if you were the one who killed him. What happened, Dan? What made you slit his throat?"

"A month ago. Heard figured out I'd knocked off Rousseau. He threatened to go public with what he knew unless I paid him for the foreseeable future." He relaxed his grip on my neck.

"How did he figure it out?" I tried to crane my head to look at him.

"He was poking around in my private life, trying to see if I merited being one of their private club of Trustees."

"I saw some printouts from the Web on his desk," I said. "They were in Farsi."

"Yeah. I was over on an Iranian cultural forum. I might have said something about clearing the world of one more gay man. He told me he used Google Translate to translate it."

"You were bragging about killing someone?" Iris's voice rose.

"Just shut your piehole, Iris. Anyway, Walter, after you left with Wojinski, Heard and I went up into the woods to take our argument off the public beach. Wojinski had brought his multi-tool to cut those fancy cheeses he brought. But he left it, and I had stuck it in my pocket. It conveniently had his name stenciled onto it and I conveniently left it there. I knew there was no way anyone could pin Heard's death on me. It was a perfect opportunity that presented itself." He waved the gun in the air.

My relief at the gun being pointed anywhere but at my brain was short-lived. Dan brought it back, to my temple this time.

"So Mary was right," Iris said. "In the pub."

"Yeah, she was right. She must have found his bank records or a letter or something and figured out why he was receiving checks from me. I had to put a stop to it, anyway. He was soaking me. I have a good life going for me here, and he was ruining it."

A drop of rainwater fell from Dan's sleeve onto my neck inside my jacket collar. The water rang a bell in my brain. I was wearing my jacket. Which was where I had put my phone. My left hand closed around it. I felt the volume buttons on the side and slid my thumb to the exact middle where the emergency call icon was. I pressed and held it for a slow count of three. And then held it another second to be sure, grateful beyond belief that I'd installed the emergency button app in the spring after the very real emergency I'd been through. I knew the phone's sound was muted, since it had vibrated with Bobby's text. The call was supposed to go to the local 911 dispatcher, and they would know where I was from my phone's GPS—

I cursed in silence. The dispatcher's voice would come through out loud when they picked up. But if I disconnected, would they know I had dialed? Desperate, I felt again for the power button and pressed it, and then pressed my thumb on the middle of the screen again. I had to connect with the Yes button under the confirmation message that read something like, "Do you really want to power off your phone?"

Iris stared at me. Maybe she'd seen my hand move in my pocket. I smiled a little. I hoped Iris's usual ESP would work. Help should be on the way, friend. If we're still alive then.

Dan looked at Iris and twisted his head down to look at me. "What are you two up to?"

"Nothing, Danny." Iris spread her hands apart and shrugged. "You won't get away with this, you know."

Good move, Iris, I thought. Keep him talking. How did Iris stay so cool, though? My legs felt like they could barely hold me up. My stomach roiled. My fingers were icy.

"I do whatever I want. You can call it getting away with something. I call it creating my own life." His voice was smug and he preened with his body, but he kept his hand firmly clasped on my neck.

"You kill any of us and your life'll be a lot worse, you know." Iris defied his confidence with her own.

"Listen, Talbot," Walter said. "Let's work out some kind of a deal. We won't rat on you and we'll give you plenty of time to leave town. What do you want, twenty-four hours? I happen to have a lot of cash on me right now, too. You can have all of it."

"Forget it, Colby. You think I trust you not to call the cops the minute I leave?"

"Hey, we go back a long ways, buddy. Isn't that worth some trust between Trustees?"

Dan snorted. "Trust. Look who's talking? You're the biggest sleazeball banker in the Commonwealth." He pointed the gun at Iris. "Got any duct tape?"

"It's in the kitchen."

Dan looked at the three of us. "Forget about it. The logistics of that are a hundred percent against me. But I'll take the cash." He addressed Walter. "Take it out with one hand and toss it on the table."

Walter reached his right hand toward his back.

"Stop right there!" Dan pointed the gun at him. "Money's in your back pocket?"

Walter nodded. I wondered if I could twist away, or knock the gun out of his hand, but his other hand still clamped onto my neck.

"Turn around. And move slow."

Walter did as he was told. He slowly extracted a fat wad of green.

"Turn around again," Dan barked.

Walter turned. He leaned forward and tossed the money on the coffee table. The wad, all hundred-dollar bills, scattered on the table. It had to be several thousand dollars. Dan whistled.

"Charles was soaking me. I can use this." He let go of my neck and leaned past me to scoop up the money. He kept the gun pointed at Walter, but Dan's eyes were only on the cash. I looked at Walter. He gave a quick nod.

With a swift move I clasped my hands in front of me, brought them up, and then crashed with all my strength onto the back of Dan's neck as I drew a focusing yell out of the depths of my center, my *ki*. At the same time, Walter flipped the end of the coffee table. It slammed toward Dan's face.

Right before the table hit him, Dan fired. Walter fell onto his side.

His head glanced off a bookcase on his way down. I cried out. Iris, a blur of motion, brought Aphrodite over her head and down onto Dan's. He crumpled and landed facedown with a thud.

Chapter Twenty

"Police! Drop your weapon!" A shout came from the kitchen doorway. A uniformed Stelios Papadopoulos stood with legs wide, weapon drawn and pointed.

"Stelios!" Iris cried. She rushed to kneel by Walter. "Get the paramedics! Dan shot Walter."

Stelios moved closer and kept his weapon drawn on Dan as he called into his radio for medical help.

Dan Talbot lay motionless on the carpet. Another officer hurried to Dan's side and pressed his foot on the forearm that still grasped the gun. Dan moaned. He released his grip on the weapon. He moved his left hand. The officer straddled him, placing one knee on the left arm. The officer's foot pushed the weapon along the floor away from Dan's hand, then he handcuffed Dan's hands behind his back. The officer pulled on gloves and drew evidence bags from his back pocket. He emptied the gun's clip into a bag and gently inserted the gun into another bag.

I took a step toward Iris and Walter. My legs threatened to buckle. My ears rang. I supported myself with one hand on the edge of the coffee table that now lay on its side. "Walter. Is he—?"

Iris looked up. Tears streamed around a smile as she pressed her hands down on Walter's shoulder. "He's breathing. He's got a big-ass hole in his arm. But he's alive." She gazed back down at him. The smile turned to a frown. Blood leaked around the bullet hole despite the pressure she applied with both hands. Walter's eyes remained closed, and his skin had the pallor of ash. A siren keened ever closer.

"You saved us, Iris," I croaked out.

"You struck first. You're the brave one."

Paramedics streamed into the room along with another officer and Chief Flaherty. Stelios pointed the paramedics at Walter. Iris moved aside so they could work on him. Walter opened his eyes and found Iris. In a weak voice he said, "Not quite as much of a sleazeball as he said, I hope."

Iris planted a loud kiss on his forehead. "No sleaze on this hero."

The paramedics loaded him onto a transport stretcher and carried him out. Iris blew him another kiss as he left.

"I'm going after. You okay?" she asked me.

I nodded and sank onto the couch. I stared at Dan, who began to struggle against the handcuffs. Stelios kept a close watch on him.

I finally knew the truth about my father. Dan had murdered him. I felt sick. And sad. And furious.

"Why did you do it?" I gripped one hand with another so they wouldn't shake. "Why did you kill my father?"

Dan twisted his head to look at me. His eyes burned a channel to mine.

"He deserved it," he spat out in a hoarse whisper. "Your father, Charles, they all deserved it."

"Be quiet, Talbot," Stelios said. "You'll get what you deserve in court." He read Dan his Miranda rights. He and the other officer hoisted Dan to his feet and led him out.

Chapter Twenty-one

Mom bustled around my kitchen the next evening. "It's after six. Where's your sister?" She set knives and forks on the four red place mats, then opened the oven door and leaned down to poke a wooden spoon into a full casserole dish.

"Maybe she's stuck in traffic. She had to work today, you know." I placed wineglasses above each knife. I straightened the silverware. Usually I didn't care about place settings, but today the ritual comforted me. The numbness in my heart hadn't eased. I'd felt distant from reality all day long.

Jackie burst through the door carrying a wooden bowl full of salad. Iris followed right behind with a pastry box in one hand and bottle of champagne in the other.

"Smells like a party in here." Iris smiled.

"I'm still having my birthday party on Friday, right, Mom?" Jackie asked.

"Yes, dear, you are."

"How's Walter doing?" I asked as I hugged Iris.

"He'll be fine. The bullet missed all the important stuff. He's already complaining about the hospital food and asking me to sneak in some Scotch for him."

"Sounds like you guys had quite the adventure," Jackie said. She set the salad on the table. She gave our mother a kiss on the cheek, then drew another bottle of champagne out of her bag. "We might as well start on this."

I frowned. "What do we have to celebrate? Finding out that Daddy was murdered?"

Mom and Jackie exchanged a look. "Honey, we're celebrating knowing the truth," Mom said. "We're celebrating a man who killed more than once being locked up, hopefully forever. We're celebrating that Walter is alive. That we're all alive."

Iris nodded. "Amen."

I looked at each of them in turn. They shared the same expectant look, the same invitation for me to join their celebration of life. "Oh, why not? Pop that baby, Jackie."

The cork hit the ceiling. "Pour it, quick!" Iris grabbed a glass from the table.

When four glasses were filled, we clinked each other's glasses.

"No more murders," Mom offered. She held her glass high.

I murmured, "No more murders," and hoped the wish would suffice.

My mom set down her glass. She grabbed some oven mitts, drew the bubbling dish out of the oven, and set it on a trivet in the middle of the table.

"Is that chicken-chili casserole?" Jackie asked. "Like you used to make when we were growing up?"

At the nod, I inhaled the delicious aroma. "Comfort food."

"I thought we could all use some comfort," Mom said.

After we all sat and she doled out servings, I extended a hand to her and to Iris on my other side. Jackie completed the circle. I closed my eyes and let the blessings wash over me for a moment. The scent of a mown lawn wafted in the open windows, and an oriole sang its rich full notes.

Jackie cleared her throat. I opened my eyes and squeezed both hands as I looked straight at my sister.

"Well, I'm hungry!" Jackie said. "You're the Quaker, not me."

We kept the conversation light as we ate, but questions kept arising. I set down a forkful of salad.

"Iris, remember what you said about Mary going away when she was younger?"

Iris nodded, her mouth full.

"I think Mark Pulcifer might be her birth son. Her child with Walter."

Iris nodded again. "He is." She refilled everyone's glasses, emptying the first bottle.

I stared. "You know this?"

"Walter told me this morning, in the hospital. Mark grew more curious about his birth parents and did some Internet searches. He had contacted Walter only a few days ago."

"When I was over at Mary's last week, Walter showed up in a big hurry. He said to her, 'Why didn't you tell me?'" I set my chin on my hand, my elbow on the table. "I thought he said the word 'mark,' but I didn't realize it was a name. But then I had a drink with Mary at Ithaki, where Mark worked. She looked at him like she knew all about him, and not simply because he worked in her brother's insurance agency."

"He must not have contacted Mary, though." Jackie leaned back in her chair.

"Right," Iris said. "Walter said Mark knew about Mary, but he wanted to talk with Walter first. Mary can be unpredictable, and Mark's probably seen that working with Charlie at the agency." She sipped her champagne. "And you know what else Walter told me? He's going to push the Trustees to start doing what they're supposed to. I think having a gun shot at him kind of woke him up to doing what's right."

"He's going to push them to pay what they owe to the schools?" Jackie asked.

Iris nodded. "They're going to have to get two new Trustees now, to replace Danny and Charlie. Walter's got some ideas for who, and one of them is James Wojinski. Another one might be yours truly." She grinned.

"I'll drink to that." I raised my glass and took a sip. My phone rang where it sat on the counter. I reached for it and checked the display.

"Uh-oh, it's Chief Flaherty. I'd better answer this." I put down the glass before I connected and said, "Hello, Chief." I listened, thanked him, and disconnected.

"What's up?" Jackie asked.

"They finally processed the video from the hospital parking lot where my tires were slashed last week."

"What?" Mom said after a sharp intake of breath. "You didn't tell me about that."

"Mom, there's actually a lot I don't tell you. I didn't want to worry you. Anyway, it took them a while because Zac is away. But the chief said it was my esteemed karate instructor who knifed my tires. Dan Talbot." I shook my head. "What a scumbag."

"He must have sensed you were on his trail," Iris said.

"Maybe. But I'm not sure I was at that time."

"Say, Bobby Spirokis was leaving the rehab center this morning when I got to the hospital," Iris said. "Guess he's doing pretty well."

"I'm glad. He must have been terrified of Dan."

"Speaking of nuts, anybody heard anything about that crazy Fiona?" Jackie looked around the table.

"James came into the bakery this afternoon," Iris said. "He's free, of course. But he said Fiona is home. It turns out the crash was an accident, after all. She was deluded about thinking she brought it on."

"I feel bad for both of them," Mom said.

"Yes, and for Daddy, too." I couldn't help it. My thoughts kept returning to an image of my father being drowned by Dan Talbot. Or maybe Dan killed him before he hit the water. I'd ask my mother about an autopsy. But not now.

"Did you ever talk to Dan Talbot's father?" I asked.

"No." Mom gazed out the window. "I didn't have the strength to. He sent me a card, but I tossed it in the trash." She patted my hand, and then wiped a tear from her cheek. "Your father loved all of us. We can hold that in our hearts."

• • •

I was nearly home from my run the next morning. At the corner with High Street, a little red car passed me and turned up my street. It stopped with squeaky brakes and honked. I turned to look.

"Yo, *gaijin!*" A head hung out the driver's-side window.

"Elise! *Gaijin!*" Our nickname for each other was the Japanese word for "foreigner."

Elise pulled closer to the side of the road and climbed out of the car. Gone was the black spiky hair, pasty skin, and trembling hand of the addict. Her hair now formed a soft cap around her grinning rosy-cheeked face. She wore her same black high-top sneakers, but now with khaki shorts and a tie-dyed T-shirt in blues and pinks instead of her former all-black attire. She'd put some meat on her skinny bones and showed muscled arms and legs that looked like she'd been exercising, too.

I strode up to hug her and then stepped back, matching my friend's smile. "You look awesome. I haven't seen you so healthy since our year in Japan."

"Hey, rehab's good for something. I'm back on the streets again, though, so watch out."

"Whoa—" I began.

"Hey, I'm kidding!" Elise laughed. "Not to worry, Lauren. I feel so good being rid of that habit. I know I still have work to do, but I'm not planning on ever going back there."

"Happy to hear it. I'm heading home to make coffee. Join me? We have a lot to talk about."

"Twist my arm."

About the Author

Agatha Award-winning author Edith Maxwell writes the Amesbury-based Quaker Midwife historical mysteries, the Lauren Rousseau Mysteries, the Local Foods Mysteries, and short crime fiction. As Maddie Day she writes the Country Store Mysteries and the Cozy Capers Book Group Mysteries.

A longtime Quaker and former doula, Maxwell lives north of Boston with her beau, two cats, and an impressive array of garden statuary. She blogs at WickedAuthors.com and KillerCharacters.com. Read about all her personalities and her work at edithmaxwell.com.